SCRAP

SCRAP

Kathy Biggs

HONNO MODERN FICTION

First published in Great Britain in 2023 by Honno Press
D41, Hugh Owen Building, Aberystwyth University, Ceredigion, SY23 3DY

1 2 3 4 5 6 7 8 9 10

A catalogue record for this book is available from the British Library.

Published with the financial support of the Books Council of Wales.

ISBN 978-1-912905-84-3 (paperback)
ISBN 978-1-912905-85-0 (ebook)

Cover design – Mad Apple Design
Cover Illustrator – Osian Grifford
Typeset by Elaine Sharples
Printed by 4edge Ltd

For my husband, Paul, with love.

Be not forgetful to entertain strangers; for thereby have some entertained angels unawares.
Hebrews 13:2

Ah, but a man's reach should outstretch his grasp, or what's a heaven for?
Robert Browning

The kid works quickly, he holds the pencil but allows his hand to move of its own accord. Sometimes his eyes are open and sometimes they are closed. He frames the page on all sides, as if he is looking through a window, then pauses and allows himself to wander out into the space beyond. He is in a small garden and at the bottom of the garden, standing by a closed gate, is a tree. He sketches the stretching curve of its trunk, the network of slender branches that veer off, reaching upwards, into a sky that is fading towards evening and, with light taps of his pencil, adds small sprays of leaves and berries. He sits back to consider what he has drawn, then leans and starts again. First, he creates a twisting pathway of thick stems that burrow down into the dark earth beneath; slim off-shoots nosing their way towards the promise of water. Then, with a nod, adds the final details: a man sitting alone staring out into the approaching dark and a small box cradled in the rooty tangle below.

He closes the sketchbook and slips it into his rucksack; then, as he turns to leave, takes the small photograph from beside his bed and zips it into the compartment on its lid.

1

The kid was in the back of the car for a week before they found him: the hottest July for years, the sun so fierce it made your head hum – some kind of personal white noise that put a distraction over everything. People drifted by at half-speed, clumsy in flip-flops and weighed down by bottles of water; drugged by the haze of sun cream, barbecues and sweat that lay like a lid of grease over the dazed city. Reservoirs shrank, lawns perished and everyone got sick of sunbathing. Mornings were bad enough: an oven blast waiting at the front door, but teatime – when things should have been letting up – some unnatural intensifying, a crescendo of mad heat that filled the papers with global warming and left families limp and incapable in front of the telly. Fires sparked and fights flared, police patrolled in shirtsleeves, wading through the town centre where sunstroke stalked the population of Swansea like a new epidemic.

And all that time, the kid was in the back of the car.

Mackie was running late, walking as fast as he could in the heat: just gone nine and the sun already going like a new invention. He crossed over on Craig Street to get out of the glare and onto the main road where there was no escaping it. He took the last stretch at a slow trot, still nurturing some hope he might get in before Tranter. He turned the final corner, rehearsing his lines under his breath – *Sorry, boss. Lauren didn't turn up, I had to take her kids to school* – and stopped. There were two cop cars parked by the yard entrance, windows down, blue lights flashing. He approached them at a slow amble, reminding himself that he was at work, and whatever they were there for was about the scrapyard, not about him. The cars were both empty. The main gates were still shut, the padlocks closed and looped through their chains, but the metal door cut into the one gate was open, draped loosely with blue police tape. Mackie looked back at the cars then clambered over the tape and walked into the yard. The sun had turned it into some kind of light show: bouncing off every windscreen and bumper, picking out hubcaps and exhaust pipes. Apart from that, everything looked pretty normal, so at that point he was thinking there must have been a break-in. The idea seemed to fit because Sharon was in her usual place, perched on her wheelie chair in front of the office window. She spotted him and scooted herself towards the office door, then leaned out and silently beckoned him over. He shrugged at her and mimed – *where's Tranter?* – but she hoisted herself out of the seat and flapped her hands some more.

'What's going on?' Mackie said.

She grabbed his arm and pulled him into the office. 'Thank god you're here,' she wheezed, then shut the door and got herself back on the chair.

He cracked the door open again.

2

'No. Close it, close it,' she said, waving her arms again, sending out a fug of perfume that made him turn his head.

'What's happened? Is it a break-in?'

'No.' she said. 'It's Trev ... he...'

'Trev? What's he done?'

'I don't know.' She reached for the box of tissues and swiped one across her forehead. 'He was in early. I didn't know he was here until he ... oh, hang on. Shit. They're coming over.'

She squeezed past him and threw open the door. He held his breath and shot out behind her. They stood and watched as Trev, sandwiched between two police officers and looking like he'd just come off the London Marathon, hobbled towards them. He looked like he'd been whitewashed.

'Can you get us a chair, love?' one of the cops shouted. 'Miss? Could you get us a ... oh, hell. Come on now, sir, just a few ... oh, bugger.'

Trev's knees buckled and he sort of drifted to the floor. The one cop got down beside him and arranged him all lined up and tidy on one side and the other cop came sprinting towards Mackie and Sharon.

'Got some water handy, love?'

Sharon spun her bulk and disappeared back into the office. She emerged with a bottle of Coke. 'This do? It's all I've got. Water's off.'

He grabbed it and took it over to Trev who, as far as they could see, hadn't moved since the cop had laid him out.

'What the hell is going on, Sha?' Mackie said.

'Trev was in early, I don't know what he was doing but he

suddenly came flying into the office shouting, "get an ambulance, get an ambulance…"'

'An ambulance? Is it Tranter?'

'No, no. Not bloody Tranter. It's … I don't know. Trev found something – someone – in one of the cars. I think it was a…'

She got no further because just as she was about to enlarge upon the situation, an ambulance shrieked up and Tranter appeared. 'Sharon,' he barked, 'get Trev's mother on the phone. And Mackie – get the keys and get those fucking gates open.'

Mackie didn't wait to be told twice. He bolted into the office, unhooked the fob from the wall, his fingers shuffling for the right key, and sprinted to the gates.

He stepped out onto the pavement and tried to fiddle the key into the first padlock, but the ambulance was backing up and the noise of its reversing alarm bouncing off the metal gates and the dizzy spin of the blue light made him clumsy.

'Which way do those gates open, mate?'

The paramedic in the passenger side was leaning out of his window.

'Eh?'

'The gates. They open inwards or out?'

'Er … in,' Mackie said, then had to think about it. He got the first padlock off and started pulling at the chains. Tranter had this awkward way of fastening them, some kind of complicated weave pattern that he thought was more of a deterrent but made them a bastard to get off.

'What's going on, mate?' Mackie shouted, embarrassed by how he must have looked: on edge, overheated. Pathetic.

'Not sure until we get in there. Someone trapped or...'
Mackie didn't hear the rest because the paramedic was already
out of the vehicle, pulling boxes of stuff from a side
compartment. The driver opened the back door and came out
with a bottle of oxygen and a large bag.

'We'll go have a look first,' she said and disappeared through
the small door in the gate.

Mackie was still fiddling with the second padlock when they
came back. They weren't panicking but he could see that
they were panicked. They moved like water. Smooth, no
friction in what they were doing. In one seamless motion,
they rolled out the trolley, pulled down a second bag, had a
quiet word on the radio, then, just as the last chain rattled
free and the doors started opening, they shot past Mackie
and into the yard. His hands were shaking as he fastened the
gates back. He dumped the chains in the oil drum and
jogged back towards the office. He could see Trev still
stretched out on the floor. One of the police officers and
Sharon were with him but there was no sign of the
paramedics. He had the feeling everyone, except him, knew
what was going on.

'Mackie,' Sharon shouted, 'They need you to go and help.'

'What?' It wasn't a question as much as a way of buying
himself some time. It didn't work, because one of the
paramedics suddenly reappeared.

'Follow me,' she shouted and bolted off like a greyhound,
Mackie trailing behind her wondering what the hell it was he

was running towards. 'Where's your boss?' she yelled, without turning or breaking stride.

'I ... I...' He didn't know where Tranter was. Truth be told he was starting to feel like he didn't know where he was himself. He might have put this down to the heat, the speed at which everything was happening – but he would have been lying.

'We're going to need him,' she shouted, as they rounded the corner.

'I'm here.' Tranter was striding towards them. He had the long metal shears balanced on one shoulder.

'We're going to need more than that,' the paramedic said. 'We need to get it down.'

'Get it down?' Tranter said.

'Yeah. We need the car on the ground. Can't do anything with it up there.'

'But ... that's ... what about the fire lot?'

'No chance,' she said. 'They're all out on that grass fire and we can't wait. We need that car down, like, now.'

'In one piece?'

'In one piece.'

2

Mackie knew what was coming.

'Right.' Tranter was already fishing in his trouser pocket. He pointed at the paramedic. 'You go with this lady, Mackie. I'll bring him round.'

The paramedic looked at Mackie.

'Magneto.' Mackie offered it like it was some kind of explanation.

The paramedic raised an eyebrow then set off jogging. Mackie fell in behind, following her the length of the first aisle, telling himself not to panic, that he could cope. The heat was stupendous: radiating off the piles of scrap cars and flowing down the corridor between them in a rolling wall you could almost see. They turned at the top end and cut across to the holding bay. *The Waiting Room* he and Trev called it – the place they stacked stuff that had just come in, or stuff they hadn't got started on. Generally speaking, this was where he and Trev spent most of their time. Where he would have been that morning if it hadn't been for Lauren.

'OK, this is it.'

They'd stopped at the foot of a pile of three cars. There was a ladder leaning up against them, wedged at the bottom with a couple of tyres.

'It's the one on the top,' she said. 'The Merc.'

Mackie looked up. 'What? Your mate's up there?'

She nodded. 'Yeah. But we need it down. Can't work with it up there.'

'So ... what ... what's going on?'

If she answered, Mackie didn't hear her because at that moment, Tranter turned Magneto's key and with a shuddering lurch, like they were on the car deck of a ferry, the ground sent up a sick vibration. It crept under their feet, across the ground and hit the piled cars like a giant tuning fork: they were engulfed in an unholy racket that set Mackie's head humming like a harmonica.

'Ye god,' she said. 'What the hell is that?'

'It's Magneto,' Mackie said. 'The magnetic crane.' *Christ.*

As if on cue, Tranter, mounted up in the cab like one of the riders of the flaming apocalypse, he appeared at the far end of the row, trundling towards them at a rate that made them both step back.

The paramedic grabbed the ladder and yelled to her partner. His head appeared from the back window of the Merc and he made some gesture with his hand that Mackie didn't understand. 'I can't leave him,' he said.

Him? Mackie felt the ground shift slightly.

'Shit,' she said. 'OK, right.' She strode towards Tranter and Magneto, which, Mackie thought, was more than he would have done, and held up her arm. Tranter stopped and jumped down from the cab. There were a couple of minutes of pointing and talking before Tranter got back into the cab and put the crane into gear.

The paramedic came dashing back, put her hand to her mouth and hollered up the ladder again. 'You're going to have to get out,' she shouted and, when she got no reply, shot up the ladder and stuck her head in the back window. As soon as their feet hit the ground they pulled the ladder out of the way then beckoned to Tranter.

'Come on, come on,' the paramedics were saying.

Mackie stood back, not sure what he was supposed to be doing and not sure he wanted to be there. He watched Tranter inching the jib into position. He got it in place above the Merc's roof; then, with the delicate precision of a surgeon, he lowered it until the magnet was touching the metal.

'Yes,' the paramedic shouted. 'That's it. You've got it. Bring it down. Come on, bring it down.' She was gesturing frantically at Tranter, indicating where he should land the vehicle, then they all stood back as he switched the magnet on and with a solid thump latched it onto the roof of the car. There was an ominous creak as Tranter pulled on the jib lever and the crane started to take the weight of the car. He lifted slowly, easing the Merc into the air, softly, softly, so it wouldn't start swinging or, worse, spinning. They watched as it detached from the car beneath and then floated out above their heads.

'That's it,' she shouted.

Tranter was working the levers like he was conducting a bloody orchestra. The Merc was *gliding* down. He caught

Mackie's eye and gestured him towards the descending car. Mackie got in place and, as soon as it was within touching distance, put his hands on it, steadying its final approach.

'Yes, yes. We've got it. The paramedics sprang forward as soon as the tyres touched earth.

Tranter shut off the engine and slid down from the cab and, in the silence that fell Mackie got a sudden urge to run. All he could hear was his own ragged breathing, the quiet tension in the paramedics' voices and the desperate rasping of an Ambu bag.

Tranter tapped his shoulder. 'Go tell the cops we've got him down.'

Mackie nodded then dodged past the Merc, keeping his eyes well away from what was going on because whatever it was, he knew he couldn't handle it. Not again.

Sharon came out of the office as soon as she spotted him sprinting across the yard.

'Mackie.'

'Hang on,' he shouted and carried on past her towards the gate.

One of the police cars had gone and there was a small crowd on the other side of the street, lined up behind a slash of blue and white tape. They surged forwards a few inches as soon as they saw Mackie, necks craning and heads bobbing. He leaned down to the cop sitting in the passenger seat.

'They said to tell you they've got him down,' he whispered, and it was like the words released something in him, something lodged between his heart and throat, and to his horror he started to cry.

'It's OK, mate,' the officer said, getting out of the car and taking his elbow. 'Just show me where to go.' He bent down to speak to the cop in the driver's seat. 'You keep your eye on this lot, yeah?'

'Bit of a shock, eh?' the cop said as Mackie steered him towards the holding bay. He still had hold of his arm, worried, maybe, that he was going the same way as Trev.

'It's down there,' Mackie said, pulling his arm free to point the way. 'Turn right at the end of this row, that's where ... oh.' The paramedics were running towards them.

They had the trolley between them. One of the paramedics had one arm in the air, holding a drip bag. Tranter was following behind, a pair of metal shears clamped across his chest, striding along like some Tarantino psycho and for a few moments, it was like everything slowed down.

The air thickened, wrapping itself around the scene, blurring the edges, hushing the sound of the trolley wheels on the dirt road, the voices of the paramedics, the crackling of the cop's radio and, as if in some dream, they hurtled past – a brief glimpse of something small and pale beneath a heaped sheet, flanked by an oxygen cylinder, a littering of tubes, syringes, half packs of gauze and cotton wool – leaving Mackie alone, staring down at his boots and listening to the thud of his own heart.

It was a kid. Trev had found a kid.

'Mackie.'

He looked up and turned towards Tranter's voice.

'Get a fucking move on,' he yelled. 'You're going with them.'

Sharon was waiting for Mackie at the gate. She gave him a small pat on the back and thrust a bottle of Coke into his hands.

'You'll be OK,' she said.

'I know.' It wasn't convincing, even to his own ears.

'Just don't ... you know ... don't *lose* it.'

'I won't. I'll be fine.'

She knew. Some of it, anyway. He'd told her more than he told most people. It was old history but still, that's what trips most of us up, isn't it? *Water under the bridge, mate.* Yeah, but you can still drown in it.

3

Mackie took a deep breath and walked through the gates. The police car had moved further along the road, the spin of its blue light throwing a wash of colour over the line of gawkers whose ranks had swelled and now seemed to include a couple of photographers. Tranter, whether he'd been commissioned or just decided to do it, was patrolling the blue tape, the metal shears over his shoulder like a rifle. Mackie walked to the back doors and looked in. The paramedic was bent over the trolley, talking in a low voice. At that point he was hoping Tranter was mistaken – that he didn't need to go with the ambulance.

But the paramedic got to his feet. 'Get in and buckle up,' he said, and pointed to a seat squeezed in between an assortment of gas cylinders and plastic boxes. Mackie backed onto it and listened as the bloke spoke into his radio. 'Morriston? You ready? Yep. On our way now ... yeah...' He lowered the radio and bent over to look at the kid. 'Young, I'd say. Twelve? Thirteen maybe?' Then he watched as the bloke pulled the doors closed, rapped his knuckles against the bulkhead and trapped himself into a seat by the trolley. He pressed a button on the wall and spoke into a microphone. 'We're ready to roll. He's GCS 3 so hit it.' He threw Mackie a small nod. 'Hold tight,' he said, and then they took off.

They took off, it seemed, on two wheels, rearing up like a mad horse and for a moment Mackie thought they were airborne. He held onto his breath, waiting for the thud as they touched down again, trying to swallow down the fear that was rising in his throat. He made himself concentrate on what he could hear: the steady blare of a siren, the hiss of oxygen, the low murmur of the paramedic's voice as he tended to the kid. Mackie told himself he was OK, but then the siren of the police escort close behind them struck up, discordant and confusing and Mackie knew he wasn't: the water that had flowed under the bridge fifteen years earlier had suddenly swelled up and was threatening to engulf him again.

'You alright there, mate?' The paramedic was looking at him.

'What? Yeah. I'm fine.' It wasn't true.

'A bit of a rough ride.'

'Yeah.' The guy had it in one.

'I...' Mackie hesitated, realising that he might have told him there and then – this stranger. He might have told him this wasn't his first rough ride – that his first one had, in fact, been much rougher because it had involved his wife – but the paramedic didn't hear him, his attention was already back on the kid. Mackie leaned forward in his seat and watched. The only part of the kid he could see were his bare feet – filthy and cut – poking out from beneath the thin sheet that was covering him.

'Come on, son. Come on.' The paramedic's voice was low and soothing. He was stroking the kid's forehead like a dad tucking his child in for the night. It made him think of Lauren, made him want to unbuckle himself and tell the kid everything was going to be alright.

'Is he going to be OK?' Mackie said, but his voice was lost in the blare of the sirens and the din of a dozen pieces of equipment rattling against the ambulance walls. He pressed his lips together hard and tuned into the low lull of the paramedic's voice and clung onto it like it was a rope flung out into a rough sea.

The radio crackled into life. 'ETA two minutes,' the driver said. 'How's he doing?'

'Just keep your foot down. Are they ready for him?'

'Ready and waiting, hang on. Here we go. Move over, move over. Oops, sorry.'

There was a screeching of tyres as they cornered hard into a swerve that catapulted Mackie's stomach up into his throat. Then they straightened up and started picking up speed. He could taste sick in his mouth. *Two minutes.* He started counting. He'd got to ninety when they lurched into another sharp turn then suddenly slowed down and cruised to a halt.

He didn't know what he would have said. That he wasn't his next of kin; that he didn't have any details; that he didn't want to be involved – couldn't cope with being involved – because next thing he knew they were slamming through the plastic doors and from then on it was like he no longer had any control over what happened and the notion of trying to keep himself together – to keep his head above water – was of no consequence at all.

He lost them as soon as they were through the doors. Or they lost him. The real truth is he lost himself – as he followed them through he walked straight back into his old nightmare. He stopped and propped himself up against the wall, watching as the medics stampeded the trolley down the corridor, all the balls of a bobsleigh team until they reached the doors at the end and disappeared. There was silence for a moment or two, then relief. Until, like a tidal wave, back it came – the memory of the night she died: the sound of the trolley wheels, the urgency in the mix of voices, the slap of shoe leather on the floor – clamouring at his throat, clawing at his face, choking the breath out of him until his eyes swam.

'Sandra', he whispered and let his chin fall to his chest.

He might have stayed there for a minute or for an hour – propped up against the wall like he'd maybe taken a rest during a long walk – he wasn't sure. But it left him with a feeling of contentment, which at the time made sense; it was only afterwards, when he was trying to account for the missing minutes, that he felt unnerved. He didn't remember pushing off the wall or walking down the corridor, he didn't remember a thing until he pushed through the doors and into the A&E department.

The noise was like a slap in the face: sharp, unexpected, staggering. Mackie hesitated at the door like a man waking from a dream, contemplating the allure of going back rather than going forward. He let the door swing closed behind him and stood for a while, trying to make sense of what he was seeing. The place was seething with people, like he'd walked into a shopping arcade or onto some crowd scene in a film. No one seemed to be sick: no apparent accidents or emergencies, just people milling around or chatting in groups, some laughter, an overlay of background music, an abnormal feeling of excitement. He looked back over his shoulder at the door he'd come through then took a deep breath and stepped forward into the throng. The heat was stupendous: a heady fug that had him dripping with sweat and undoing the front of his overalls within moments.

Two things struck him as he crossed the room. The first was the smell of smoke. Not cigarette smoke, fire smoke: a sweet, toasted smell that had something of childhood in it. The second was that everyone he could see was young: teenagers, early twenties maybe, and they were all half-dressed. They were in a heat wave, he knew that, but these kids looked like they'd just flown in from Marbella.

He carved a path through the crowd and, ignoring the string of kids lined up at reception, chatting and laughing like they were waiting to order a pint, walked to the front of the queue. The woman on the desk looked up at him.

'Oh,' she said. 'You're not with this lot, then?'

'No,' he said, 'What's going on?'

She leaned across the desk. 'Well, it's not for me to say,' she said, 'but what a flipping morning. Off their heads, the lot of them.'

He turned round and scanned the waiting room. 'What do you mean?'

'Smoke inhalation. Hah. Inhaled a lot more than smoke if you ask me.'

'So, what...?'

'The fire,' she said. 'Up on the Gower. The rave? Set the bloody grass alight. Still burning, apparently. There's decent people with caravans up there, you know. I was talking to one paramedic – like Armageddon he said. Well, they shouldn't be here if you ask me. Anyway...' She straightened herself up, picked up her pen and smiled at him. 'How can I help you, Sir?'

'A rave?' he said, trying to remember if Lauren had said she was going to the rave. 'Was anyone hurt? Has ... has anyone been admitted?'

'Not a single one,' she said and Mackie felt his shoulders drop an inch or two. 'Mind you, there's still four ambulances up there. God knows what they're going to bring back. Anyway,' she glanced over his shoulder at the small queue that had suddenly formed. 'How can I help you?'

'I came in with – with a young boy. In an ambulance?'

She gave him a look that suggested she'd just changed her opinion of him.

'Name?'

'Ah ... I'm not sure, I. From the scrap yard. Tranter's?'

She hit the keyboard.

'Tranter's. That's the name, is it, of this boy?'

'What? No. That's where we've come from. I just came with them a few minutes ago, I...' He stopped, suddenly unsure of how long he'd been in the corridor.

She peered at the computer screen then did some more tapping. 'Can't see anything here. Sure it was this hospital?'

'Yes, I'm sure.'

She was still shaking her head when the paramedic from the back of the ambulance appeared.

'Alright there, mate? They've taken him straight up to ICU.'

'Oh, ICU.' She pushed herself back from the counter and leaned over for the phone. 'Why didn't you say that in the first place?'

'Don't bother ringing,' the paramedic said. 'I'm going up there now. I'll take him with me.'

Mackie followed the paramedic onto the ICU – hanging back slightly, trying to ready himself. It wasn't fear, as much as the fear of fear. It made no sense, he knew that, but there it was: some need of protection or armour. He re-fastened the front of his overalls and kept walking. It was exactly as he remembered: low ceiling, no windows, a refrigerated twilight zone, the soft shoe silence punctuated by submarine clicks and pings, the background wheeze of artificial breathing like some great sleeping animal, the feeling of life suspended. This was where his life ended. His proper life. The one he had before.

They stopped outside the door of a dimly lit room. 'Go in,' the paramedic said, 'I'll let the nurse know you're here.'

'OK,' Mackie said, then found he couldn't bring himself to cross the threshold. Instead, he watched the paramedic disappear down the corridor then stood in the doorway peering into the gloom.

'Mr Mackie?' The nurse was on her way back. 'I can let you see him for a few minutes. Is it alright to take a few details from you?'

'Well...'

She handed him a form. 'Just your name and contact details, that kind of thing.'

He took it off her, then followed her into the room.

'He's had a rough time,' she said. 'So don't expect too much.'

I don't know him, he wanted to say, but instead found himself watching as she leaned over the lad and touched him on the shoulder.

'Alright, son. Your dad's here.'

'Oh, I'm not...' he started, then stopped as she came across and reached for his arm.

'It's OK,' she said. 'He's not conscious, but you know, it's OK to talk to him. It's good if you talk to him.'

Mackie approached the bed slowly, looking at everything except the kid: the circle of soft light falling from the lamp, the abstraction of tubes and wires criss-crossing the bed, the way the fan was lifting the edges of the thin curtain, billowing it out like a sail. And then he made himself look. The kid was small – maybe twelve or thirteen, like the paramedic had said. His thin arms were bandaged, and his hair, which lay low on his forehead, was black and matted. His lips were cracked and bloody and there was a faint scarring that suggested previous injury. Like he'd been in a fight, Mackie thought, or put in a boxing ring. He had a graze on his cheekbone, a cut above his eyebrow and, beneath his left eye, a track of dried tears. Mackie couldn't help himself. He reached out his hand and stroked the kid's forehead.

'It's alright, lad, you're safe now,' he said.

The kid's eyelids flickered for a moment or two, then opened. His eyes were green, the colour of tarnished copper. Mackie stood stock-still as the kid scanned his face from forehead to chin, until some feeling of electricity, a feeling of being *read*, made him step away from the bed.

The kid kept staring. Mackie found himself unable to look away.

'It's you,' the kid said, then closed his eyes.

'What...?' Mackie took another step back and steadied himself against the door frame. 'What did he mean?' he said to the nurse.

'He didn't mean anything,' she said. 'It's just the meds.'

Mackie mulled this over for a moment or two. 'I better get off, now,' he said. 'Get back to work.'

'Oh, OK. The form,' she said. 'Have you filled it in? We'll need to get in touch with you.'

'What? No. I...' He picked it up off the small table where he'd left it. Someone had already filled his name in the next of kin box. *Mr Mackie.*

'I think there's been a mistake,' he said. 'I'm not his next of kin.'

'Oh. I thought A&E said his dad came in with him. I thought – what he said just now – I thought he knew you.'

'No,' Mackie said. 'I work at the scrapyard where he was found. I came in with him, but I'm not his dad. I don't know him. I don't know anything about him. I...'

He didn't know why he said what he just said.

'It's alright,' the nurse said. 'But if you wouldn't mind

leaving your contact details? Social services will be in at some point and it might be useful if there was someone, you know, who could give a bit of background information.'

He scribbled his address and phone number on the form and handed it to her.

'You've no idea how he ended up in the scrapyard, then?' the nurse said, gazing over at the boy.

'I haven't got a clue,' he said. 'Not a clue.

4

Nine days earlier.

They were on the motorway: the soft rubber ripple of the tyres drifting up through the seat, carrying the hum of the road, like a song, into his aching back. He had been asleep, folded in on himself, neat as an envelope. He shifted position, waiting for the warm sting of blood to reach his cramped legs, then slid the blanket off his face.

Marco and Drake were talking about what was going to happen when they got there. Marco's voice was fast. Electric. The drawing was on the dashboard, with Marco's research: pages printed off the internet, maps, telephone numbers. Clues. They would look at it when they got closer then wake him up. Get him to finish the job. Get him to find Eileen.

He was concentrating on car headlights, counting the seconds between the sweeping beams as they came from behind, projecting silent movies onto the ceiling of the car, cartoon flickers that caught his eye and made him wish he was at home. He held his breath as they passed, releasing it when the car settled back into darkness and resumed his counting. He got to twenty before the inside of the car lit up again. High headlights, a dark rumble as it pulled alongside to overtake. He lifted his head to watch it pass. A Land Cruiser. It was close, he thought. Maybe too close. Something about it was adrift. He watched the driver lighting a cigarette then letting down the window, one hand on the wheel as he exhaled into the night air.

The lurch was slight: a small stumble that didn't quite correct itself. The driver dropped his cigarette and grabbed the wheel with both hands, fighting as the Cruiser veered towards the crash barrier. The kid sat up. 'Marco?'

The Cruiser was suddenly alongside them – a fleeting moment of metal against metal, before it shuddered away, straightened momentarily, then, in slow motion, tilted away from them, wheels peeling off the tarmac as it rose into the air and hurtled towards the crash barrier. He heard the screaming shear of metal as it hit then watched as it ricocheted off, back across the lanes and straight into their path.

When he woke the night was a weave of light: blue and orange. He was lying in long grass. The sound of running water and voices. The smell of oil and petrol. He rolled onto his side trying to remember why he was there. He raised himself up and looked towards the voices. A paramedic was wheeling a trolley towards an open ambulance. Beyond that something blue and twisted – flattened metal and shattered glass, a tyre or maybe a wheel...

It was Marco's car.

He was half off the ground, hauling himself towards it when the paramedic closed the ambulance doors. 'We'll leave you to it then, mate.'

'No problem. Shouldn't be long. I'll get the Cruiser on then I'm off.'

He lifted his head and watched the ambulance go, its sirens cracking the night in two, then crawled towards Marco's car. A door slammed and he sank low, watching as a breakdown truck reversed past him, then he crept forward until he was level with Marco's Astra. The passenger door was hanging open.

'Marco,' he whispered. 'Marco.'

His voice flew out into the night like a small bird. He got off his knees, leaned into the car and ran his hand over the dashboard. His drawing wasn't there. He felt the seat – it was wet and covered in glass. He could hear the truck driver loading the Cruiser. He knew he needed to go but he had to find his drawing. He got down on all fours and patted the grass around the car. When he heard the truck door slam he leaned back into the car for a final look and, in the revolving orange light, saw it – there, on the back seat. He pushed it inside his shirt then, keeping low, ran towards the breakdown truck. The driver was already in the cab, his head down over paperwork. He crouched low and crept past, climbed up onto the trailer bed and, as the driver put the truck into gear, slid himself through the back window of the crumpled Cruiser.

He was woken by the hiss of air brakes and the slam of a door. A bright light suddenly flooded the vehicle and he slid himself silently off the back seat and into the footwell. He could hear voices and then the rough rumble of chains being loosened.

The kid tried to push himself further under the driver's seat and waited, concentrating on the sounds outside: footsteps, more chains rattling free, then the metal grind of the ramp rolling out somewhere beneath him.

'That'll do, mate. Leave it there. The lads'll sort it in the morning. Sure the cops were OK with this?'

'Sure. Said they'd come here to see it.'

The window of the Cruiser was smashed and the voice was very close. The kid gripped the bar beneath the seat. He squeezed his eyes shut and concentrated on the feel of the metal, its cool smoothness, then on the hot scratch of the carpet beneath his cheek, the smell of mint and cigarette ash. He held on until the creak of metal gates and the rattle of chains told him it was alright to let go.

He rolled onto his back, lay for a few minutes, listening, then hauled himself onto the back seat, feeling the gritty crunch of shattered glass through his jeans as he leaned his face out into the night and sniffed the air. It was heavy with salt and rust and oil and he thought, perhaps, he was by the sea. He listened for the lap of water but heard none – only the soft zip of tyres on a nearby road. He narrowed his eyes and waited for them to adjust. He was surrounded by towers of metal and steel. Haphazard shapes jutting out against the dark sky, shy flashes of chrome and glass. With a small nod he sat back in his seat. He was in a scrapyard.

The kid stuck his head back out into the dark and considered the space around him. They were coming back in the morning – that's what the man had said. That meant he needed to get out of there – or find somewhere better to hide. He eased himself through the window and out into the blackness, waited for a moment until the spinning in his head slowed down, then stepped away from the Cruiser. It was a mistake.

A high voltage light suddenly burst into life. It blazed down on him, holding him there, his mouth open, his hand shielding his eyes, until the message travelled from his brain to his feet and he set off running towards a large shed at the other side of the yard. He flattened himself against the plank wall and waited until the light went off; then, moving slowly, he felt for a door. When he found it he fit the handle into the palm of his hand. It turned eagerly enough, a loose rattle that sounded promising, but yielded nothing. He tried again, putting his shoulder against the door but it still held. He didn't know what to do. He could feel the tears coming. *Get your fucking smart on,* Marco would have said. *Get yourself a fucking plan.* But Marco wasn't there. The kid scanned the area behind him: a wall of cars rose up in unsteady columns, shanty towers of faded metal and steel – a lot of places to hide. He crept to the foot of the nearest tower – its base was a Toyota. He stepped up onto its empty window frame, grabbed hold of the roof of the car above and pulled himself up. He imagined Marco was below, hissing instructions, speeding him on. He checked over his shoulder before he reached for the next car: another half metre and he might trip the security light again. He took a deep breath and snaked his arm up and climbed until he reached the car at the top. A blue Merc. He grabbed the hanging strap and hauled himself up; then, as quickly as he might dare because he could feel the tower below him moving, pulled himself in. He waited for a minute or two until the cars settled then lifted his head and looked down at the yard. He had a plan. He would hide there until morning and then, when the gates were open, sneak out. He had the drawing and he would use it to find Eileen. He would find her and warn her about Marco.

5

Mackie got out of ICU and headed back down to Reception. It wasn't until he reached the main foyer, and caught a whiff of Costa's, he realised that in all the commotion with the kid, he hadn't eaten. He was starving. A coffee and muffin would do it, he decided, and a chance to sit somewhere quiet and try get his head back on straight. It was firing off in too many directions. 'It's you,' that's what the kid had said, like he knew him; recognised him.

'Mackie?'

He spun round, slopping the foam off his latte onto the table.

'Trev. Shit. Oh, sorry, Bertha – I mean, Mrs Tyndall.'

Mackie loosened the muffin from its paper napkin and dabbed at the table. Bertha made a noise like a tyre going down and started rooting in her handbag. She threw a packet of paper hankies at him then whipped them back and ripped them open.

'So,' she said, and sat down next to him. 'What are you doing here?'

Mackie took a quick bite of his muffin to buy a bit of time. The last thing he needed was a grilling from Bertha.

Trev's mother was something of a legend at the yard. They

were all scared of her – even Tranter. He'd had a run in with her, years back, after Trev backed the tipper into Tranter's van and had his wages docked. Bertha paid a visit, slogging across the yard: square and solid in what looked like a man's overcoat, her handbag slung across her front like an ammo belt. She had a greasy black beret jammed on her head. There was something Soviet about her that made you think of gulags: miles of icy wilderness and no escape. She'd marched across to Tranter's private office and disappeared inside. There'd been a long silence and then Tranter had come trotting out with a handful of cash for Trev.

'I just came in with the ... the ambulance,' Mackie said. This was a lame attempt to separate himself from any semblance of being in the know: partly because he didn't want to talk about it and partly because of the way Bertha was looking at him – like she was quietly selecting which instrument to use to get the information out of him.

'Go on...'

'Well...' He tried to catch Trev's eye, but he'd gone big with a chocolate milkshake and was giving it his full attention.

'They brought you in too, then, Trev?'

Trev let the straw drop from his mouth and wiped the foam off his lips with the back of his hand. Bertha tutted and skimmed a paper hanky at him.

'Yeah,' he said, looking at his mother. 'It was my blood pressure. Went too low. I'm alright now, though.'

Bertha gave a snort. 'You, alright? Hah. That'll be the day.'

Trev rubbed the back of his head. 'It was a hell of a shock

though, Mackie, my god, I – He found the straw with his lips again and took a long pull on the milkshake.

'Go on. Spit it out. Tell him what you were doing.'

Trev, to give him his due, didn't even bother trying.

'On his own, he was. Weren't you Trevor? On his own up a ladder...'

Trev raised his eyebrows at Mackie while Bertha set off with her account of the story. Mackie listened until she got to the part about coming in to talk to Tranter about compensation, then made a big show of looking at his watch, got up and excused himself.

Work, he'd said. He needed to get back to work. This was only partly true. What he really needed was to talk to Sharon.

'Watch out, mate. Move over.'

Mackie leapt to one side as a trolley, flanked by two paramedics, hurtled towards him. A nurse jogged up and grabbed the end of the trolley. 'Another one off the Gower?'

'Yeah, straight up to the Burns Unit...' And then they were gone.

Mackie's knees dissolved. Lauren. He'd been so caught up with the kid he'd forgotten about her. He wrestled his phone out of his pocket and tapped the screen. There was a missed call and a message, both from a number he didn't recognise. He opened the message first. "Hi, Dad, just to let you know, I'm OK. On my way to pick..." He closed his eyes and mumbled a few words of thanks, then logged into the answer machine. The caller had left no message but no matter, she was alright. She was on her way – he checked his watch – on her way, no doubt, to pick the twins up from school. All was well. Panic over. He could go back to the yard, have a catch up with Sharon, maybe make a start on the stockpile and stop worrying about Lauren, the twins, school ... and what the kid had said. He let out a long sigh of relief, took a couple of deep breaths, and set off towards the bus stop.

Mackie had a theory about relief. Enjoy it while it lasts, that was his theory. Don't shrug your shoulders and pretend you weren't worried. No, stick your damn hand up and say, *yes, I was scared shitless,* then feel the relief and fucking enjoy it. There'd been moments when he'd imagined imparting this advice, this pearl of wisdom, to other people; envisaged himself as a counsellor, a life coach maybe. A nice little room, two comfy sofas or a small circle of chairs even, a clutch of troubled souls hanging on his every word. Listen to me, he would say, because this is not out of a book. No – this is out of my life which has been just about as shitty as a life could be: relief is the gulp of air you snatch when your head suddenly breaks free of deep water, glorious and unexpected. So learn to breathe deep, get a lungful, because you don't know how long it will have to last.

He was still running on full when he reached the carpark and decided to get a taxi rather than join the Marbella crowd who were queueing for the bus and looking a lot less perky. They'd just pulled out of the hospital grounds and into traffic when his phone rang. It was a number he didn't recognise.

'Mr Carpenter.'

No one called him by his proper name except ... he took a big gulp of air and felt the water close over his head. 'Miss Jones,' he said.

'Sorry to bother you,' she said. 'It's just that we weren't sure who was coming for the twins?'

'Me,' he said, without hesitating. 'I'm on my way now. Sorry. There's been some big fire over on the Gower? The Mumbles Road – it's all backed up.'

'Yes, yes, we know,' she said. 'And don't worry, you're not the only one who's been held up. We've got quite a handful of little ones still here.'

'Well, I'll not be long,' he said. 'Ten minutes tops.'

He tapped the taxi driver on the shoulder and gave him the school's address, then scrolled back through his phone messages. He tapped in the number Lauren had called him on and waited. It went straight to voicemail. No personal message to give him a clue whose phone it was. He left a message and then redialled. This time it was engaged so he rang off and sat, phone in hand, willing it to ring. It didn't.

'You alright, mate? You want me to open the window?'

'What? Yes. No, I'm fine. Thanks.'

'Bloody hot, eh?'

'Yeah. Yeah, it is.' Mackie wiped his face on his sleeve, checked the screen one last time, then tapped a message to Sharon. He kept it vague, said he wouldn't be back in but he'd call her later.

By the time he got to school the 'handful of little ones' had been claimed and Lauren's kids were the only two left in the playground. Miss Jones appeared as soon as his hand was on the gate.

'Sorry,' she said. 'I wasn't sure what to do. Who to call, you know?'

'My fault,' he said. 'I should have told you this morning.'

'Mum away?'

'What? Lauren? Oh, no. She's got something on, you know.' He was tempted to make something up, invent some clever job interview or college course but the twins were round his legs.

'Well, OK, see you in the morning, then,' Miss Jones said. 'Unless, mum...'

'No, it'll be me,' he said, too quick, forcing a smile.

'Well, lovely. Ooh, and don't forget. Last week of term now. Fancy dress tomorrow, but remember,' – pantomime hand to the mouth – 'nothing too warm!'

He nodded, took the twins' hands and left before he said something that could later be used in evidence.

'Where's Mummy?'

This was a bloody good question. Mackie had re-read the message he'd had from Lauren and couldn't see any other meaning to it than the one he'd assumed – that she was on her way to collect the twins. He'd tried to call her again – an unproductive exercise at the best of times – and got the 'number unavailable' message each time. Consequently, he fudged the answer and the walk back was pretty joyless, the twins whacked out and whiny and him too wrapped up in his own thoughts to pay them proper attention and put their minds at rest. His mind kept drifting back to the hospital. The way the kid had looked at him. What he'd said.

'Is she at home?'

Another good question – and one he hadn't really thought of. Of course, that's where she'd most likely be – at home, stretched out on the sofa, sleeping off the after effects of something illegal. The realisation – as depressing as it was – put a spring in his step.

'Come on,' he said, in a voice that sounded worryingly like Miss Jones'. 'We'll go and see. We'll remind her about those fancy dress outfits, too. What is she making, do you know?'

The twins looked at each other and then at him and gave a little synchronised shrug.

'Is she making them now, you mean?' Amber said. Her lips were pursed into a little bow like she was weighing up the idea of this. Like she was carefully reconstructing a world where her mother, who most of the time couldn't be arsed making a decent meal, was at the kitchen table sewing fancy dress outfits.

'Well, probably,' Mackie said. 'Let's have a guess at what they'll be...' It was starting to take on a bedtime story kind of feel. That make-it-up-as-you-go-along scenario, struggling to keep track of the plot when all you want to do is get downstairs and crack a can.

'A cowboy.' Amber let go of Mackie's hand and did a short gallop along the street.

'Yes, a cowboy. We'll be cowboys,' Tylo said and trotted on after her. Mackie almost joined in. Stopped himself at the last minute. It was the kind of thing he'd done when Lauren was small not realising how desperate he must have looked. Twenty-three years old, wife already dead, cavorting round the playground with a three-year-old.

You alright, Mackie?

Yeah, sound.

He thought people were being supportive. He was probably scaring the shit out of them.

Lauren and the kids lived on the Mercer Estate. It was nice. New build. Not easy to get a place there but they did, given Lauren's circumstances. Her circumstances being that she was the single mother of twins – courtesy of Lloyd Price, a no-good arse whose life plan consisted of two things – getting wasted and playing Xbox with his stoner mates. How he'd drummed up the energy to get her pregnant in the first place had always been a mystery to Mackie. To date, his only role in the twins' lives was as a threat she could suddenly fall back on if he didn't toe the line.

Mackie had cried when she got the offer from the council. It was tidy and pleasant, good neighbours – no scrap cars, barking dogs, unnerving gangs of kids etc – plus it was just round the corner from him. *Perfect place for a fresh start, love,* he'd said. Still full of hope at that point, see, not allowing for any slippage or for the fact that the hope was all his, not hers. But the steady trail of social workers, health visitors, community police officers – her support network had her marked out quicker than Blind Pew and his black spot and, before long, the people who had been so interested and charmed by her and the twins were starting to cross the street and distance themselves from her. And it was Mackie, not Lauren, who was mortified.

'Come on, Grandad.' The kids cantered up to him, side by side, straining on imaginary reins and making clicking noises, and waited for him to open the gate. He concentrated on the front door, determined to ignore the general wreckage of the garden. The living room curtains were open and he didn't know if this was a good sign or a bad sign.

'She's in, she's in,' the twins shouted when they got to the front door and found it off the latch and slightly open. They'd pushed in and Mackie followed behind.

'Mummy. We're home. Grandad's here ... Mum?'

She wasn't there. He clocked that as soon as he got through the door. No music on, no fag smoke hanging in the air. The place was a tip, but that was normal.

'She's not here, Grandad.' Amber was in the kitchen, staring at the kitchen table, contemplating the accumulated debris: a compendium of shitty stuff that never got washed, moved or put away.

'And they're not here,' she'd said, kneeling up on a chair and shifting a couple of cereal boxes to one side.

'What?' He was scanning the kitchen trying to get a reading. To the untrained eye the place looked abandoned or derelict or maybe the wrecked aftermath of some malicious break-in. But this was how she'd always lived. For some reason he couldn't fathom, Lauren thrived on it. The kids were another story, of course.

'Our cowboy outfits. They're not here.'

'Oh. Right, erm, let's have a think.' He was getting nothing from the room. The kettle was cold, the fridge was empty, the bread bin yielded a packet of sweaty crumpets. He flicked the light switch. At least she'd put some money on the electric. She might have just left or she might have gone a week ago. He'd weaved his way through the junk on the floor and into the living room, pulled back the curtains then closed them again. It wasn't the mess that got to him really because that could be sorted. Used to get sorted. He'd come round, willingly, for months after she moved in – *help you keep on top of things, love* – he'd wash the windows, tidy the garden, peg the clothes on the line, do all the things people do to show they're OK, they're managing. He'd stopped in the end: turned up one morning, with the Flymo and strimmer for god's sake, ready to really impress the neighbours, and found the police there. *Breaking up the party*, they said. He took the twins back home with him and waited for the knock on the door.

'Grandad.' Tylo was sitting on the bottom stair, his chin resting on his small fists.

'What, lad?'

'What will we do about our fancy dresses?'

'Did you check upstairs?' he said. He might have said he was humouring the lad except there was no humour in the situation at all as far as he could see.

Mackie followed behind as he clumped up the bare wooden treads. 'Mummy? ... Mummy?

She wasn't there. Mackie went into the twins' bedroom, gathered an armful of clothes off the floor and bundled them into a carrier bag. 'Come on,' he said, putting a perkiness in his voice that he neither felt nor trusted. 'I've got a good idea.'

6

Good ideas can be pretty easy when you're a kid. This was one of the things Mackie reminded himself of when he started getting complicated. *Trust in the little things, Mackie,* his counsellor used to say. Melody, her name was. Like a song. He used to wonder if her parents wanted her to be musical. She made him tell her all the things he liked doing when he was young: the things that he looked forward to, like what did he do when he got home from school. Watching cartoons then keeping out of his dad's way didn't seem like much of an answer, so he made things up. Things he thought you might like to hear if your name was Melody. He had no doubt she saw through him but she let him off the hook. After all he was the damaged goods, the one who needed his hand holding.

Anyhow, his good idea at that point had consisted of walking down to Tesco's: two birds with one stone, he'd thought – pizza and chips for the twins and, hopefully, a pair of cowboy outfits. The trip had been a bullseye from that point of view, but Tesco's, like it always did, had left him feeling unsettled, out of step, trying to work out how everything had changed so quickly – how the corner shop of his youth had been replaced by this juggernaut of a super-store. He'd traipsed round, dodging mothers, buggies and screaming kids, wondering – like some old codger – if this was what they called progress.

He got the kids bathed and in bed, then took himself out into the back garden trying to think of something to do that would take the fizz out of his head. He'd called Lauren's mobile on repeat then had to give up because it was making him feel worse. He settled himself on the bench and concentrated on what he could see. *Staying in the moment,* as Melody would have said. Next door's washing was still on the line: Dougie's work jeans, stiff-legged and crisp from the day's sun. Beyond that a string of pigeons were lined up on the house roofs – the sky above them trailing pale clouds that looked, if he moved his head in the right place, like snow on the rooftops. It worked for about five minutes and then his mind drifted back to Lauren.

It wasn't unusual. It's what she did all the time – swanning off somewhere without telling him, generally turning up the next morning unrepentant and amused by his anger, cocky because she knew he wouldn't show it in front of the twins. Eventually, he went inside and turned the telly on. He tried to engross himself in a film, but his mind kept butting in.

It's you. Why the hell had the kid said that? And why had it – he searched for the right word, the right feeling – why had it unnerved him so much? Did the kid know him? He shook his head to dismiss the thought then took himself to bed where he lay, fully clothed, staring at the clock, checking his phone and listening out for the twins.

Kids can be a great tonic. He actually used to believe that –

after Sandra died and it was just the two of them, him and Lauren. He'd hung his hat on that child, held onto her like he'd dived to the bottom of the ocean and fetched her up like a pearl. They were a great team – anyone would have told you that: cycling on a weekend, badminton club, judo. They did it all and they did it together. He went to sleep every night knowing what she was doing and where she was. Thought it would never change, even had this fantasy that one day, maybe after she'd finished at Uni and she was off travelling the world, he'd be able to shift up a gear – still have her under his wing, of course – but maybe start looking at what he wanted to do: drop the crappy jobs, do some training perhaps.

He looked back on this old version of himself sometimes: sifted back through the years and tried to find this man he used to be, like he could dust him down, breath some life into him. He'd even gone as far as sending off for a prospectus – *Counselling and Mediation.* He didn't even get it out of the envelope. Because it did change, of course. Or Lauren did. At thirteen she got awkward and moody, *hormonal* he'd thought, preparing himself to saddle up and ride it out. But by fourteen he was lagging behind and fifteen – by then she was more or less out of control, running a different race altogether, one he didn't recognise, and she got away from him – away up the field until he'd lost sight of her altogether. Nothing great about her then, his little pearl. *Challenging.* He took advice from professionals, read books, trawled the internet, but learned nothing that took the edge off, nothing that changed the fact that he'd lost her – and that he missed her.

He eventually did fall asleep because he was woken by his own cry, the sheet tangled in his hands and the pillow wet with tears. He'd dreamed his dream. The one that had stalked him for years after Sandra's death.

He is wading out to sea and it is dark. He has a torch but is struggling to keep it above the water because he's pulling a small dinghy behind him and the sea is choppy. There is something in the bottom of the dinghy but he can't see what it is. He strides further out until he can no longer feel the seabed and has to drop the torch and start swimming. The dark doesn't frighten him until the sea begins to swell higher, landing mean waves that slap against his face and slop over into the dinghy. He keeps going but the rope he is holding is burning his shoulder, and he can feel his legs starting to tire. 'We're almost there,' he shouts, although there is no one to hear. 'We're almost there.' Then the sea rises up like a wall and the dinghy tilts and the rope slips from his hands and the moon comes out from behind a cloud and he screams and thrashes through the waves towards the dinghy. But he is too late. It is empty.

Mackie hauled himself up and sat on the side of the bed, leaning forward as if he might make some more space in his chest, some room to reel his heart back in. He swayed gently, like he could still feel the rise and fall of the sea and buried his face in his hands, pulling the breath in between his fingers, slow and deep, drawing the air down into his lungs. Eventually, when he felt calmer, he went down to the kitchen and made a coffee. The sky was already fading towards day, fingers of paler blue breaking through the dark, so he unlatched the back door and took the coffee outside. The birds were already up and interested, dark silhouettes flitting in and out of the loose branches of the tree. A Rowan – *perfect for the suburban garden*. He'd planted it a few months after Sandra had died. So he wouldn't forget. So he could watch it growing and always remember. They used to put fairy lights in it at Christmas, him and Lauren, but it was too tall now.

He leaned back on the bench and sipped his coffee and allowed himself to think about the dream. Not properly, because he didn't trust himself to do that. Instead, like he had one eye closed and the other half open, he scanned over it quickly and realised that the intervening years had not changed it one bit. Neither the dream nor how it left him feeling. *Guilt feelings, Mackie,* Melody used to say, smiling at him over her cup of chamomile tea. They're *only natural so don't be afraid of them.* He knew what she'd be saying now. *Use your devices.* His devices. There was a time in his life when he thought that was something you aimed at the telly or maybe plugged into the computer – when the very mention of visualisation or mindfulness would have put a smirk on his face. But that was before. *After?* He clung onto the buggers like a drowning man.

7

'Grandad!'

The twins were at the back door, grinning at him. They looked like they'd walked off the Milky Bar Kid advert.

'Well, howdy there,' he said, in his best western drawl. 'You're looking mighty fine, this morning, pardners. Where d' you leave the hosses?'

'In the field,' Amber shouted.

'In the field? OK. Well, let's rustle you two cowboys some grub and then we'll saddle 'em up and ride into school.'

By the time he got into the kitchen they were already setting the table.

'Come on, sit down. I'll do that— '

He took the cereal box from Tylo and pulled a chair out for him. They had a way of seeing to themselves in the morning that made him want to weep. *Would it be too much, Lauren, to get up and make your kids their breakfast?* Apparently so. Apparently, the kids liked to get their own breakfast: it made them feel grown up.

'So – last week of school. I wonder what you'll be doing today. I wonder what Miss Jones will have up her sleeve?'

This was a bit of a double-barrelled question because Miss Jones, he knew, had plenty up her sleeve – her full quota of

45

Child Welfare Training for one, which meant his relationship with her was an uneasy mix of friendliness and caution – not unlike the one you might have with a neighbour's Alsatian, although he wouldn't say that to her, of course. When it came to Child Protection, she had a firm grip on her end of the rope – plus a bloody good team behind her – whereas his end was frayed and unreliable and there was only him pulling on it.

'Is Mummy back?'

Is Mummy back? That was another thing that made him want to weep – how Lauren treated them like some kind of afterthought but was still the centre of their small universe.

'Oh, I'm sure she will be,' he said. 'But she's probably still asleep? We'll ring her on our way to school, eh? Anyway— ' he was changing the subject, 'I've got a question for you both.'

Tylo straightened himself in his chair and put his spoon down. 'Do we need to put our hands up, Granddad?'

He took everything so seriously – five years old and already concerned with doing things right. It made Mackie want to breed it out of him, the way a horticulturist might: some gentle tweaking that would ensure stronger, healthier growth so that he wouldn't spend the rest of his life stunted by the fear of getting things wrong.

Like he had been.

'Hands up? Nah! That's for school. Let's have fingers on buzzers...'

Amber flashed him a big grin, ready for action. Tylo solemnly moved his bowl to one side and put one hand on the table – his finger poised over some imaginary button.

'So – your starter for ten – what's a cowgirl's favourite hairstyle?'

Silence. Then, from Tylo, 'Does it mean a cow – who's a girl?'

'No,' Mackie was beginning to wish he'd not said anything. 'It means a cowboy who's a girl. That's a cowgirl. Do you want a clue?'

He went to the kitchen drawer and got the hairbrush out – and a hair bobble – and put them on the table. The kids looked at them – and then back at him.

'OK, OK,' he said – because time was moving on – 'your final clue.' He tucked the tea towel into the back of his jeans and did a gentle trot around the kitchen table. Amber's face lit up.

'I know, I know,' she yelled. 'It's a tail. A horse's tail.'

'No it's not, Am,' Tylo said. Mackie could see the relief on the boy's face. 'It's a ponytail!'

Miss Jones was ready for him when he arrived. Her opening gambit was gleaming with the polished edge he'd come to recognise – suspicion dished up as friendly interest.

'Ah, Mum still away then?'

He wasn't ready for her. On the walk over he'd tried Lauren's phone several times and discovered that her mobile was not simply switched off, but no longer in use and, despite his best efforts, this new development had thrown him. On the one hand, he reminded himself, she had been in touch. The Gower thing might have panicked him, but she'd been in touch since then. Also – this was normal behaviour for her. She always came back eventually, so why would this time be any different? But the other hand kept tugging at him. Like what if he'd become too blasé about her behaviour – the boy who shouts wolf type scenario, that was suddenly going to end in disaster – so, by the time he arrived at school he was wondering whether he should maybe call the police – just to be sure...

'What?'

'Mum.' Miss Jones was keeping it breezy. 'She's still away?'

'Erm, no. She's busy.' He was praying the twins wouldn't butt in.

'Ooh, there's lovely.' She ushered the twins off to join the queue of kids lining up by the school door.

This was his cue to fill in a few details but he had nothing ready. They stood for a few moments, smiling awkwardly at each other, until, without warning, his phone rang.

'Ah, here we are,' he said, without looking at the screen. 'That'll be her now...' He turned on his heel and fled.

'Lauren?'

'Pardon?' A woman's voice, but not Lauren. 'Sorry,' she said. 'I was looking for, erm...' she paused. 'A Mr Mackie?'

'Yes?'

'Is that you?'

'Yes.'

'Ah, fabulous. It's Elaine here, from the unit? I think we met yesterday?'

The unit. It was the hospital. 'Oh, right.'

'Just to let you know – the young lad has woken up. He was asking for you.'

'What?'

'We were hoping you could pop up this morning?'

'Erm, well, no,' he said. 'Not really. I've got work...'

'Oh.'

It was the wrong thing to say, he could hear it in her voice. He could have stood his ground – simply reminded her that he didn't actually know the kid, that his involvement had been purely circumstantial, coincidental even. But he didn't.

'I'll do my best,' he said, thinking he was leaving his options open. That was the story of his life.

8

'She's not your fucking mother, kid, so fucking back off, right?'
Marco never called him by his name. It was like his mouth had
become too sharp and cold to say it. He didn't like it when the
kid cuddled up to Eileen on the sofa. He didn't like it when
she tucked him into bed.

'He can do that himself,' he snarled, when Eileen ran him a
bath or got this breakfast ready.

'True, true,' she said, in her lovely voice that sounded like
she was singing. 'But I just love to do it for him, don't I, pet?'
Then she would cup his cheek in her hand and Marco would
stomp out. 'It's just a phase,' she would say. 'He's missing your
dad.' And they would have a cup of tea and sit at the kitchen
table. Eventually, she admitted, it wasn't just a phase. It was
something else: something that sucked all the air out of the
house. Her house.

So they started playing a game, which wasn't a game really
because, although it made them feel better, they both knew it
was serious. They talked about the future, planning what they
would do when Marco had moved on. Because Marco was
definitely moving on. *Yes: he was going to move out and get his
own place, he was going to get a car and learn how to drive so
Drake wouldn't have to drive him everywhere.* Mostly though, he

was going to find his dad. He was going to do a lot of things but he never did any of them. And for this, the kid blamed himself.

It was a Friday the first time it happened. Eileen had picked him up from school early because he wasn't feeling well. He was in bed with a temperature, listening to a humming sound that might have been inside his head or out in the street. Afterwards he couldn't remember falling asleep except he must have done because Eileen woke him up as she was pulling the curtains. He could smell toast. She perched on the side of the bed and put her hand on his forehead.

'Now then, Mr Sleepy. How're you feeling?'

The kid considered the question. Strange, he might have said, but he didn't, because it didn't cover the sensation in his head: the humming sound had gone but in its place was an emptiness. Like a room stripped of furniture and brushed clean. Like there was a door open and cool air was blowing through his brain.

'Hungry?' he said. It was the right answer.

She produced the plate of toast with a flourish and helped herself to a slice.

'Guess what?' She held her hand underneath her chin as she took a bite.

He looked at her. 'Marco...'

Eileen nodded and chewed faster so she could get the toast down and the words out; it was unnecessary because somehow the words were already lined up in his head. He could see them standing side by side in the empty room.

'He's not come home,' the kid said.

'Absolutely right.' Eileen looked at her watch. 'Nine o'clock and not a peep.' The kid closed his eyes and concentrated on the empty room inside his head. The words had gone but he had his eye on the open door, waiting to see what would come in next. Nothing.

'What do you suppose? Do you think he's gone and done it at last?'

This was part of the game. It was his cue to make the next step.

'No,' he said. 'He's coming back.' It was the briefest flicker, too fast for him to catch, but, as soon as the words were spoken, a picture flashed through his brain: a dark place, bright lights in the distance. He shuddered.

'Are you alright, pet?'

'Tired,' he said and let his eyelids close. He heard her tiptoe out of the room then concentrated on his head. There was nothing there – no humming, no empty room, no picture – just the sound of the radio downstairs and the tick of the clock on the landing. He rested against the pillows and let himself drift off to sleep.

When he woke next morning, his sketchbook was on the floor beside the bed.

Marco was gone for three nights. They waited it out, clench-jawed and pale, trying to enjoy the lull and not think about the impending storm. It came nonetheless: Monday night the kid was woken by Marco's voice outside his bedroom door. He shuffled further down the bed so his head was under the duvet, then held his breath as the bedroom door opened. He didn't move. The light went on and Marco came in. He kicked the edge of the bed.

'I need some paper,' he hissed. He was on the phone. 'Yeah, yeah, give me a fucking minute, man— ' He booted the bed again then pulled the duvet off the kid's head. 'Paper,' he said. 'Get me some fucking paper, now.'

The kid slid out the other side of the bed. His school bag was hanging on the wardrobe door. He unhooked it and crouched down to open it.

'Fucking hell...' Marco barged over and snatched it off him and emptied it onto the bed. He picked up the kid's sketchbook.

'No,' the kid said, then shuffled through the pile and handed his maths book to Marco.

'Fuck off,' Marco batted it to one side. He sat on the bed, flicking through the sketchbook for a blank page. The kid squeezed his eyes closed and held his breath. *Don't see it, don't see it.* 'Yeah, hang on I'm ... fuck me.' Marco went quiet. The kid could hear him turning the pages. 'I'll phone you back, bro, OK?'

The kid waited. He suddenly needed the bathroom.

'What,' Marco said, slapping the page with the back of his hand, 'the fuck is this?'

The kid didn't need to look. It was his drawing, the one he'd done when he was ill – the one he hadn't known he'd done until he opened his sketchbook at school.

'I don't know,' the kid said, because it was the truth. 'It's just a drawing.' He looked down at the page in Marco's hand. It was mostly dark blue, a view through a car windscreen: a dark night outside, a row of streetlights, a platform strung up with lights that led out across a choppy sea and, in the near distance, a tower. He recognised it because he had looked at it so many times that day. But try as he might, he couldn't remember drawing it.

Marco stared at the page. 'Do you know where this is?'

The kid shrugged. 'No.'

Marco smiled and for a minute the kid felt himself relax. 'This is fucking unreal,' Marco said and he put his hand out and placed it on the kid's shoulder. 'Fucking unreal.'

He tapped a number into his phone and got off the bed. He turned at the door. 'I'll be back,' he said giving the kid a thumbs up and another smile and the kid, thinking it was some kind of praise, smiled back.

9

The kid was asking for him. The very thought had set Mackie's heart banging. He'd been halfway to the yard, head down, walking fast, trying to work it all out when, as he made the last turn towards the yard, he was struck by a sudden thought. He knew it was a clutching-at-straws kind of thought that Melody had cautioned him against, but he felt there was a certain logic to it. The thought was that maybe the kid did know him. Maybe they'd met at one of those overpriced, over-jolly Christmas dos the social services put on for foster families and the kid had recognised him. He might have stopped himself there because he could feel his mind beckoning him to a place he'd learned not to tell people about: a place that allowed him to slip down black holes and land at the feet of solutions and theories that had no bearing on reality. Melody had disapproved: *That's not a safe way to think, Mackie.* But Melody wasn't there to pull him back so he let himself go with it, following the helter-skelter of his mind until he dropped out at the bottom with the answer, like a winning ticket, clutched in his hand.

He would go and see what the kid wanted, and, if he did know him, he would fill in the blanks for the hospital, then walk away. It was a good idea and he grabbed it with both hands.

He sent a quick text to Sharon, then before he could change his mind, headed for the hospital.

The unit hadn't changed from the day before but the nurse on duty had. She regarded Mackie through the glass panel in the door – the expression on her face made him suddenly aware of how he looked: scruffy and a tad wired. He pulled his T-shirt straight and hoisted his jeans up.

'Can I help you?' Her voice came through a small intercom on the wall.

'Erm ... someone phoned me? Asked me to come in? To see the young boy. The lad from the scrapyard?'

'Are you family?' He made himself take a deep breath. She wasn't going to let him in and his idea, his good idea, was going to disappear down the drain.

'I was the one who brought him in,' he said, hoping that might gain him some ground.

She gave a small frown and consulted a clipboard. 'Mr Mackie?'

He was going to correct her, tell her Mackie was his nickname, not his proper name, but she already had him down as a bit suspect so he just nodded. She buzzed the door open and stood to one side to let him pass.

'He had quite a good night,' the nurse was referring to her charts, 'but he's not out of the water yet.'

He's not out of the water yet. The words pinged a small arrow into Mackie's heart.

'You'll need to put this on,' She handed him a long cotton

gown. He struggled getting his arms into it. 'Here, turn round.'
She fastened the tapes at his neck and the casual brush of her
fingers against his skin brought a flush of heat to his face.

'Thank you. I won't be staying long, I've got to get back to
work.' She gave him a stiff nod and held the door open for him
to go in. He hesitated a moment then walked up to the side
of the bed.

He couldn't tell if the kid was asleep or unconscious. Either
way he was still lying in a nest of wires and tubes, his face pale,
even against the white of the hospital sheets. He had a blood
drip in one arm and a bag of clear fluid going into the other.
A pair of slender tubes hissed oxygen straight into his nostrils
and although the bedside fan was on, his hair was still matted
and plastered to his head. Mackie shivered. The window blind
was down and the sun behind it lent the room a feeling of
warmth which wasn't actually there.

The kid looked cleaner, like someone had given him a wash,
but there was still an air of neglect about him, some sad
greyness ingrained into his skin.

'They said he'd woken up, that he was ... was asking for me?'

'Well, he did,' the nurse said, looking up from her clipboard,
'but he's gone off again. We're not sure what's going on. He'll
be having a scan later.' She hung the board back on the bed.
'I'll leave you for a minute or two, shall I? Make yourself
comfortable.' She indicated a chair positioned at the bedside.
'Give me a shout if you need me, yes?'

When she'd gone Mackie sat down and stared at the kid's
face, looking for something familiar. There was nothing. He

didn't know the kid at all. The scarring on his top lip was more evident now some of the dirt had been washed off. The cut above his eye had been dressed and the graze to his cheekbone was pooling into yellow and Mackie wondered if he'd been right the day before – maybe the lad had been put in the boxing ring.

The thought made him shudder. He knew all about being put in a boxing ring.

You need to give this game up, son, that's what they used to say to him: the doctors in A&E knew him by name. *Good god, Mackie, you're going to get yourself killed.* And they were right, of course. Nearly right. His last fight. It was touch and go, that's what Sandra said afterwards. *Touch and go, Mackie. You've got to give it up.* He didn't remember everything about it, of course, which was just as well because having a hole drilled in your head to get the blood clot out never struck him as something you would want to know about. When he woke up nearly a week later it was like his head was trapped inside a bell. Every movement of his eyes set up a reverberation that felt like his skull had been smashed with a hammer. A normal side-effect, apparently, of having the hole patched up with a metal plate. Eventually, he found that although he couldn't remember everything about it, he did remember the important thing – the thing that happened after he took the punch that knocked him senseless, that sent him down like a sack of wet sand. He remembered his face hitting the floor, watching a spray of sweat and blood fan out in front of his eyes as he suddenly lifted up out of his body, and rose towards the

58

ceiling. He remembered looking down at the ring: his father's face contorted with anger, mouthing words he could not hear; the ref with his hand in the air, the countdown long finished; Sandra up on her feet pulling at the ropes, and beside her, his arm around her shoulders, his mouth too close to her face, like some over enthusiastic understudy, his best mate, Spencer. Mackie watched him stroking her back, like he was rehearsing for the real thing. *Sandra*, he shouted, and that one word rocketed him back down to the boxing ring, back down into his body. Back to Sandra.

Mackie put his hand on the kid's bandaged arm, avoiding the tube taped to the back of his hand.

'Hello, they said you wanted to see me ... so I've, erm, I've just popped back to ... to see how you're doing.' He was wondering what else he could say when he felt a tiny movement beneath his fingers, a quiet sliding of tendon against bone. He looked at the kid's hand. His middle finger was raised slightly off the sheet. It held there for a moment or two then dropped. Mackie looked at his face, then back at his finger.

'Are you waking up, lad?' he said.

The finger moved once more and Mackie's heart picked up pace. He was out of the chair, on the verge of calling out for the nurse when a strange sensation at the back of his neck made him stop. He turned slowly – like a man in slow motion – to find the kid awake and staring at him.

'Oh, Christ,' Mackie said, 'hang on.' But the kid reached out as if to stop him.

'Wait,' he whispered and Mackie waited. The kid considered him for a long time – the same searching look that Mackie hadn't been able to pull himself away from the day before. His gaze was calm and unblinking; something otherworldly about it that made Mackie think of new-born babies – and the word came before Mackie could stop it – angels.

He pictured the look on Melody's face. More dangerous thinking. Or, worse still, magical thinking. *A natural part of childhood*, she'd informed him, but, like Santa and the tooth fairy, one we grow out of. She'd been asking him about his father, tiptoeing towards territory he'd not ventured into for years. *Inner child work*, she'd called it, but to him it was a no-man's land of tangled barbed wire, half-buried things he didn't want to look at too closely. He'd told her that he used to think someone might rescue him and she'd nodded – until he explained that he wasn't hoping for a concerned neighbour or the police, but for some kind of caped crusader. Some superhero zooming in and picking his dad up by the scruff of his neck and taking off with him. Melody had managed a small smile then launched into her magical thinking lecture. He had just listened, because how could a woman called Melody understand what it was like living with a father whose idea of a Friday night cool down was ten pints then beating the shit out of his kid? That the only escape on offer was to join the local boxing club so that he could learn how to beat the shit out of someone else?

The nurse suddenly appeared in the doorway.

'Everything alright?' she said. 'His alarm went off.'

'He ... he...' He glanced back at the kid and saw his eyes were closed again. He should have told her then about the kid moving his finger and opening his eyes – but he didn't – and he wasn't sure why. Part of it was he still didn't know why the kid had asked for him, and part of it – the part that would have put a big frown on Melody's face – was he couldn't shake the feeling that, although he definitely didn't know the kid, he somehow recognised him. He had no idea what that meant, but he knew he was on dodgy ground.

'Actually, I better get going.' He nodded towards the clock above the locker. 'Work ... you know— '

'I know.' She rolled her eyes and smiled. 'On a day like this too, eh?'

'Yeah.' He gave a short laugh. 'Right, then I'll...'

'Oh... You wouldn't do me a favour?'

'A favour?'

'His clothes. You wouldn't be able to wash his clothes, would you? Bring them back on your next visit?'

'Oh. Er, yeah. OK, yeah, I can do that.'

'Just give me a tick, I'll go get them.'

The kid opened his eyes as soon as she was gone and, with a small movement of his arm, beckoned Mackie over. Mackie's heart set off like a freight train but he couldn't resist. He went across and sat down beside the bed.

The kid blinked once, a slow motion, close and open, like the turning of a page, then took in a deep breath.

'Will you...' His voice rustled through dry lips.

61

'What?' Mackie could hear the nurse coming back.

The kid blinked again. 'Will you help me?'

Mackie looked down at the floor. *Don't get involved* Sharon had said and she was right: Lauren, the twins, Tranter – his plate was full enough already. He glanced over his shoulder, urging the nurse along, then back down at his feet: anywhere except the kid's face. And then the kid reached out and put his hand on Mackie's arm. It was the softest of touches – weightless, almost – but it sent a warm rush of blood coursing through Mackie's body: through his lungs, into his brain and then, in a rush of something golden, into Mackie's heart.

'OK,' he whispered. 'Yes.'

'My rucksack...,' the kid croaked. 'I need my rucksack.' Then he made a small noise in the back of his throat and closed his eyes again.

10

Mackie's head was ringing by the time he got back to the yard. This was not a good sign. The headaches weren't as bad as the early days, but still felt like someone was trying to hammer a metal bucket onto his head. He'd tried to explain it to the neurologist once, but the guy had given him a watery smile and told him he'd have to learn to live with it, spot the signs, avoid triggers, try nipping things in the bud with Anadin Extra, blah, blah, blah.

'Mackie.'

He'd timed it well. Sharon was just setting out the chairs. She'd got her leopard print ensemble on and her hair was pinned up in fat rollers which meant she was singing at the club later on. He could smell the coffee.

'Is he...'

'You're alright. He's not in. Phoned just after you, so I didn't say anything. He's gone to pick a machine up from some factory. He won't be in 'til after dinner.'

Mackie pulled one of the chairs further into the shade and sat down, grabbed the packet of digestives and ate two before Sharon was back out with the tray. She put it on the table then bobbed back into the office. He heard the crackle and whistle of the tannoy, then Sharon's voice – she could have made a fortune on a sex chat line – floated out across the yard. 'Come and get it, boys.' She was laughing when she sat down at the table. 'I am naughty,' she said.

'But nice,' he said, which was the right answer.

'Extra nice,' she said, waggling a Tesco's carrier bag. 'Doughnuts.'

'My god, Sharon, you know how to please a man.'

'Don't I ever,' she said, but there was a flat edge to her voice that said they both knew the truth about that and weren't going to talk about it. Sharon was 'romantically involved' (her words) with Barry Sowerby – the bloke who owned the club where she sang. A secret involvement, of course, seeing as Barry was married and, as far as Mackie was concerned, pretty devoid in anything he might call romance.

'Here,' she said, passing the bag over. 'Tuck in before Trev gets here, you know what he's like on a doughnut. Then,' she re-arranged herself on the chair, 'start spilling the beans.'

Mackie took a slurp of coffee then launched into the story he'd prepared. He'd got to the part about arriving at A&E when Trev sauntered up.

Sharon swallowed down a mouthful of doughnut. 'We're talking about the kid you found, Trev. Did they know who he was, Mackie?'

Mackie shrugged his shoulders. He might have said the kid seemed to know who he was, but he kept it to himself. Her question had thrown him off script. 'How would they know?'

'Missing persons,' Trev offered. He was keen on cop dramas. Generally had a Michael Connolly on the go.

'Well, they didn't seem to know who he was. Thought I was...'

His dad, Mackie was going to say, but he couldn't get the words past the lump in his throat.

'What?' They thought you were what?'

'I don't know. Thought I knew him.'

Trev was still in detective mode. 'What about his clothes, couldn't they identify him from his clothes?'

'Apparently not.'

Mackie could have mentioned the fact that the kid's clothes were in the carrier bag stuffed inside his overalls – but that would have involved explaining to Sharon why he had them – and he hadn't got that part of the story quite clear in his head. Soft, she'd call him – but she hadn't seen the state of the poor kid. He'd had a quick look in the bag when the nurse handed it over, then shoved it inside his overalls. There was a T-shirt and a pair of jeans. No underwear, no shoes – nothing that could be described as a rucksack. The only place it could be, he'd decided, was the Merc. His plan was to look for it as soon as he'd finished his coffee.

'My mum reckons I could probably claim,' Trev said.

'What?'

'Claim. You know, accident at work. The trauma.'

Sharon helped herself to another doughnut. She gave it a squeeze and licked the jam off the side. 'Actually, Trev, the most traumatic thing about yesterday was when your bloody mother turned up.'

Trev ran his fingers around the inside of his roll-neck. It was still pristine. Bertha ironed him a fresh one every morning. They lent a reverential air to his oily boiler suits. They reckoned she must have had hopes for him taking the cloth.

'What happened, then?' Mackie said, embracing the opportunity to change the subject. 'After I left?'

Sharon let out one of her low rumbling laughs. 'Pin your ears back, Mackie boy, and I'll tell you.'

The second ambulance arrived, apparently, not long after Mackie had left with the first ambulance, and just before Bertha got there. This, according to Sharon, was a godsend because not only did it swell their ranks, it meant that when Bertha stormed the gates, Trev had a pair of paramedics fussing over him.

'Trevor,' she'd bellowed. She was wearing an apron. Leather. 'Mum...'

Bertha had inserted herself between the two paramedics who, unaware of who they were dealing with, calmly shuffled her to one side so they could get on with what they were doing.

'We won't be a minute, dear. If you could just stand back...'

'She just ignored them,' Sharon said. 'Then she hollered, "Trevor, stop all this nonsense and get off the flaming floor."'

She had barged between the paramedics and glared down at Trevor who, Sharon admitted, was starting to get some colour back in his cheeks, then grabbed hold of Trev's arm and hauled him up like he was a dog on a lead. He'd stood for a few seconds, suspended, Sharon reckoned, by fear, then the whitewash effect reappeared and he sank to the floor again. Bertha, undeterred, stuck her hands on her hips and, looking at no one in particular, yelled, 'Get Tranter over here. Now.'

This didn't take much doing because Tranter, according to Sharon, was hovering in the office, watching the proceedings.

'Mrs Tyndall,' he called. She spun on her heels and steamed across the yard, leaving Sharon and the paramedics looking down at Trev who opened one eye, gave them a jittery smile, then wet his pants.

'Wait here while we go get the trolley,' one of the paramedics said, and shot off leaving Sharon gawping at Trev and trying to hear what was happening to Tranter.

Whatever it was, Tranter was saved by the bell because the two paramedics came back and in less than a minute, they had Trevor loaded and strapped down under a red blanket. They set off across the yard at a lick, hoping, no doubt, to lose Bertha. A good plan, but futile.

'Oy. Where the hell do you think you're going?' Bertha had shouted. They kept moving. One of them looked back over his shoulder.

'Taking him to Morriston, love. You'll have to get a move on if you want to come.'

'Well, she was out of the office and across the yard like she'd been shot out of a cannon,' Sharon said. 'Honestly, Mackie, I thought I was going to...' She stopped mid-sentence. 'Oh, shit. His nibs is back early. Quick.' She got to her feet, grabbed the doughnuts and started stacking empty cups on the tray. 'Go on, lads,' she said, without looking at them. 'Look lively.'

Mackie folded the chairs and leaned them against the office wall, listening to the grind and wheeze as Tranter angled the lorry through the gates, then set off towards the stockpile aisle. He knew Tranter was crap at manoeuvring, so if he was lucky he'd have time to check the Merc before he'd managed to get the lorry parked up.

'Mackie.' Sharon was coming after him. 'Are you OK?'

'I'm fine,' he said. 'Had a bit of a headache.'

'What about your Lauren?'

'I don't know. She's...'

'Dropped you in the shit again.'

'Yeah. Something like that.'

'Suppose that means you can't come down the club tonight.' She swept her hands down the front of her outfit.

'Why don't you come round after?' he said. 'We could have a proper catch up.' He wasn't entirely sure what that meant except he'd only managed to tell her part of the story before Trev butted in. He'd been relieved at the time but now, back in the yard – back in real life – the hospital, the kid, and the idea that he could help him, all seemed like part of a dream.

'Sorry, mate. I've had a better offer.'

'Barry?'

'Got it in one.'

11

The Merc was still where Tranter had dropped it, garlanded with a double row of blue police tape. Mackie noticed that the hubs were gone. So much for Trev and his bloody trauma. He walked around the car, avoiding the stuff the paramedics had left behind then, without touching the bodywork, leaned his head in through the back window.

'Can't touch that.' Tranter's voice came out of nowhere.

'Shit.' Mackie stood up too quick and caught the back of his head on the door frame. The inside of his skull struck up like a church organ.

'I was wondering where you'd got to,' Tranter said.

Mackie waited. He was pretty sure where Tranter was heading.

'So. Yesterday. What time d'you get back in?'

There it was. You had to hand it to the man – true colours through and through. No interest whatsoever in the kid – his only concern was how much he could get away with docking off Mackie's wages.

'Er...' Mackie didn't know what to say. 'I...'

'We'll call it half a day, then. I'll tell Sharon. Oh, and by the way, the police are coming back so keep off that Merc.'

'Right you are,' Mackie said. He waited until Tranter was out of sight, then went over to the car.

Trev said the kid had been on the back seat. He could see nothing other than an empty crisp packet and a banana skin. He ducked his head back in through the window and looked at both footwells. At first glance they looked empty but, when he walked round and pushed his head in the opposite door, he spotted something underneath the driver's seat. He stood up carefully and looked back to where Tranter had disappeared, then pulled his sleeve over his hand – too many cop shows – leaned into the Merc and drew out a small rucksack.

'Mackie.'

He swivelled round at the sound of Tranter's voice. 'Mackie. Where the fuck are you?'

'I'm coming,' he yelled, already jogging away from the Merc. He tossed the kid's rucksack through the smashed windscreen of a Golf and legged it towards the lorry.

The afternoon went quickly thanks to Tranter's new purchase – a couple of machines from some engineering works that were being demolished. Christ knows who'd loaded them on but it took the two of them, three if you counted Tranter – who was reffing from the sidelines – to get the buggers off.

'Christ almighty, Mackie, look like you're bloody trying.'

'It won't budge.'

'Get out of the sodding way, then.'

Mackie watched as Tranter wrestled with the fastening.

'Oh, for fuck's sake,' Tranter snarled. 'Mackie.'

Mackie jumped to attention.

'Go and get the big knife off Sharon.'

Mackie swivelled on his heels and hot-footed it to the office. Sharon had been listening. She was in the doorway with the knife at the ready.

'Do you need to get away for the twins?' she said.

He nodded. 'Christ knows how I'm going to do it. I'll ... I'll just have to tell him. Ask him. He's already docking me half a day.'

'Rather you than me,' she said, nodding her head towards Tranter. He was hitting the ratchet with a lump hammer. Trev had backed right off.

'Time for his tablets,' Sharon said. 'Oops. Better get a move on, Mackie.'

Tranter had flung the hammer on the ground and was standing on the back of the trailer, hands on his hips, yelling for the knife. Mackie jogged over.

'Quick cup of tea, was it? Here, give me that fucking knife.' Mackie handed it up and stood back as Tranter unleashed the blade from its leather scabbard, held the knife aloft and brought it down onto the strap. It cut through in one, releasing the tension in the webbing and the ratchet end whipped through the air and clocked him on the side of the head.

'Whoa...' Mackie jumped up onto the back of the trailer and grabbed hold of Tranter.

'Christ's sake, get the fuck off.' Mackie stared at him. It was unbelievable that the bloke was still on his feet.

'Are ... are you...' He was still waiting for him to keel over.

'What?'

'That was a hell of a knock.'

Tranter looked at him like he didn't know what he was talking about.

'Well?' he said, hands on his hips again. 'What the fuck are you two waiting for. Get this unloaded.' He booted the machine. 'Now.' With that he leapt down from the trailer and walked off across the yard.

'Christ. He must have a thick skull,' Mackie said. It had been a long time, but he could remember what it felt like to take a knock like that.

'Either that, or he's got a fucking guardian angel,' Trev said.

'What?'

'You know,' Trev said, and made some kind of flapping motion with his arms. 'A guardian angel, yeah?'

'That's magical thinking, Trev,' he said, although the words had set his heart racing.

'Yeah, well it wouldn't go amiss, Mackie, would it?' He gazed around the yard. 'I mean, look at this place. Look at us lot. I reckon we could all do with a bit of fucking magic.'

Mackie didn't reply. He had never challenged Melody's lecture on magical thinking because, basically, he wasn't well enough at the time: the medication and the crippling slog with psychiatrists and social workers had been enough to cope with, never mind trying to explain himself and run the risk of landing deeper in the shit. Nonetheless, there was an explanation. He just didn't tell people about it.

He thought about what Trev had said. *A guardian angel* – because the words had not only set his heart racing – they'd conjured up an image of the kid.

It was knocking on three o' clock by the time they got the machines off the trailer. Tranter had been back and forth, *overseeing,* which meant that Mackie hadn't had a chance to try Lauren again. He waited until Tranter was out of the way then dodged behind the lorry cab and got his phone out. He checked for messages – there were none – then rang her number. He was waiting for the answer machine to kick in and realised that the line had connected: her phone was ringing. He listened to it ring – once, twice, three times – then, with a small warning beep, his phoned died. He jogged over to the office.

'Sharon, can I use your phone?'

She handed it over. She'd just done her nails. 'School?' she said, looking at the clock above the desk.

He nodded, and tapped in Lauren's number. 'Come on, come on,' he said. The phone didn't connect. 'Shit.' He tried again and the answer machine picked up. 'Lauren,' he yelled. 'Where the hell are you? Ring me for god's sake.'

'You OK, Mackie?'

'Yeah, yeah. I'm going to have to go get the twins.'

'How long has she been gone this time?'

'Too bloody long. Friday night. I said I'd have them 'til Sunday. She didn't come back.'

'You're too soft on her, you know.'

'I know, I know,' he said, 'but what am I supposed to do, Sharon? What am I supposed to do? You can't just turn your back on people, I...'

He made himself stop. 'Where's Tranter?' he said. 'I'll have to go break the bloody news.'

'He's round with the Merc. The cops came to look at it.'

'OK. Wish me luck.'

'Hey, hang on.' She chucked a Tesco's bag at him. 'Them doughnuts were on special offer. You and the twins can have these on the way home.'

He waited until he was out of sight, then slipped the kid's clothes out of his overalls and put them in with the doughnuts.

There were two cops: one in uniform and one in jeans. They had their backs to Mackie but Tranter was watching as he approached – which foiled Mackie's plan to grab the kid's rucksack out of the Golf.

'Ah, this is the bloke who accompanied the lad to hospital,' he said.

The cops swivelled round and Mackie's heart sank. He knew the uniformed bloke, or he knew him. Them. He knew Lauren – her situation. He gave Mackie a slight nod.

'Ah, we were hoping to have a word with you,' he said. 'You've met our mystery lad, I believe?'

'Erm, yeah. I went with him, you know. In the ambulance. Have you found out who he is?' Mackie said.

The officer shook his head. 'No. But we might have something to go on.'

He stepped forward and held out a couple of photographs. Mugshots. 'Do you recognise either of them?' Mackie tucked the Tecso's bag under one arm and bent to look at the photographs. Two blokes. One in his early twenties, maybe – small wiry-looking guy with dark eyes. A *fuck-you* expression on his face. It was harder to tell with the other guy because of the mess his face was in. He was a bit older, maybe, although that might have been the bruising round his eyes.

'No,' Mackie said. 'Who are they?'

'They were picked up from a motorway smash a week or so ago. This one was the driver – he pointed at the bruised guy. But this one – this is the one we're trying to get hold of.'

'Oh?'

'Yeah. We think he might be able to tell us something about this kid you found?'

'Right.' Mackie was working hard to reel himself in. He was trying to work out how to ask more without asking. 'So...'

'He was asking about a kid, see? When they took him to the hospital? He was a bit out of it and he kept asking if they'd found a kid.'

'Have you been to the hospital then, and asked the kid about it?'

'Yeah. But he hasn't woken up yet. We're going back after we've finished here.'

'Could I have a word, boss?' Mackie said, and walked away a few steps more, hoping Tranter would follow. He didn't, so he had to say his piece in front of the cops which meant he ended up fabricating an entire scenario that involved Lauren attending an interview that had overrun. By the time he'd got to the end of the explanation, he was running with sweat and the three of them were looking at him like he was some half-assed comedy act.

'Sounds like you better go then,' Tranter said.

'Yes. Thanks,' Mackie said and, for some reason gave the three of them a small wave. 'I'll see you in the morning, then...'

'Most obliging of you,' Tranter said. He put his hands on his hips and turned so the cops could hear him. 'Sounds to me like we need a bit of a chat, lad. I don't do part-time, so maybe if that's what you're looking for you need to get yourself down the Job Centre. I'll see you in my office first thing.'

'Right,' Mackie said. He wanted to stroll away slowly but time was ticking. He set off at a jog knowing it made him look pathetic.

Trev was right – they could all do with a bit of magic in their lives.

12

The kid was concentrating. He was trying to block out the sounds around him – the soft hiss from the oxygen tube; the quiet beep of the machine that sat beside his bed and sent messages to the nurses; the steady whirr of the fan that blew cool air over him – so that he can hear the voices outside his door. He couldn't hear what was being said, only that there were men – two men – talking to the nurse. There was only one explanation he could think of – one terrifying explanation: Marco and Drake had found him. He closed his eyes as the door opened and he waited to hear his brother's voice.

'So, has he said anything yet?'

He was wrong. It wasn't his brother. Nevertheless, he lay completely still, kept his eyes closed and listened.

'Not really. Nothing real, if you know what I mean. A bit of rambling, that kind of thing. The meds – and the dehydration of course. How about you – any leads on who he is?'

'Any leads?' They were police officers.

The kid imagined simply opening his eyes and telling them everything: who he was, where he was from, what had happened. Telling them about Marco and Drake, the accident,

77

how he got to the scrapyard. But he knew what would happen if he did that because Marco had drilled it into him often enough. Go to the police and social services would jump straight in. Then there'd be a lot of talking and a swift trip into foster care. Then how would he ever find Eileen? How would she find him?

So, he kept his eyes shut and kept listening.

'Have either of these two visited him?' the police officer said, and the kid heard the slight rustle of paper.

'No. He's only had one visitor. A Mr Mackie – from Tranter's. The scrapyard?'

'Yeah, we know. We've just had a word with him."

'So – who are these, then?'

'Not sure. But this one' – the kid heard him tap the paper – 'this one was brought in after an RTA. Got a bit chopsy in A&E and they called us in. He was off his head on something but started ranting on about a missing kid. Then this young beggar turns up and we maybe put two and two together, so...'

'So where is he now?'

'We've been trying to get hold of him. Need him to come up and check this kid out. See if it's him he's looking for.'

The kid couldn't stop himself. He let out a gasp – and his machine started beeping.

He imagined sitting up and telling them everything. Telling them about Marco – what he'd done, what he was going to do if he found Eileen, but the nurse was busy at his side. He felt the give in his head as the fluid she was injecting into his arm swam out into his bloodstream. He held on for as long as he could, but he was slipping. Slipping. Slipping back again into the past.

Six weeks earlier. The kid had intended to leave the scrapyard the next morning. He had unfastened his rucksack, hoping that the drawings in his sketchbook – and Marco's research – would lead him to Eileen. But the rucksack was empty. He unzipped the compartment in the lid and checked that the photograph was still there, then climbed out of the Cruiser and went looking for the way out. The gates were padlocked and chained – and too high to climb. He contemplated the fence that circled the yard – its top unreachable and laced with barbed wire. The heat and the pain in his head sent him looking for water but, as he was scooping his hands under a hosepipe, he heard a car pulling up nearby. He scooted back across the yard and dodged behind a stack of scrap cars. Without thinking he stepped up onto the door frame of a mini and reached for a hold on the car above. He could hear the rattle and grind of the gates opening so, trying to ignore the pain in his wrist, pulled himself up. Up and up he climbed, until he reached the car at the top. A blue Mercedes. He grabbed its roof with both hands, threw his rucksack in then swung himself through the back window – just as a car drove into the yard and parked below him. He watched as a woman got out and walked across the yard to a small wooden building. Before he knew it, days had gone by and he had made a home in the Mercedes. It was the colour of the sky and perched, like a crow's nest, on the top of the tower. The sun beat down on it all day and, as it ticked and throbbed around him, his head grew lighter, emptier – as if he were on the edge of sleep. Sometimes he let his gaze lift above the high fence and he contemplated the horizon like a sea captain surveying an uncharted stretch of water. Sometimes he watched the people down in the yard. He watched the woman as she set out chairs for tea break. She wore shiny pink leggings and a top with sequins on. Her blonde hair was stacked on her head and bobbed like a small cloud. She looked, the kid thought, like a mermaid. She called the men on a microphone then brought out the coffee and biscuits. One man was small and he looked sad. The other wore a white top under his overalls that made him look like a vicar. He had a van by the back wall of the scrapyard where he hid a small store of car parts and, sometimes, food. The kid watched them as they ate. He tried to switch his hunger off but it was gnawing a hole in him.

At night he crept down and drank at the tap, splashing water onto his face, hunched over, ready to disappear into the shadows. He had learned to move around the yard without tripping the light sensor.

He spent hours staring at the photograph, hoping it would direct him to the white room. It didn't. He thought about Eileen, trying to catch some thread that would lead him to her – but she felt so far away.

The drawing made things worse. He remembered waking to the sound of Marco shouting at Eileen: his voice like a machine gun, a spray of words that rattled around the kitchen and didn't stop. Eileen stayed quiet: tired of it, the kid knew. Also frightened. They were both frightened but his fear was that she would leave – that he would come home from school to find her gone and Marco at the helm. He heard the kitchen door slam and turned sharply onto his side. Marco came in and sat on the bed and touched the kid's shoulder. A wash of acid rose into his throat.

The kid rolled onto his back and Marco leaned in closer. His mouth smelled of cigarettes. He had the sketchbook in his hand. 'You know what this means, don't you?'

The kid shook his head.

'It means you're like mum, a *Clairvoyant*.' The kid didn't know what that meant.

'It means you can see things — like she could.' The kid looked at the drawing, unsure of what Marco wanted him to say. 'So ... I've got you something because we need to start practising.'

Marco emptied a carrier bag onto the bed. It was another sketchbook– a proper artist's sketchpad. The kid opened it and stroked his hand across the paper. The feel of it beneath his fingers ran a cold thread through his heart.

When it started it was like a game. *Like hide and seek,* Marco said. *I'll hide somewhere and you see if you can find me.* The kid didn't understand the first time because, while his eyes were closed and he was counting, he heard Marco go downstairs, then out through the gate. He got off the bed and watched as Marco got into Drake's car and they drove away.

When he came back a couple of hours later his clothes smelled of rain even though it wasn't raining.

'Go on then,' Marco said, opening the drawing book at the first page.

'What?'

'Where did I go?' The smile on Marco's face put a knot in the kid's stomach.

He pushed the drawing book away. 'I don't know. I thought we were playing hide and seek. But you went out.'

'Course I went out. That's the whole point, isn't it?'

'I ... I don't—' The kid didn't know. He didn't know what the point was.

'Come on, Riley.' Marco pushed the drawing book back towards him.

The kid felt another wash of acid in the back of his throat. Marco never called him by his name. He swallowed hard and picked the sketchbook up.

'Like last time ... just draw a picture of where I've been. Here—' He tossed a pencil across the bed.

'But I—' He didn't know how he did it last time. Part of him didn't believe he had done it.

'How the fuck did you know?' Marco had said.

'Know what?'

'That we were in fucking Blackpool?'

'You'll have to go out,' the kid said. 'I can't do it if you're here.'

'No problemo, kid,' Marco was smiling again. He patted the kid on the side of the face. 'Keep at it, yeah. No arsing around. I want to see it as soon as I get back.'

The kid took the drawing book to the small desk under his window and sat down. He understood now what Marco wanted him to do but he didn't know how to do it. It happened by itself last time. He had a vague memory of a strange empty feeling in his head and closed his eyes trying to bring it back. He thought about Marco: how he would be smiling when he came back through the door, expecting a result. How his face would change when he saw the blank page. He looked out through the window and gazed down the road. He counted streetlights and garden gates; parked cars and people; trees and car headlights. Then he got up and went downstairs to Eileen. She was in the sitting room, doing one of her puzzle books.

'Ooh, I'm glad you're still awake,' she said, tapping the page. 'I'm stuck. Come and give me a hand.'

He sat down and eased himself into her side.

'Where's Marco gone?'

'He didn't say.' She bent down and rested her chin on the top of his head.

'Are you OK?' he said. This was the question constantly in his mind.

She gave a funny little laugh. 'OK? Course I am. Always OK, me.'

He knew this wasn't true.

'Don't you be worrying. Things will get better, you'll see.'

He knew this wasn't true either. He could feel it in the air – even when Marco wasn't there: something tight that made him want to hold his breath.

Afterwards, he wondered if it was this thought that made it happen because, all of a sudden, his head started to hum and a picture flashed past his eyes.

'Oh.'

Eileen peered down at him. 'What?'

'I ... I think I need to go to the toilet.' He jumped off the sofa and ran up the stairs.

'Have you been at the fizzy drinks again?' she shouted after him, but he didn't dare answer because he didn't want to stop whatever it was that was happening. He shut the bedroom door, sat down at the desk, closed his eyes and waited. He concentrated on the humming sound: how it filled every part of his head, how it took away everything except itself. Then without warning, it stopped.

He opens his eyes and finds himself in a brilliant white room. He can hear nothing. A cool breeze is blowing across his face and he turns towards it. In the corner of the room is an open door. He approaches it and, without hesitating, steps through and floats out into a bright cloudy sky. He stretches his arms out and swims through the clouds, feeling their cool breath on his hands and face as they part before him, up and up until his head suddenly bursts through into brilliant sunlight and at the same time his feet find solid ground.

He looks around and, although thick clouds lay at his feet, frothing and surging like a carpet of foam, the thought comes into his head that he can see everything.

He raises his arms as though they are wings, springs up into the clear air and glides out into the blue sky – out like a bird, feeling the heat of the sun on his back and the strength in his arms. His eyes scan the carpet of cloud and, without understanding it, he knows what he is looking for. A clue. In the distance something is sticking up through the swirling white. A lighthouse. He tucks his arms into his sides and, like a dart, aims himself towards it. He travels quickly but the lighthouse disappears before he gets there: it sinks away beneath the clouds, leaving in its place a neat, round hole. He glides to a halt, landing gently on his belly, at the rim of the hole. He peers down and there he is: Marco.

The kid picked up the pencil and drew without looking at the page, as if he was still above the clouds in the place where he could see everything. When he finished, he went back down to Eileen.

'That was quick.' She put her arm round him. 'Everything OK?'

'Yep.'

'I've been thinking,' she said, then stopped – a sudden burst of bass beat drifted in from outside. Marco was back.

'Quick, you go up to bed. I'll tell him you're asleep.' She followed him out of the sitting room and went into the kitchen. The kid noticed that she unlocked the back door. He ran up the stairs and was just getting into bed when Marco came into the bedroom.

'You done it then, kid?'

The kid flicked his eyes over to the sketchbook. Marco picked it up, considered it for a moment or two then tossed it onto the bed.

'What the fuck is that?'

The kid didn't say anything. He lets his eyes rest on the open page.

'It's ... I don't...'

'That's not what you were supposed to do,' Marco said, picking the drawing up again. 'This – this is Drake's fucking car. I mean, anyone could draw that. And this, what's this supposed to be?' He leant over the kid and pointed at the lines drawn around the edges of the page.

'It's a window,' he said. 'I saw you through a window. You were parked outside in the street waiting for someone – looking for someone,' he added, before he could stop himself.

'What window?'

The kid took a deep breath and closed his eyes. 'A café, I think.'

Marco grinned and walloped the kid on the back of the head. 'Fuck me. You've got it. One hundred fucking percent ... shit, wait 'til I tell Drake...' Then he was out of the bedroom, out of the front door, already talking on the phone. Excited: whatever the drawing meant, Marco was excited by it. The thought slid like ice down the back of the kid's neck.

13

Mackie jogged the entire distance to the school and reached the gates on the stroke of 3.30pm, so he was puzzled to find the playground empty. He pushed through the gate and made for the main entrance wondering if his watch was wrong when Miss Jones, who must have been on lookout, bustled out through the double doors flanked by the twins. They were drooping.

'Am I early?' he said.

'Late, I'm afraid,' she said, with a smile that looked more like a wince.

'But it's...' he pushed up his sleeve, ' ...it's just gone half past.'

'Early finish today, remember, Mr Carpenter, early finish. Mum did have a note.' She arranged her mouth into a little bow. 'Ready for our early start tomorrow? The school trip. Perhaps you'd like me to write another note for Mum. Or give her a ring, perhaps?'

'What? No. My mistake. She must have told me and – this heat, you know.'

She didn't know. She didn't have a fucking clue.

'OK, kids?' He held his hands out and the twins shuffled towards him. 'My goodness, Miss Jones. Looks like these two have been rode hard and put away wet.'

'I beg your pardon?'

'Like they've – it's a cowboy saying, you know – about horses—'

'Oh.' She gave him a smile that barely lifted the corners of her mouth.

He soldiered on. 'Anyway,' he said. 'Not long 'til the big holidays now. Hope you've got something nice planned.'

It would be something wholesome, he reckoned, like cycling round Brittany, or bird watching in the Pyrenees. He couldn't see her giving it large in Ibiza.

'I have,' she said. 'But how about you? Are the twins with you again?' Mackie had to stop himself re-running Lauren's interview story. 'Oh, no. Not like that. They are at the moment, of course, just for a couple of nights.'

'Nothing official, then?' she said. She was referring to the respite fostering arrangement, the one that had eventually been set up for him and Lauren. It had frightened the life out of him at first – given his history – but had turned out to be a good idea for most people: it ticked a box for social services, stopped people like Miss Jones getting too antsy and meant the twins were always safe. He never let himself look too closely at what he got out of it, but it certainly didn't involve any respite.

'Anyway,' he said. 'Better get these two cowboys home. Packed lunches tomorrow, is it, Miss Jones?'

'No need, Mr Carpenter, no need. The coach is leaving at 8.30 sharp. Home at 6pm. OK?'

'Brilliant,' he said. Because, at the time, he thought that bit of leeway, that slight release of pressure would make the next day so much easier.

The evening started well because the twins were whacked and more or less offered to go to bed, which then made it hard because, without the distraction of their company, Mackie started to unravel. Not in a big way, the kind that would have put the little crease in Melody's forehead, but enough to make him put the can of lager back in the fridge and put the kettle on.

He took his mug of tea outside and sat on the bench under the tree and made himself think ordinary thoughts. He thought of Sharon. She'd be 'backstage' now, (Barry Sowerby's name for the store cupboard when he had a live act on) revving herself up with a couple of glasses of Prosecco. *Crazy Sharon*. She was his star turn. She did Patsy Cline covers and the punters couldn't get enough. He'd had posters made specially – Sharon on stage, eyes closed, breathing into the microphone like she's giving it life support. When she sang, no one moved. It was like she cast a net over the audience, hauled them in and took them with her. She earned Barry a fortune.

'Alright, Mackie?'

Jan Jeary was standing by the gate at the end of the garden.

He gave her the thumbs up. 'Fine, Jan yeah. You having a bit of a do, then?'

She lifted her arms so he could see the carrier bags. 'Got some reduced steak,' she said. 'You fancy coming over? Derek's got the barbie going. He's filled the paddling pool.'

He flicked his head towards the bedroom windows. 'They're already asleep. Bushed.'

'Come on your own then, you could keep nipping back to check on them.'

'Nah,' he said. 'Thanks for the invite, though.'

'Well, if you change your mind...'

'Yeah, I know.'

'You want me to pick 'em up in the morning – early start for the trip, isn't it?'

'Oh, yeah. Why not. Thanks.'

Jan Jeary was his fall back when it came to the twins. Part of the support system that kept the whole Lauren show on the road: so much mortar holding the whole thing together, it should have felt safe. Instead, it felt like a house of cards – ready to crash down at any minute.

He sat there a while longer, nodding and waving at various people as they walked past on their way to the barbecue until he couldn't stand it anymore and made himself get up and go inside. It was one thing to feel lonely, it was another to have every bugger in the street feeling sorry for you.

He got the can of lager back out of the fridge and necked half of it before he'd closed the door, apologised to Melody, got a second can and went and plonked himself on the sofa in front of the blank telly. His reflection stared back at him. Unsparing. He didn't need a crystal ball to predict his future because he was already halfway there – if he didn't do something about it, he was going to end up with Lauren's kids full-time. Agreeing to foster them was one thing – it had got them out of a fix – but now? Now they were with him more than they were with her. *I don't want to bring them up,* he'd said to Sharon once – half because it was true and half because he wanted to see how it would feel if he said it out loud. It felt crap. *Stop stepping in then, Mackie,* she said. *Stop filling the gap every time your Lauren messes up.* She was right. *Let social services step in*, she said. They'd have to step in if there was no one else. *You don't need to tell me that,* he'd wanted to say, but he didn't because that was part of his life that he just didn't talk about anymore – not even to Sharon.

It was the third can of lager – and the thought of the crystal ball – that had him sliding back into dodgy territory. He leaned back on the sofa, as the alcohol teased the knots out of his brain and closed his eyes. Before long he was thinking about the kid again – about seeing him in hospital – what he'd said, how he'd looked at him, *what he'd thought.*

He'd dismissed it at that point, of course: *fanciful thinking, Mackie,* as Melody would have said and he would have nodded his head in agreement. But now, his brain bobbing along like a balloon off its string – he would shake his head and tell her what he chose not to tell her at the time. He would tell her about the picture.

Mackie's grandmother had died when he was three years old. He had no memory of her other than the few facts passed onto him by his father: that she was strict Chapel, she didn't approve of enjoyment in any form and she hated men – him in particular. The picture had belonged to her. His mum had come back from the funeral with it, gone to his father's shed for a hammer and nail and, still in her coat and hat, hung it above the kitchen door. It was a quote from the bible: *Be not forgetful to entertain strangers; for thereby some have entertained angels unawares. Hebrews 13:2*

The words were framed by a loose trail of flowers and he got to know them by heart. Not just know them, but, young enough at that point to embrace Father Christmas and the tooth fairy, to believe them.

The truth was, despite Melody and the psychiatrist, and, for that matter, Section 63 of the bloody Mental Health Act, he'd never really stopped believing them. Which made the next step easy:

The way the kid had looked at him, how he'd made him feel – *what he'd said.*

Maybe the kid was an angel?

The thought put a smile on his face ... then the thought of Melody and what she would say wiped it off. *Oh, Mackie,* she would have said, *keep yourself right away from that edge.* He lifted his hand and gave her a little thank you salute. He often took her name in vain, he knew that, but there'd been a time when he thought she was an angel – because she'd been the one who'd saved him. She'd carried him through the early days at Cefn Coed, when he'd thought the metal plate in his head was picking up radio signals, when he'd had to be put in isolation because he decided one of the nurses had stolen his daughter; the weeks and months that followed his discharge and nearly had him at breaking point again; then the long slow haul that turned out to be a recovery of sorts. And even though he didn't see her anymore, she was still with him – all these years later. A steadying song in the back of his mind.

14

There was nothing quite so sensible and steady about Mackie the next morning. Shame would have been his first choice of word because he was still on the sofa when Jan Jeary turned up.

'Two minutes, Jan,' he croaked, then shot up the stairs to wake the twins. Their beds were empty. He found them in the kitchen – fully dressed and eating cereal.

'Alright, Grandad?' from the pair of them, like finding him on the sofa surrounded by lager cans was nothing out of the ordinary.

He waved them off, necked two Anadin Extra, and set about loading the washer. He unpacked the clothes the nurse had given him, shoved them in with a few other bits and pieces, then made a strong coffee and took it outside and tried to get his banging head in order. Shame was only half the story. The rest was alarm – pure alarm that he'd let himself get so – *stupid* – the night before. So close to an edge he wasn't safe being close to. There was only one thing to do – he needed to make a plan and stick to it.

By the time he got to the yard he had it all in order. He was going to see Tranter – hopefully get a bollocking as opposed to the sack, retrieve the kid's rucksack from the Golf then, as soon as he'd finished work, take it and the clean clothes back to the hospital. Then he was going to get to the bottom of the *It's you* malarkey, because no doubt there was some sensible, normal, sane explanation for it, and then he was going to get on with his own life – or what passed for his own life.

He went straight to the office to see Sharon.

'How did it go, then?'

'What?' She looked knackered. In fact, she looked like she'd been crying.

'Last night,' he said. 'The club.'

'Oh, you know...' She turned back to the computer.

'Is he in, then? Tranter? I have to see him about leaving early yesterday.'

'He's in his office.'

'You OK, Sha?'

'Yeah. Fine. Go on, bugger off.'

Mackie didn't want to see him but knew he'd chew on it until it was done, so he set off towards the big shed. Tranter's den, as they referred to it, was a partitioned-off corner: a gloomy, oily hole they all avoided.

'Now then,' he said, when Mackie walked in. 'What brings you to my lair?'

Mackie waited for him to remember but Tranter said nothing.

'I – erm, you said you wanted to see me. Yesterday, when the police were here? I had to go early and...'

'Oh,' Tranter said, putting a hand to the side of his face. He had a hell of a bruise. 'Did I? Well, it's your lucky day, lad, because I'd forgotten.'

'Right,' Mackie said, then stood waiting.

Tranter looked at him for a moment or two. 'Well, go on, then,' he said.

'What?'

'Go get some fucking work done.'

Mackie went back to the office to see Sharon. She was still hunched over the computer.

'Good news,' Mackie said. 'He'd forgotten.'

'Fabulous,' she said, without turning round.

'Sure everything's OK, Sha?'

'I'll see you at coffee, Mackie,' she said. 'I'll give you all a shout.'

'Yeah, OK. See you at coffee,' he said and left her to it. The bin was half full of paper hankies. Barry Sowerby had a lot to bloody answer for.

As it happened, he didn't see Sharon at coffee because the police turned up again and wanted to have another look round, which foiled Mackie's plan to retrieve the kid's rucksack out of the Golf – and put Tranter in a shite mood. They spent a lot of time in the office going over records: which cars had come in when, that sort of thing, then they went and had a look at the 'Waiting Room' – in particular, at a Land Cruiser that Tranter had taken charge of a couple of weeks earlier. Mackie and Trev hung around in the stockpile area, out of sight, listening to what was being said.

'Thomas Motors brought it in,' Tranter said. 'Must have been, what, last Sunday? Early hours, maybe half midnight, one? I came and opened up.'

'Did anyone check it over?'

'No. The driver dropped it then we both buggered off. Why?'

The police officer ignored the question. 'You done anything with it since?'

'Nope. Been waiting for you lot, haven't I? I was given permission to take it in – and told that someone would be coming to look at it. So what's this all about?'

'We need to check a few things out.'

'This to do with that kid, then?'

'No.'

Mackie raised his eyebrows at Trev. *Not about the kid?* Then what was it about?

As soon as they'd gone Mackie went over to see Sharon. 'What did they want to look at on the computer?'

'They went through the last couple of weeks. Wanted to know if we'd had an Astra in. Dark blue. Registered up north.

He ran through the stockpile in his head. 'We haven't.'

'No, we haven't. I told them that. Wanted to know who else might have taken it.'

'You any idea what this is about?' he asked.

She shook her head. 'I assumed it was about that kid, but they didn't ask about him. You seeing him again?'

'Yes. I'm going straight after work. They asked me to wash his clothes. I've got to take them back.'

She mulled this over. 'What about your Lauren? She back yet?'

'Nah. Haven't heard a thing, but it's OK. The kids are on a school trip. I don't have to pick them up 'til 6pm.'

He considered her face. She had the defeated look she often had after a night at the club. 'Bad night, last night?' He wasn't referring to her singing, but to whatever she'd got going with Barry Sowerby.

She shook her head. 'I don't know who's the biggest fool here, Mackie. You – or me – but we both need to bloody do something about it.'

'You're right,' he said.

'Catch up tonight, then?'

'Brilliant.'

'I'll bring the wine.'

The kid was asleep when Mackie got there. The tubes and wires had been removed: he looked lost without them, like nothing was anchoring him to the bed. His hair had been washed and combed away from his face and the bruise under his eye was creeping down towards his cheek. Mackie counted five stitches in the gash on his forehead.

He was unpacking the carrier bag when subtle change in the air told him that the kid had woken up. He turned to find the kid staring at him – or not him, but the clothes in his hands.

The kid gave a small groan and held out a hand.

'Can I— ?' His voice rasped out through cracked lips.

Mackie passed the clothes to him. 'I found the rucksack,' he said, 'but I couldn't bring it.' He was going to launch into an explanation about the police being at the yard, but the look of defeat on the kid's face stopped him.

'Is there something in it you need?'

The kid nodded and Mackie waited to see if he was going to elaborate. He didn't, so Mackie launched into the next step of his plan. 'I was going to ask you something,' he said, 'that thing you said yesterday...' He got no further because the door opened and the nurse came in.

She smiled at the kid. 'There's someone here to see you.'

The kid grabbed the clothes, pushed them underneath the sheet and scooted himself back against the pillows, like he was scared.

'Maybe I should go,' Mackie said to the nurse, but the kid's hand shot out and grabbed his arm. He was shaking.

'What's the matter?' Mackie said, but before he could answer the door opened again. His heart drooped.

'Oh hello, Mackie. This is a nice surprise. Coincidence even.' It was Tracy Cooper. Social Services. Lauren's key worker. 'Just had the call.' She was all sweetness and light.

'Hello Trace, how's things?'

'Oh, you know how it is, Mac. She smiled at the kid who was still hanging onto Mackie's arm.

'Hello. They told me you'd woken up.' Then she swivelled back to Mackie. 'Do you two know each other, then?'

'Not really,' Mackie said. 'I got sent in with him – in the ambulance, you know? Anyway ... I was just going.'

He grabbed the empty carrier bag because he knew why Tracy was there – and he knew how she worked: she had an any-port-in-a-storm approach to placing kids, especially if there was somebody like him on hand. A pushover. She followed him out into the corridor.

'So, how's things with your Lauren?'

'Fine. Yeah, good.' It was the wrong thing to say.

'Really?' She paused for a moment. 'So, I guess that means you've got a bit of space, then.'

'No,' he said. 'I haven't. Summer holidays coming up and all that.'

'Oh. She's going off somewhere, is she?'

'No. I meant, you know, I might get away for a week or two.'

She clasped her hands in front of her belly, put her head on one side and gave him her best lingering look. 'Poor little thing. Look at him in there ... can't imagine what he must've gone through, can you?'

Mackie looked over at the kid – his skinny arms against the white sheets... 'I can't Trace, I'm sorry...'

'But you've had all the proper checks, you're so good with the twins.'

Mackie hesitated.

'Come on Mackie, it wouldn't be for long,' Tracy pleaded. 'You know what it's like getting an emergency placement.'

He couldn't give in. One minute in the house and she'd know that Lauren was AWOL.

'Sorry, Trace,' he said. 'I can't. I just can't.'

He looked over his shoulder and realised the kid was

watching them. It was the hope on his face that scuppered the rest of Mackie's plan. He ought to have asked his question then been out of there and away. But no, before he could stop himself, he was at the kid's bedside leaning over him.

'I'll come back,' he whispered. 'I'll come back with your rucksack as soon as I can.'

Then he left, before he could say anything else.

15

Mackie was folding clothes when Sharon arrived.

'Don't tell me they're in bed already.' She plonked a box of Mini Magnums and two bottles of Merlot on the table.

'Been snoring a good hour. Thought I wasn't going to get them home. Had to carry Tylo the last bit. Absolutely knackered. I'll have to bath them in the morning.'

'Nothing from your Lauren, then?'

'Nope. But no news is good news and all that.' He put a bit of bravado in his voice to hide the fact that he was starting to feel a bit antsy about it. Lauren had a track record when it came to buggering off, but it was Tuesday evening now: any normal parent would have been down the police station.

'So, how'd you get on with the kid?' She was tipping a family bag of crisps into a bowl and filling a couple of wine glasses.

'OK.'

'Come on then, spill the beans. What happened?' She clapped a heap of crisps into her mouth and waited for him to answer. He had to give it some thought because he didn't quite know where to start.

'There's something a bit funny about him.'

She snorted. 'He came to the right bloody place then. *The scrapyard*. Joined the heap with the rest of us sad buggers.'

'No.' Mackie shook his head. 'He *said* something funny. When I was at the hospital.'

'What?'

'It was nothing, really. It just...' He suddenly wished he'd kept his mouth shut.

'What?'

'Well...' He pulled a face to show that he hadn't really taken it seriously. 'He said, *it's you.* I don't suppose it meant anything. He'd only just been admitted. It was the medication – that's what the nurse told me.' He turned his back on her so she couldn't see the flush rising in his cheeks.

'*It's you?* Like, he knew you, you mean?'

'Yeah.'

'Well that doesn't make any sense.'

'I know ... I think he's scared.'

'Well, that does make sense.'

'I'm not sure ... it was when Tracy Cooper showed up.'

'Oh, what did *she* want?'

'He was OK once he saw her, but you should have seen him when the nurse told him he had a visitor. He looked like he'd seen a ghost. He grabbed my arm. I could feel him shaking.'

'Perhaps he's been in care.'

He'd already thought about this but it didn't add up. 'His clothes weren't marked. If he was in a home they'd have had his name inside.'

'Foster care, then?'

'But Tracy would have known. He'd have been reported missing.'

'Not if he's from up north like that Astra the police were asking about.'

'What?'

'Those cops, when they came to look at the records. That car they were looking for, the Astra, it was from somewhere up north.'

'I thought they said that wasn't about the kid, though.'

'That's what they said, but I didn't exactly believe them.'

'Why not?'

'Because they were also asking about that Land Cruiser, the one that came in a couple of weeks back. Sounded to me like they were *investigating*.'

'The motorway smash, you mean?'

'Yeah.'

'But what's the connection?'

She shrugged. 'No idea.'

They both thought about this for a couple of minutes, then Sharon suddenly jumped to her feet.

'Well smack my bloody arse.' This was one of her favourite sayings and as far as he knew, no one had taken her up on it. 'It's obvious, Mackie, the kid must be something to do with that accident.'

'Nah, that would mean...'

'That would mean he's been in the Merc for what – a week?'

'Impossible. It would have been like an oven. He'd never have survived ... although...' Mackie was thinking about his first glimpse of the kid in the ambulance. The touch and go panic of the journey to ICU. 'He was pretty far gone when Trev found him.'

'Well, there you are then. There's your bloody answer.'

'What?'

'You said the kid recognised you. Well that's why, isn't it? He'd probably seen you – seen us all – in the yard.'

Mackie swallowed hard. She was right, but he didn't want her to be right. She'd dived in and come up with a better answer than his. A logical answer.

'Don't believe me, Mackie?'

He held his tongue for fear of what he might come out – a brief rendition of his angel theory, for example.

'Here.' She threw her car keys on the table. 'Go back now – ask him, then back off, yeah? I don't like the look of you, pal. You've got enough problems of your own. You need to get your head straight. You don't need this kid in your life.'

'You're right, Sha,' he said, and made a big deal out of sliding the keys back towards her. Then for no reason he could explain, he changed his mind. He grabbed the keys and got to his feet. 'Actually, I *will* pop over. I'll be as quick as I can.' Then he left before he had chance to talk himself out of it. By the time he got into the car he knew that Sharon was only half right – because although he might not need the kid in his life, he couldn't shake the feeling that the kid needed him in his.

The kid was trying to work out what to do. The man – Mackie? – had still not been back to see him, but the social worker woman had, asking him questions he pretended he didn't know the answers to. He knew she had been talking to the police because she asked if he'd come to the scrapyard with anyone else, and did he know of anyone who might be looking for him. He told her nothing.

They had moved him to a different ward. A good sign, the nurse told him as she wheeled him into the lift. He said nothing because he was too busy concentrating on which button she would press, whether they would be going up, to where he would feel safe, or down. He held his breath as the lift shuddered and started to descend. The mechanical voice called out after each floor they passed and, by the time they reached the first floor where the doors pinged open, the kid's head was spinning.

'Now this is more like it, isn't it?' the nurse announced, as she wheeled him into a small side ward. 'No bells and whistles to keep you awake all night. And – look what you've got here...'

She showed him a small television attached to the wall opposite the bed. But the kid wasn't interested. He got up from the wheelchair and peered out of the window.

'Am I allowed to sit here?' he asked, as he scanned the carpark below.

'Well, I don't see why not. You know what they say about a change of scenery ... now, give me a minute while I go and find out who to hand you over to...'

The kid rested his forehead against the window. The glass was warm from the sun, but there was no comfort in it. The scenery was the last thing on his mind. He couldn't shake the feeling that time was running out. He leaned on the windowsill and surveyed the carpark below – watching as cars left and arrived; as people headed towards the hospital entrance, just one floor below him. This would be his lookout post because he knew without a doubt that Marco would be getting closer and he knew how bad it was going to be when he did: bad for him, but much worse for Eileen. Marco was angry about what she'd done. He was angry and he wanted to punish her.

Six weeks earlier.

Marco didn't come back until the next day. They were sitting in the kitchen having some breakfast and he suddenly burst in through the back door.

'What?' he said, because they were both staring at him. His lip was swollen and bloody and he had blood down the front of his T-shirt. The kid looked at his hands – knuckles were grazed and raw.

'Marco.' Eileen hesitated. 'Are you OK?'

He didn't answer because he had thrown his jacket off and was pulling his T-shirt over his head. He stepped out of his trainers and took his trousers down. When he bent over to shove everything in the washing machine the kid could see his back was a raw mess of cuts and bruises. The imprint of someone's boot across his shoulder blades.

'What happened?' The kid was shaking.

'Nothing happened,' Marco snapped, stepping closer to Eileen until his face was nearly touching hers. 'You got that, woman? If anyone asks, nothing happened.'

Marco was in bed when the police arrived. Eileen was too afraid to tell them where he was. 'I'll go get him,' the kid offered. 'He's upstairs.'

'What the fuck do you want?' Marco didn't open his eyes. There was blood on his pillow.

'The police are here.' The kid stood back as Marco pulled on his tracksuit, slid open the bedroom window and climbed out. He hung off the sill and dropped onto the garden below. He looked up at the kid and put a finger to his lips, smiling like it was a game. When the kid went downstairs the police officers turned to look at him. Eileen had made them some tea.

'He's gone,' the kid said and they put their cups down and left.

'Sorry,' Eileen called at the door, although she didn't know what she was apologising for because they hadn't told her what Marco had done. One of them gave her a small white card. 'Let us know when he comes back, will you?'

'He jumped out of the window,' the kid said, when the air had settled back down. Eileen didn't reply at first. She put the kettle on then turned to face him.

'Sit down, pet... We need to have a talk.'

He didn't want to sit down because he knew what she was going to tell him. He stayed where he was, so she couldn't say it. 'I've been having a think.' She paused. 'I don't know how much longer we can go on like this.'

He could feel his head getting heavy. She was going to say the words anyway.

'I have a sister,' Eileen explained. 'She's a good way from here and – well, I was thinking we could go and stay with her.'

'What? I mean, who?'

'You and me, pet. We could just pack a few things and go. Stay with her for a bit then work out what to do. We can't go on like this...' Her words trailed off. She was trying not to cry.

'But when? When would we go?'

'I was thinking we'd go today. Now.'

The kid looked at her. Her neck was red and her face was damp.

'What do you think, pet?'

She was trying not to hurry him. *What about Marco?* he wanted to ask, but he knew she was past being able to think about Marco.

'OK,' he said and she let out a long stream of breath and pulled him towards her.

'Come on, I'll help you pack.' He could hear the rush in her voice, even though she was trying to hide it.

She followed him up, placed a small suitcase on the bed and started putting things in. When he looked out on the landing, he saw her suitcase was already standing there and he wondered how long it had been packed and waiting – waiting for this moment.

'That's it,' she said, pulling the suitcase off the bed. She then picked up her own case and he followed her down the stairs. Although he didn't recognise it at the time, that was the point where things might have gone differently: if they'd gone straight out the front door and to the car; if he hadn't suddenly remembered his sketchbook and pencil and left her in the hall while he ran up to get them; if, just as they were passing the kitchen door, Marco hadn't walked in through the back door and caught them. Eileen made a small squeak and dropped the cases. She took a step back and tucked the kid behind her.

At first Marco said nothing, but the kid was waiting. He could feel the pressure building – like some wild electricity that might be in the air or in his head.

'What's going on?' Marco demanded. He came out of the kitchen, into the hall and looked at the two suitcases.

'I said: what's going on?'

'Me and Riley are going on a little holiday, that's all.' Eileen put her hand behind her back to feel for the kid's shoulder.

'On holiday? What do you mean, *on holiday?*'

'Oh, it's a surprise! A mystery tour, isn't it, Riley?' Eileen gurgled, without turning round to look at him.

'He's got school.' This took them both by surprise.

'Oh, I can call school, you know— ' She trailed off as Marco bent down, opening the suitcases. He checked the contents then handed her one case.

'You better get going, then,' and for half a second the kid felt some hope in her. She held her hand out for the second case but Marco smiled then tossed it into the kitchen. It hit the table then flew open – the clothes he'd just packed strewn all over the floor.

She turned away from him, keeping the kid tucked in front of her, her suitcase at his side like a guard rail. 'Come on then, pet.' She steered him towards the front door.

She felt herself jerk backwards as Marco grabbed her. The kid tried to catch hold of her hand but she was falling. Her suitcase lifted into the air as she toppled back, then scraped along the wall, knocking the mirror. It swung on its hook for a second then fell hitting the radiator and exploding into a thousand jagged pieces. He saw Eileen was on her back and Marco was standing over her. The kid ran to the front door and opened it because the air was choking him. He ran out into the garden, down towards the gate. *Help,* he wanted to shout, but the word would not come. He wanted to run through the gate and keep running but he couldn't. He couldn't leave Eileen.

He watched as she came out through the front door, walking very fast, tripping over her shoes because Marco was holding her at the back of the neck. She was crying and her face was bleeding.

'Open the fucking gate,' he shouted. The kid couldn't move.

'Open the gate, pet.' Eileen nodded at him. His fingers struggled with the latch but he managed to loosen it and stood back as Marco shoved her through and slammed her against the car.

'There you are,' he growled, throwing the suitcase at her. 'Enjoy your fucking holiday.' Then he grabbed hold of the kid's arm.

'Go on,' he shouted, as Eileen got into the driver's seat. 'Fuck off. Fuck off and don't bother coming back.'

The kid didn't take his eyes off her as she started the engine. The car moved forward and she rolled down her window. 'I'll come back for you, pet,' she shouted. 'Don't worry, I'll come back.'

Marco let go of him and ran at the car. He grabbed for Eileen's hair but the window was already going up, so he kicked the door and banged his fists on the roof.

'Get in the fucking house,' he snarled. The kid ran up the path, up the stairs and into bed. It wasn't until the morning when he realised that his hands were bleeding.

16

Mackie drove slowly, rehearsing his lines, because he was suddenly feeling at sea again. He knew Sharon had worked it out: the kid had recognised him because he'd been in the Merc longer than they'd realised; he'd seen them all. And thank god she had, because he was already worrying her. She knew him better than anyone else, but Christ knew what she'd have made of it if he'd launched into his angel theory. At the same time, he knew he wouldn't quite let go of this idea until he heard it from the kid himself.

He stopped at a petrol station and bought a bag of mints and, as an afterthought, some sweets for the kid: the police visit had meant he'd not managed to get the rucksack out of the Golf and he didn't want to turn up empty-handed. The hospital carpark was busy: visiting time by the look of the small groups of people heading towards the main entrance. *Heading towards what?* he wondered, as he popped a couple of mints into his mouth and joined the flow of visitors. *Life, death or the everything in between?*

When Mackie got to ICU the kid was no longer there.

'Gone? But I've got something...' He held the bag up to show the nurse, hoping she wouldn't ask to look inside – and find two packets of sweets.

'Three floors down,' she said, and gave him a ward number.

He took the stairs, to try and buy himself a bit of time. Sharon was right, he didn't need the kid in his life – so why had he felt so panicked when he thought the kid had gone?

The kid, it had to be said, was looking better. Whether it was the softer lighting in the ward or the fact that there were other people around – patients, visitors, a group of nurses at the desk – there was something more solid about him. He didn't see Mackie at first – he was busy with a plate of toast.

'You're looking a bit better, lad.' Mackie pulled up the chair beside the bed and launched into his script. 'I can't stay, I've borrowed my friend's car. I've just popped back to tell you that I've not forgotten about your rucksack. I couldn't manage to get it without – without anybody seeing me.' He left it at that.

'That's OK,' the kid said, and smiled.

'Blimey, you must be feeling better.'

'I am.'

'Oh, I brought you these, though.' Mackie put the sweets on the bed and stood up, ready with his next lines. 'So ... I was just wondering ... just wanting to clear something up, sort of. Well, you probably don't remember this, but – that day in Intensive Care...?'

The kid was staring at him.

'Well, you said something.' Mackie stopped and cleared his throat. 'You said something that made me think you knew me. You said,' he gave a small cough, '*it's you*, like you recognised me.'

'I did,' the kid said.

'What? Recognise me?'

'Yes.'

'But how?'

'Because I've been looking down on you all.'

He'd been looking down on them all? Mackie sat back down, realising what a field day he could have had with that particular notion.

'Because you were in the Merc?' Mackie said, and at that point he wasn't sure what he wanted the kid to say.

'Yeah. I could see you when you were having your tea break.'

'Right. OK. Well, I'm glad I've got that cleared up. So...' he stood up, 'like I said, I have to get straight back...' But the kid wasn't really listening – he was rummaging under his pillow. 'I've got something for you,' he said and Mackie watched as he pulled out a sheet of paper. From what he could see of it, it was a hospital chart. He folded it in half and handed it to Mackie.

He hadn't been prepared. That's what he realised later. He'd expected something like a thank you card, maybe – not that he needed thanking – or perhaps something similar to what the twins brought home from school. So, when he'd unfolded the page – the smile and thank you already on his lips – he wasn't ready.

'What's this?' he'd said, although it was more than bloody obvious what it was. A band of sky, heavy with clouds and sea gulls, a wide stretch of choppy sea, and, perched on a slender plinth, her arms reaching out across the water – an angel.

The kid had drawn an angel.

'I'm not sure,' the kid said.

Not sure. Mackie didn't know what the hell that meant. All he knew was that his heart was going like the clappers and he was heading for the helter-skelter again. 'Well, what is it for?'

'I think it's to help you find someone,' the kid said.

'What?' He'd not got any further than that. *Find who*? he might have said, but he couldn't get the words out. It didn't matter anyway because the kid was somehow ahead of him. He'd closed his eyes for a moment then looked at Mackie. 'Your daughter', he said. 'She's in the sea'.

Mackie didn't know how he got back home. One minute he was reeling across the carpark, trying to catch his breath, the next he was parking outside his front door.

'Thank god you're back,' Sharon said, 'thought I was going to have to finish the bottle on ... good god, Mackie. Are you OK? You're as white as a sheet. Here...' She shifted over on the sofa and patted the cushion beside her. 'Come on. Park yer bum and tell Aunty Sharon all about it.'

He sank down beside her on the sofa. 'Well you were right, Sha...' That seemed like a solid place to start. 'It seems the kid knew me because he'd seen me, seen all of us, actually, when he was in the Merc.'

'Told you.'

'But...' He didn't know how to say the next bit. 'I think I might have been right too – about him being a bit strange.'

'Go on.'

'He gave me this.' He pulled the drawing out of his pocket and handed it to her.

'Very nice. He's got skill, I'll give him that. Hang on, I think I recognise her. It's a statue, I think ... I've seen it before, but can't remember for the life of me where...'

'He said it would help me find someone.' He gave a small laugh.

'He said what?'

'I know. Doesn't make any sense, does it?'

'Find who?'

'My daughter. He said she was ... in the sea.'

'What? Your Lauren, you mean? Did you tell him she's gone AWOL?'

'No. Well, she's not exactly gone AWOL, Sha, has she? Not by her standards.'

Sharon took another gulp of wine while she digested this information, then suddenly clapped her hand to her forehead.

'Hang on a minute, Mackie. "She's in the sea"? What about that rave on the Gower? That would have been right up her bloody street. What if she was there? What if something happened to her?' She was looking at him like she'd just solved a Miss Marple.

He rubbed the back of his neck – it was prickling with sweat – and went to stand by the back door. 'No. I've already thought of that, she's scared of the sea.'

The truth was he'd taught her to be scared of it – and who could blame him after what happened to Sandra?

'Anyway, she texted me. Monday afternoon, I had a text – well half a text from her...'

'But it's Wednesday now.'

'I know.'

'Right.' Sharon heaved herself up off the kitchen chair. 'I think you need to get back over there now and ask him. Ask the kid what the hell he meant. "Your daughter's in the sea?" For Christ's sake, Mackie. You can't just ignore something like that. I think you need to go and ask him – and then get in touch with the police.'

He swallowed hard. She was right. He'd left it too long. He'd been telling himself he was protecting Lauren but what if she was in trouble? What if she actually *was* in the... He had to stop himself, because what the kid had said did make sense, or had, a long time ago. But it wasn't something he talked about.

'I can't go to the police, Sha. Not without thinking it through properly, you know? She's that close,' – he pincered his thumb and index finger almost closed – 'that close to Child Protection.'

'And?'

'And I can't do that to her, can I? I can't do it to the twins. I'll give it another day and then...'

She shook her head. 'I don't want to say the wrong thing here, Mackie, because I know you have it hard, but isn't that a bit bloody defeatist? I mean, what about you? You're hanging around in case your Lauren suddenly needs you, but what about what you want? Isn't it time you moved on and had a bit of life for yourself?'

118

The irony of what she'd said painted a flush of red across her face and she gulped down a mouthful of wine to cover it. People bonded over different things, that's what Mackie had learned: walking clubs; keep fit; football; kids; pets, even. For him and Sharon it had been their respective brush with mental health – both problems and services. *Damaged goods we are, Mackie,* she'd said to him once, after a particularly gruelling heart to heart that had involved a bit too much wine.

She'd had a bit of a troubled childhood. That's how she'd put it. She didn't go into the details but she'd ended up living with her nan from the age of nine. After that everything was marvellous until she was eighteen when, influenced by what all her mates were doing, she left Swansea to do a degree at Bristol University. *Accounting.* It was OK for a couple of weeks but after that it wasn't. She'd hated it – said she always felt she was on the edge of things, like she didn't fit in. So she stopped eating. Not at first. She'd flirted with making herself throw up for the first term but then, after the Christmas break, upped it a notch and more or less stopped eating. The only real help she got was her nan who, after a phone call from one of her friends, made an impromptu visit, took one look at Sharon and the empty fridge, and hauled her back to Swansea – and arranged an appointment with the GP.

From what Mackie could work out, it was all downhill from there: she ended up drifting for a couple of years until she unfortunately washed up at Barry's club. The rest was history – sad history. Mackie swirled his wine and let his eyes trace the outline of the Rowan. Its branches were stretched out and still and, backlit by the streetlight it looked unreal, like it was part of a stage set.

'You're right,' he said, knowing that the acknowledgement would be as far as he got because he was beyond changing things: the fight had gone out of him a long time ago. She'd hit the nail on the head earlier: he'd found his bloody place in life. Like her and Trev, he was on the bloody scrap heap – broken down and going nowhere fast. He leaned over and clinked his glass with hers.

17

Sharon was waiting for him when he got to the yard. Not just waiting – she was on lookout. She spotted him the minute he set foot in the yard and beckoned him over.

'Aberystwyth,' she announced. 'It's in Aberystwyth.' There was a note of triumph in her voice that suggested he should know what she was talking about. He hadn't got a clue.

'Your statue. Your angel. She's in Aberystwyth ... look.' She swivelled the computer screen towards him. 'I came in early and did a bit of research. Have you got the picture on you? I'm pretty sure that's her.'

He did have the picture on him – crumpled to buggery now because he'd looked at it so many times. He'd had to put it away in the end because his distraction started putting the twins on edge. He didn't realise how badly until they got to the school gate and Tylo started crying and asking about Lauren. Mackie had appalled himself by trotting out a lie.

'She's coming back later,' he'd said, hoping that would suffice, but Miss Jones had detected there was a problem and was heading towards them.

'Everything alright, here?' She smiled down at Tylo, who by that time was hanging onto Mackie's leg.

Mackie tried his best smile. 'A bit tired, that's all, after yesterday.'

'Ah, well. Not long now 'til the end of term, eh? Come on, Tylo.'

And off she'd gone, Tylo in tow, leaving Mackie wondering what the hell he was going to do about half term if Lauren didn't come back soon.

'Mackie!'

'What?'

'The picture – do you have the bloody thing or not?'

He got it out of his jeans and handed it over.

'Haha. I'm right. Look.'

Mackie looked at the screen – there she was, the angel in the kid's drawing: wings outstretched, and perched so lightly on her plinth it made you wonder if she had just landed or was about to leave.

'So,' Sharon rubbed her hands together, 'here's the plan...'

It was a good plan – and a tempting one at that: a day at the seaside – fish and chips, a walk along the front, locate the statue and, with a bit of luck, Lauren. But there were a few flies in the ointment.

The first was the realisation that it would serve as a sort of distraction therapy – something that made him feel like he was trying to find Lauren – but didn't involve him having to go to the police just yet. He swatted that away.

The second was that it was crazy. Setting off to Aberystwyth on the strength of some strange kid's drawing. He ignored that one.

It was the third one he couldn't stop buzzing round his

head. The twins. It made him feel bad – but he didn't want to take them with him.

'So, Mackie, boy. Whaddya think? Tomorrow? Is it a date?'

They set off early. Jan Jeary had jumped at the idea of having the twins because the football was on and her husband had asked a couple of his mates round to watch. This was a double result because it meant she was going to look after them at Mackie's. She turned up at 8am, armed with an inflatable paddling pool, a beach umbrella and a pile of comics. By the time Sharon arrived half an hour later, the three of them were up to their elbows in a mixing bowl full of flour. The twins hardly noticed him leave.

'I can't believe we're doing this,' Sharon said, as they drove away. 'Did you bring your sunhat and suncream?'

She was all smiles and Mackie was glad of it. He wasn't the only one struggling and he knew that: she just hid it a lot better than he did. She talked sometimes, like he did – but they both had a repertoire that was never really expanded on. All the same, she was the best person he knew – he admired how she polished herself up every morning, putting her best smile on for them all; how she quietly mothered him and Trev; how she believed that one day some talent scout would spot her and she'd be signed up to some swanky venue. He just wished she wasn't tangled up with Barry Sowerby.

'A bit of music, Mackie?'

He was looking out of the window, marvelling at the change in scenery. They'd not been gone much more than half an hour and there they were, skirted on both sides by green fields and sheep. He'd never realised it was all so close.

'Why not.'

'Any requests?'

'Well, you know I like a bit of Dolly.' He was expecting her to put a CD on, but instead she wound down her window and started in on 'Jolene.'

He lasted 'til the end of the first verse – and then joined in.

It took a lot longer to get there than anticipated. This was due to the decision to join the A482 at Llanwrda. To be fair, the woman on the sat-nav had sounded pretty confident. *Take the next right*, she urged, as they left Lampeter, and they obeyed, only to be left in the lurch ten minutes later, seemingly miles from anywhere. Especially Aberystwyth!

'Christ almighty, Mackie. If we ever reach civilisation again I swear I'm going to get down and kiss the bloody earth. Where the fuck are we?'

Mackie had the road atlas on his knee, tracing his finger over the page as if he knew what he was doing.

'Straight ahead, Sha.' This wasn't particularly enlightening because that was the only option on offer. He turned out to be right because half an hour later Cardigan Bay came into view; a glittering expanse that made Swansea Bay look like a fish pond. It put the smile back on Sharon's face.

'So, what shall we do first?' Mackie said.

They'd parked the car and were walking to what they assumed was the centre of town. He was hoping Sharon would say fish and chips – not because he was hungry – but because he'd suddenly got the feeling they were making a huge mistake. He'd been mulling it over on the journey – not so much what would happen if they found Lauren, because that was pretty easy; he'd give her the bollocking of a lifetime and drag her back home. No, what was troubling him was what would it mean if they did find her there. What would it mean if they'd followed a drawing done by some strange kid – and they found her?

'What do you mean, Mackie? We'll do what we came to do. Go find the statue and then hope your Lauren's standing underneath it.'

She wasn't, of course. They gave it ten minutes, then wandered off to find some food. They parked themselves on a bench opposite the statue where they could keep an eye on it and scan the beach and sea at the same time.

'Perhaps we're being a bit too specific,' Sharon said, eventually. 'Perhaps the statue is just a clue, you know. A *somewhere in the vicinity* kind of thing.'

With this in mind they walked along the front until they'd almost reached the cliff railway at the other end of the beach. Mackie's gaze never left the water.

'Hang on a minute, Mackie. Look over there.'

She was pointing at a small group of women walking back in from the sea.

Mackie's heart leapt to attention. He studied the women – his eyes searching for the familiar shape and slant of her, some tug on the thread that connected them to each other.

'Nah, Silver Surfers. They're a lot older than Lauren.'

'No, I didn't mean that, Mack. I meant, just look at them – how happy they are.'

Mackie could see she was right. The women were all wet hair and smiles, laughing and joking as they picked their way back across the sand.

'Sounds like you wouldn't mind giving it a go, Sha.' He was joking really but she took him seriously.

'I might ... except for this.' She gave herself a poke in the belly.

'Well, I reckon there's nothing wrong with a bit of padding. It'd keep the cold out.'

They walked back to the statue in silence, weaving their way round groups of students, old couples, dog walkers, joggers. Mackie got the drawing back out and studied it for clues that he might have missed. He turned it over and looked at the form on the other side – a temperature chart.

'Oh. I didn't see that before. It's got his name on. The kid. He's called Lee. Lee Thorpe.'

But Sharon didn't take any notice. She was gazing out at the sea, lost in thoughts of her own. They waited another half hour and then decided to head home.

It was almost dark by the time they got back to Swansea. The journey had been a quiet one: none of the excitement they had on the way there. Sharon was still lost in her own thoughts – she stuck to the main roads and put a CD on. This suited Mackie because he was struggling with thoughts of his own, like what he should do about Lauren. The thought of it had his heart jumping, because it surely had to be telling the police that she was missing. Then he'd have to deal with the consequences. Not just him, of course, but the twins too, because school had finished for the summer.

This was where his mind was when Sharon turned the car into the end of his road and drove towards the house. He could see straight away that something was wrong. The upstairs lights were on and the front door was open. There was also a transit van parked by the gate.

'Stay there, Sha.' He got out and walked towards the van, straining his eyes to see if he recognised the number plate. He had his hand on the gate when a bloke stepped out of the house. He was carrying a cardboard box.

'What the bloody— '

'Dad!' Lauren was hot on the bloke's heels, carrying a rolled-up duvet and a pillow. The twins were in the doorway watching.

'Lauren?' He was too stunned to say anything else.

'Well, we're back.' She was all smiles. She wasn't wearing any shoes. 'Dad, this is Eddie. Eddie, this is my dad.'

He ignored the introduction. 'I can see that,' he said. 'Back from bloody where?'

She had a grin on her face because she could hear the edge in his voice.

'From Cornwall, like I told you. I texted you – I texted you on Monday, didn't I, Ed? I used his phone.'

'You were supposed to be back on Sunday.'

'I know, I know. But I texted you to let you know there'd been a change of plan.'

'Well, I didn't get it.'

'Well, I sent it, you can't blame me if you didn't get it.'

Can't blame me – this is how it went. He could already feel himself backing down; he didn't want to upset the kids or make a scene in front of the house; he didn't want to alienate Lauren. Truth be known, he didn't even want to embarrass bloody Eddie.

'Anyway, I'm here now. We're taking them back.'

We? 'Back? Back where?'

She put her finger up to her lips and turned her head away from the twins who were now standing by the gate in their pyjamas. They had that look on their faces he'd seen so many times before – a kind of dazed confusion while they try to figure out what to think. Something like buffering. 'Shhh, It's a surprise. Hold on— ' She beckoned Eddie with a nod of her head; they strode past Mackie and disappeared into the transit. He followed. The inside of the van took him by surprise and he made the mistake of letting it show on his face.

'It's lovely, Dad, isn't it?'

'It's like one of those *amazing spaces,* George whatever his name has.' He was putting on a show for the twins – scattering a few crumbs, as it were, to reassure them, because they were behind him now, holding onto his legs.

'The kids'll love it.' She was all smiles.

Well just hold your horses a minute, he was going to say, but the twins, following his lead, were peering into the van.

'Oh, it's a little house.' Mackie could see the pleasure on Tylo's small face. A little house. Something small and secure. It would be right up his street.

'Like the Wendy House at school,' Amber said. She climbed inside and started investigating.

'It's not a little house.' Lauren could never resist an opportunity to pull rank on them. 'It's a camper van. Look, it's got a steering wheel.'

'The kids will love what?' Mackie asked, eventually.

'Cornwall. We're taking them back down for the summer.'

'What?'

'Ice cream.' She pronounced it like it was some kind of secret password.

'Ice cream?'

'Eddie sells it. Sheep's ice cream.' Mackie put his hand over his mouth so he couldn't say anything. 'Look—' She picked up a small leaflet and stuck it under Mackie's nose. 'That's the trailer. You won't believe it but we've got a pitch right by the sea.'

'The sea...'

'Yeah, we go in every morning.'

'You go in the sea? You've been in the sea?'

'Well, yeah,' she said, like her middle name was Flipper. 'We love the sea, don't we, Ed?'

'Totally.' He flashed Mackie a smile. 'Anyway, Lori...' *Lori?* 'I reckon we need to hit the road. Weather's gonna be good tomorrow.'

'Hang on a minute,' Mackie said. 'What about...' *What*

about the twins, he was going to say, but he was being ridiculous because he could see that Amber had done the clever little thing she always seemed to do – she'd moved swiftly on, like a small stream that meets each obstacle by simply changing course. And Tylo simply went along with her.

'What about Jan? She was babysitting for me.'

'Oh, I told her she could go. I was here, so there was no point in her hanging around, was there?'

'Did you pay her?' It was a silly question but he was trying to buy himself a bit of time. He was aware that, despite struggling with the twins all week, he was trying to delay the moment Lauren would take them away from him. He was grappling with this when Sharon suddenly appeared.

'Well, smack my bloody arse... Oops, sorry, kids, but if it isn't the famous disappearing woman.'

'Pardon?'

'You. Your poor dad has...'

But Mackie stepped in and stopped her.

'It's OK, Sha, she's here now, so...'

And that was it, decided: Lauren loaded a few more things into the van while Mackie took the kids back into the kitchen. He wrote his mobile number onto two slips of paper and put one into each of their pyjama pockets. 'Grandad's number, in case you need me, yes?'

They nodded solemnly then skipped down the path towards the campervan. Mackie stood for a few minutes, trying to compose himself because he didn't want to cry in front of them.

'Right, let's do it.' Eddie was already in the driver's seat; Lauren was waiting for him at the kerb.

She circled round Mackie for a second or two then tackled him into a hug.

'See you when we get back. I'm … I'm sorry you didn't get the text. Anyway, say goodbye to Grandad, kids.' They were tucked in bed, side by side underneath a knitted blanket and she was beaming down at them like the Madonna posing for a Christmas card.

'Look after them.' His voice cracked.

'Oh, I will, don't worry.' She skipped round to the passenger seat and hopped in.

'Text me when you get there, yeah?'

His last thought, as the van pulled away, was that the kids weren't strapped in.

'That's the bloody mystery solved, then. Cornwall.' Sharon poured the wine and was emptying a family size bag of crisps into a mixing bowl. 'Shall we go in the garden?'

'Why not?' He was too gobsmacked to say anything else.

'So, what did you think of Eddie?' she said, chortling into her wine glass.

'Well, he's not like Eddie down the club.'

'You're right. No cardi. Liked the nose ring, though. And the dreads.'

'He sells ice cream.'

She chortled into her glass again.

'Sheep's ice-cream.'

She sprayed a mouthful of wine over her knees. She flat-handed a pile of crisps into her mouth.

'Bloody hell though, Mackie, you've got to hand it to your Lauren, she knows how to live. I mean, can you imagine just upping and offing and getting away from it all?' She waved her arm in front of her face. 'From all this.'

He could. He'd imagined it many times. Today, for example. Fields, sheep, a massive stretch of sea. And he knew Sharon had felt it too. But somehow, like her, he was always the one who had to stay – or decided to stay. Dependable or too fucking scared to rock the boat. But that was an old chestnut and he tossed it to one side because the relief of Lauren's return was kicking in and he wanted to relish it while he had the chance.

18

The kid was watching the door. It was nearly nine o'clock and the night staff had arrived. They'd closed the blinds on his window and he could no longer see out. He slid himself further down the bed when the nurse came in. He listened but gave no indication that he was awake. He felt the sheets tighten across his back as the nurse tucked him in, then heard the soft click as she turned on the night light above his bed. When he heard the door close he counted to twenty, pulled himself up and unhooked the clipboard off the end of the bed. He was getting ready. He rested back against the pillows and prepared himself. He still couldn't believe he got back to the white room. It had been such a long time he thought he had lost his way there. But he hadn't, and now he needed to go back and see if it would show him the way to Eileen. He rested the clipboard across his legs, closed his eyes and let himself remember.

Four weeks earlier.

'Forget her,' Marco said, after Eileen had been gone for over two weeks. 'She's a fucking cow and she doesn't give a shit about you.'

But the kid could not let himself believe this because Eileen was his only hope. He knew that he wouldn't survive much longer if he stayed with Marco: he could already feel the edges of himself starting to blur, like he was losing his outline, changing shape. He wondered if she had written to him and Marco had ripped up the letter. Or maybe she had sent a letter to school not realising that Marco would not let him go to school, that he needed him on the job, available at all times.

Marco was like a cockerel, strutting about Eileen's house like it was his own. He had moved his stuff into her bedroom and tipped everything out of her drawers and left them in a pile on his old bed. He had thrown all her things out of the bathroom and put his razor on the glass shelf above the sink.

Marco and Drake went out every evening, leaving the kid in his bedroom with the sketchbook spread open on the desk.

'Have it ready for when we get back,' Marco said and the kid felt the swill of acid rise in the back of his throat, because the drawings did not come easily anymore. Or the white room. The only thing that came easily was fear. They took him out at night armed with the sketchbook– and god knows what else – and they hunted down their prey.

Sometimes he was lucky and they left him in the car. He'd curl himself into a ball on the back seat and pretend everything was OK; even when they came back laughing, and the air in the car crackled with the electricity, and Marco's knuckles were raw and bloody. But other times he had to make himself fucking useful. That's when they edged him through narrow windows and waited outside while he weaved silently through dark spaces to find a way to let them in; or they sent him up drainpipes, urging him on when he looked down at their pale faces. Marco's voice was like a low hissing snake beneath him.

He did not know how to make it stop. Until one morning something happened that changed everything.

The kid woke early: it was light outside but the house was quiet. He was in bed listening. A car pulled up outside but he did not move. His face was hurting. Last night's mission had been unsuccessful because his drawing was wrong so Marco hit him. Drake had laughed.

He heard the car door open followed by the rattle of their garden gate. He waited for the knock on the door but instead heard the sound of hammering. He rolled himself out of bed and went to the window. There was a man in their garden, hammering a post into Eileen's rose bed. He steadied it with one hand then hit the top with a small hammer. He tested it for firmness then walked back to the car. He came back with a large sign, attached it to the post, then stepped back. The kid twisted his head but couldn't see what the sign said. He waited until the man had driven away and went quietly down the stairs. There was an envelope on the door mat. He checked over his shoulder then tore it open. *Could you please contact the office to arrange a convenient time for the agent to take the interior photographs.* He screwed it up, put it in his pyjama pocket, then walked down the path in his bare feet and looked at the sign.

For Sale.

Eileen, he thought. She had given up on him. And his heart sank like a stone.

Marco was like a storm. The kid hid in his bedroom, watching, as he kicked the post over, smashed the sign and stamped on Eileen's roses. He was talking to someone on his mobile. His voice was a high scream and his arm was swiping the air in front of him like he was swinging a sword. Mr Paisley from next door was watching from the other side of the hedge. Marco swung round and the old man shuffled away.

The kid could feel his own heart beating like it had risen to the surface of his chest and was trying to break free. The air in his room was screwed up tight and he could not breathe it in. He didn't dare open his window because he didn't want Marco to know he was awake, but it didn't matter because the front door slammed and seconds later Marco exploded into the bedroom. He grabbed the kid by the arm and yanked him to the window.

'Look what she's fucking done,' he screamed. His eyes were small and black; there was spit on his chin. 'Fucking look at it.'

He clamped his hand round the back of the kid's neck and forced his head towards the window. The kid could feel the blood pulsing through Marco's fingers. He suddenly yanked him backwards and spun him round.

'Did you fucking know about this?' He held the kid by the shoulders.

'No.' His voice was too small and the room swallowed it up.

'Did you? Fucking did you? Did she write to you again, the fucking cow?'

Marco let go of him, yanked the desk drawer open and tipped it over. 'Where is it?' he yelled. 'Where the fuck is it?'

'She didn't—'

But Marco didn't hear him. He emptied out the kid's school bag and kicked the books across the floor, ripped his clothes out of the cupboard, and then, with a roar, tipped the mattress off the bed. He spun round and grabbed the kid by the hair. 'She's not going to get away with this,' he said. His finger was an inch from the kid's eye. 'Sell the fucking house? The stupid bitch.' He let go and pushed him backwards towards the bed. 'Get this fucking mess cleared up,' he said, 'then get ready. Get ready because we're going to fucking find her.'

The kid dragged the mattress back onto the bed and sat down. *Did she write to you again?* That's what Marco had said. Did she write to him again? He pulled the words in and felt them settle in his chest and all of a sudden, he could breathe. Eileen hadn't given up. She had written to him. A small flutter rose from his belly to his throat and he opened his mouth to let it out. 'Eileen', he said, and he watched as her name flew into the room and out through the open window.

'Here.' Marco was back in the doorway. He skimmed the sketchbook at him.

'Get on to it,' he said. 'Now.'

For a moment, the kid thought he could perhaps make a drawing up and put Marco on a false trail; but before he could give it any more thought, before he had even picked up his pencil, the picture came to him, like Eileen was asking him to find her, like she was leading him towards her. He closed his eyes, felt for the pencil and let the drawing come. When he opened his eyes, Marco was at the bedroom door watching him. He snatched the sketchbook and took it into his bedroom. The kid followed. Marco had the computer ready and waiting: he hunched over it, his eyes flicking from the drawing to the screen, then he switched on the printer and the kid watched the blank sheets going in and maps, photographs, road numbers coming out.

'Nice one, kid,' Marco said. 'Let's go and give the bitch a nasty surprise. Get your fucking bag. Drake's here.'

Ten minutes later, they were on the motorway.

The kid opened his eyes and looked round. The ward was quiet, but a gentle hum had started in his head. He smiled and let himself relax; all at once he was in the white room.

He waits, ready to feel the breeze on his face which will lead him to the open door. But all is still. He opens his eyes but cannot see the door. He crosses the floor and puts his hand against the wall, then traces a path until he has spanned all four walls – and realises the door is not there. His heart floats up towards his throat. There is a slow movement to his left and he glances in its direction. The wall is gliding towards him. He backs away until he realises the wall behind him is also moving, creeping silently closer. He swings wildly round and holds his arms out, but the walls keep rolling in. He closes his eyes and starts a low moan. It grows and grows until it fills his head and then the room and then, without warning, a picture explodes behind his eyes.

It is Marco. He is in a very large room, standing in front of a long desk. He is leaning against it, drumming his fingers on the countertop. There is a lady behind the desk and she is looking at a computer. Another lady is walking towards him, smiling. She lifts her arm and points behind her. She is wearing a blue uniform. She is a – a nurse. 'No,' the kid says, because he suddenly understands. And then the picture starts to fade and the kid shouts out. 'No, no, no,' he shouts. 'Please, no,' and then he throws back his head and screams himself awake.

Marco had found him. He was here. He was in the hospital.

'Oh my goodness.'

The nurse was by the bed, holding his hand. 'Are you alright, pet?' She switched the big light back on and, for a moment, he thought he was still in the white room.

'Oh,' he said, and tried to sit up. The clipboard slid off his knees and onto the floor. The nurse had her fingers on his wrist, taking his pulse.

'I was dreaming,' he said. He could tell by her face that she was not convinced but that didn't matter because he was thinking about Marco. Marco had found him, and if he didn't leave now, there would be no escape. He would have to help him find Eileen. And if he found Eileen... The kid shuddered. He had to get out of the hospital.

The nurse let go of his wrist. 'I'm going to give the doctor a quick call, I think we need to get you checked over.' When she had gone he got out of bed and pulled his clothes out of the locker. He had no shoes, only the spongy blue slippers he had been given to wear. He tiptoed into the bathroom and locked the door. He was putting on his clothes when he heard the nurse come back in.

'You alright in there, love?'

'Yes.'

'I'll come back in a minute, then. The doctor's popping up to see you.'

'OK.'

When he came out he took the papers from the clipboard, shoved them inside his T-shirt and peered out into the corridor. He glanced at the clock on the wall opposite. It was 10 o'clock. The nurses were in the kitchen getting the milky drinks ready. He couldn't hesitate. He walked out, grabbed a jacket off the back of a chair as he passed the nurses' station, and headed for the door. He was almost there when the door buzzer suddenly went off. He leapt back and dodged into the nearest room.

'Oh, hello.'

The kid spun round. An old man was sitting up in bed smiling at him.

'I was wondering when you would come,' he said, and patted the bed.

The kid stared at him.

'How's our Brenda?

'Er ... she's OK,' the kid whispered. He could hear the nurse talking as she walked along the corridor. He stepped further into the room, glanced across at the man and put his finger to his lips. The nurse was at the ward door now. He could see her but she couldn't see him. She reached over and pressed a green button on the wall and the door swung open. He heard a man's voice and his heart nearly gave way.

'Hello,' the old man shouted. His voice was thin and high. It scraped the air.

'Hang on a minute.' The nurse stepped into the room. The kid pressed back against the wall and held his breath. 'Give me a minute, Jack,' she said. 'The doctor has just come. I'll be back down to you in a tick, OK?'

'Where's he gone?' the old man says.

'Who, Jack, the doctor?'

'No – our David. Where's our David gone?'

'Ooh, I don't know. But just give me a minute and I'll come back and we'll see if we can find him.'

The kid stepped away from the wall and looked out into the corridor. The doctor and the nurse were walking towards his bed. He couldn't wait, he had to do it now. He took a deep breath and, without thinking about it, strode out of the room, pushed the green button and walked through the door.

19

Nothing wakes you faster than a knock on the door in the middle of the night. That cold grip of fear as you surface, realising it's still dark, and the sound can signify only one thing: something bad has happened. Again.

Mackie hadn't been asleep very long. He and Sharon had finished the second bottle of wine and, after rolling out a couple of her Patsy Cline numbers, she'd gone home and he'd gone to bed feeling, he had to admit, pretty *sorted*. Lauren was home and, for the moment at least, his head was back above water. He'd let the wine shave the edges off the finer details – like how long it would last and whether the twins would be safe by the sea and the fact that she'd not texted him.

His worry about the kid was another matter, but he parked that, because, somewhere during the second bottle, he and Sharon settled into their usual *moving forward conversation*: Mackie with his ideas of *doing a course* and Sharon resolving to lose a bit of weight and start looking for work on the cruise ships. They'd both spent a fair amount of time smiling into the dark, picturing a future that could, if they just made a move, be theirs for the taking. It was fiction, the lot of it, but hell, it made them feel better.

There was a knock on the door. *It definitely wasn't the police, who always knock loud*, he thought as he came down the stairs. It was late. His heart pulling like a racehorse, he rushed to meet whatever it was waiting for him on the doorstep. He had his hand on the lock when a second thought lurched into his head and his throat clamped shut. *The kids weren't strapped in!* He peered through the glass pane but could see no one silhouetted outside and no blue flashing lights, so he took a deep breath and opened the door.

At first he thought it was some kind of prank because there was no one on the doorstep. There was a car idling by the pavement; the fumes from its exhaust swirling in the light of the streetlamp. A taxi. *Shit,* he thought and started walking towards it, expecting Lauren to step out of it at any second.

'He's gone round the back.' The taxi driver had rolled his window down.

'What's that?' The bloke's words made no sense.

'He's gone round the back. Your boy. He didn't have any money. Said you would pay.' He leaned back into the car. 'It's eight pound fifty, mate.'

'Right.' Mackie left him waiting while he went back inside and got his wallet. *My boy?*

'He's a bit young, isn't he?' the driver said, as he handed over the cash.

'I don't...'

'Just saying, like. None of my business, but I'd have thought he was a bit young to be out on his own at this time of night.'

Mackie nodded. 'Where did you pick him up?'

'By the park.'

'OK, thanks, I'll … thanks.' Mackie walked up the path feeling the driver's eyes on his back all the way. He closed the front door, walked straight through to the kitchen and unlocked the back door. There was a small figure sitting under the Rowan tree, staring out into the dark. The kid.

'Hello again.'

The kid looked up at him and burst into tears. Mackie's first instinct was to feed him, tuck him straight into a warm bed and let him sleep. But it was obvious the kid was too on edge for that, so he lit the gas fire in the sitting room and took him in there. When he came back with the toast, the kid was at the window, peeping out through the curtain. Mackie got him settled on the sofa, then waited. The kid was wearing a fleece jacket he'd not seen before. It was zipped up to his neck and there was some bulkiness at the front that suggested he had something tucked underneath it.

'Have you phoned the police?'

'No.' *Not yet*, Mackie should have said, because that was what he was going to do – after the kid had calmed down a bit.

'So?' Mackie took a bite of his toast to give the kid space to say something. He didn't, so Mackie, borrowing one of Melody's favourite openers, leapt in. 'Well, this is a bit of a surprise. Do you think you can you tell me what it's all about?'

'He found me.' Those three small words told Mackie all he needed to know. All he thought he needed to know. He'd been right. The kid *was* scared – and he was scared because someone was after him.

'Who?' At this point his mind was sifting through the news stories: modern day slavery, County Lines, trafficking, child prostitution. It added up: the kid's injuries, the obvious neglect, *the fear*. Someone had this kid in their grip and they wanted him back – back because he was useful or back because he knew too much.

'Marco.'

'Who's Marco?'

'He's my brother.'

'Your brother?'

'Yes. Half-brother. He came to the hospital and found me – nearly found me. So ... I ran away.'

'But how ... how did you get here? I don't mean the taxi.'

The kid pulled a bundle of papers from beneath his jacket.

'From the hospital, it's got your address on.'

'OK. So why? Why did you run away from him?'

'Because he wants me to do a drawing.'

Do a drawing. The kid said it like it made some kind of sense. 'I don't really understand,' Mackie said.

'He needs it to help him find someone.' The kid stifled a yawn.

Mackie leapt at the cue. 'I tell you what,' he said. 'You're tired, why don't we leave it there and you can tell me all about it in the morning?'

He took the kid upstairs and showed him into the spare room.

'Don't phone the police, will you? They'll tell him where I am.' Mackie was pushing the door closed. 'Or the hospital?'

'I won't phone anyone.' He couldn't believe what he was saying. 'You go to sleep. I'm going to bed now myself. We'll work out what to do in the morning.'

As soon as Mackie got into bed his head settled into a groove he couldn't get it out of: it kept looping round the same stuff, and the more it looped, the faster it went. Number one was obvious – he was on dangerous ground, insanely dangerous ground: *harbouring a minor* or whatever it would be called. He could see it on the front page: *Missing Boy Found. Former Psychiatric Patient Questioned.* He'd not only be mincemeat but his life, his past, would be on show for every bugger to read.

Number two – the hospital hadn't discharged the kid. What would happen if he relapsed? And number three, the taxi driver: one mention of a kid missing from the hospital and he'd have no problem doing the maths.

But it was number four that really snagged him: Marco wanted a drawing because it would help him find someone. Which was exactly what the kid had said when he handed over the angel picture.

He had no idea what it meant – or whether he was really up to finding out.

He got out of bed, sat by his window, and looked down on the back garden. At the Rowan tree. It had been Melody's idea, of course – some symbol of laying the past to rest, to focus his thoughts on going forward into the future. It wasn't in the perfect position according to the gardening manual, but, seeing as it was the only position available, he'd planted it there and counted it as some sort of small victory when it had grown. Thrived even. Which was more than he could say for himself.

The sky was just beginning to lighten by the time he got into bed and fell asleep. Nonetheless, his dream was as dark as it ever had been.

He is walking into the sea, striding through a tangle of seaweed, heading out towards deep water. A broad swathe of moonlight lays a path of gold across the freezing water and he follows it, feeling the burn of the rope on his shoulder and the tug of the dinghy he is pulling behind him. He walks until his feet leave the ocean floor and he has to swim. It is easy at first because the sea is calm and the way ahead is clear. The first sign is always the same: the moon is suddenly obscured by cloud and as darkness swallows him up, the waves start to swell. He looks back at the dinghy and lifts his voice above the sound of the waves. 'It's alright,' he calls, but he is already bracing himself for what is going to happen next. He turns to face it – to face the wall of water that rises up in front of him. He swims up the face of it, feeling the slip and tilt of the dinghy behind. 'No, no, no,' he yells and thrashes towards it, knowing that he will be too late. He is always too late. And it is always empty.

20

Despite falling asleep so late, Mackie woke early. He spent the best part of an hour lying in bed trying to work out what to do about the kid.

The rational part of him – which he had to acknowledge was not as substantial as it might be – told him he ought to ring the emergency social worker and at least get the situation documented. That way they would pick the kid up and he'd be able to go to work next day like nothing had happened. Except it had and that's where the irrational part pulled rank – because he wanted to know. Yes, he wanted to know the mechanics of it: how the kid ended up in the scrapyard; whether the police had it right about the motorway smash; but what really interested him – the part of the story he couldn't get out of his head – was how the kid talked about the drawings. There was no doubt that Melody would have cautioned him to walk away. Instead, he could feel himself edging towards the helter-skelter.

He got up, checked that the kid was still asleep and went downstairs. The hospital paperwork was in the sitting room where the kid had left it. Exhibit number one: the yellow sheet he'd half-filled in on the day the kid was admitted. Even his name looked incriminating – they'd put him down as Mr

Mackie and he hadn't corrected them. It hadn't seemed important at the time, but now? He could feel himself setting off on another loop of the circuit, so got up and put the kettle on. It had just come to the boil when two messages pinged through on his mobile phone. The first was from Lauren – a photograph of the twins sitting on a beach, the pair of them smiling and holding up ice cream cones. He whispered quiet thanks then opened the other message. It was from Sharon. A photo: she'd just got up and done herself a fry-up. *Diet starts tomorrow, honest!* He pressed 'call'. She answered straightaway.

'What am I like?' She had her mouth full.

'You're gonna hate yourself tomorrow.'

'Nothing new there, then. Anywho, why are you up so early? Thought you'd be enjoying a lie-in.'

'Good question, but you're probably not going to like the answer.'

'Hah! She's back already. Your Lauren. Young Eddie has sent her packing.'

'No,' although he had to admit it was a bloody good guess. 'It's the kid.'

'Oh, Mackie, you didn't go back? You told me...'

'No, I didn't go back.' He stopped. 'He came here.'

He heard her put her fork down. 'You what? You are bloody kidding me.'

'I'm not. He turned up in a taxi a couple of hours after you'd gone.'

'Well, smack my bloody arse. So where is he now?'

'Upstairs in bed. Asleep.'

'And what's the plan?'

'I don't know.'

'What did he say?'

'How long have you got?'

'All day,' she said. 'Get the kettle on, I'm on my way.'

He was poring over the hospital paperwork and the kid's angel picture when she arrived. The idea was to give the impression of a man who knew what he was doing. She saw straight through it.

'Well, you look like shit.'

'Cheers.'

'Is he still in bed?'

'Yep.'

'Come on, then. Spill.'

He told her everything the kid had said: the taxi; Marco. It went well until he started trying to explain what the kid had said about the drawings.

'It all sounds a bit far-fetched, don't you think? A bit Mulder and Scully...'

He was about to agree – bow to her better judgement – when she took a long slurp of her tea and picked up the angel picture.

'But this, mind you, I was thinking about this last night. I mean – I know it wasn't completely right. A bit of a wild goose chase and all that – but it was kind of right, wasn't it? Because your Lauren came back, didn't she?'

'I know. Almost like the kid knew something we didn't know...'

He stopped himself and waited for her to pull him back from the brink of whatever he was about to say. She didn't. She put the picture down and looked at him.

'Have you ever been to see that woman in the indoor market? The fortune teller?'

He hadn't, although he'd considered it in the early days when the ache of losing Sandra had been too much to handle; when all he'd wanted were answers to the questions he'd not had a chance to ask.

'No.'

'Well I have, over – you know, over Barry. So, it was a bit weird at first because there we were in a little booth – very atmospheric, like, scarves draped everywhere – except I could hear everything going on in the market. Felt a bit stupid but I was too embarrassed to get up and leave. Anyway,' she gave a small sniff, 'she told me some stuff that no one else could have known and ... well, let's just say I changed my mind.'

Mackie thought about this for a moment. 'What stuff?'

'Oh, you know. Just stuff. Nothing important. Anyway, it's the kid we're trying to sort out – not me. So...' she took another mouthful of tea, 'want to hear what I think?'

'I'm not sure.'

'I think first thing you need to do is get in touch with Tracy Cooper, your social worker woman. Tell her the kid is here...'

'I can't do that, Sha. I told the kid I wouldn't.'

'Hear me out, Mackie, for god's sake. Tell her the kid's here and that you'll hold the fort until they find somewhere for him to go.'

'Oh, well, ta very much. I've only just got rid of the twins and now you want to saddle me with more bloody complications ... oh...' He could feel the colour in his cheeks. 'I didn't mean it like that. Sorry, Sha, it came out wrong. But you know what I've had off Tranter all week.'

'Fair comment, Mackie. But it's the only way – unless you want to end up in the bloody newspapers.'

'And work? What about work?'

'I've got an idea to get us around that.'

It was the *us* that swung it: that, and the fact that the kid suddenly walked into the kitchen. Mackie could tell by the look on his face that he'd overheard the conversation.

'Well!' Sharon exclaimed. 'You must be the kid I've heard so much about.'

She jumped up from her chair and stuck her hand out. 'Sharon Devereux, at your service.' She gave him a small bow. 'The last time I saw you, you were hurtling past on a stretcher. Come on,' she patted the seat beside her, 'park yer bum next to me. Hungry? Mackie – what've you got in that bread bin?'

And so it went on. Sharon chatting away to the kid like she'd known him all her life, the pair of them bonding over a plate of crumpets while Mackie watched from the side-lines.

'So,' she said, eventually. 'Mackie and I have been trying to work out the best thing to do.'

The kid shot a worried glance in Mackie's direction.

'I know, I know, Mackie's explained that you don't want the social worker to know anything – and I completely understand that. But Mackie is my friend – my best friend, actually – and I don't want him to get into trouble, so...'

Mackie turned to look out of the window to hide the sudden flush of heat her words had brought to his cheeks. He leaned against the draining board and listened as Sharon talked the kid round. Ten minutes later, he was on the phone to Tracy Cooper. An hour later, she was at the door.

'Thank god he came here, Mackie. I mean, the kid's kicked up a complete shit storm.' She was as white as a sheet, her eyes rimmed with old makeup. 'I've been up all night trying to work out what to do, the police are trawling the bloody streets and the hospital's no doubt launching an enquiry into how a young lad can simply walk out of one of their wards undetected. Where is he?'

'Kitchen.'

'Is he ... is he OK?'

He wasn't sure how to answer that one. 'As far as I can tell, he's only been up a couple of hours.'

'What's he told you?'

'Not much. Thought I'd leave all that to you.'

Sharon had been right. Calling Tracy – getting it all above board – turned out to be exactly the right thing to do. By the time she left, a couple of hours later, they had the kid's story more or less straight. As Mackie suspected, it was a pretty sorry one.

The kid's name was Riley Wheeler (Lee Thorpe – the name he'd given the hospital staff – was a kid in his class at school).

He was thirteen, almost fourteen years old, his father was dead and he lived in Yorkshire with his stepmother Eileen Kavanagh. Or he had. The kid had gone pale when Tracy showed him the mugshot photographs the police had brought round, but he confirmed that the dark-eyed, *fuck-you* character was his half-brother, Marco, and the bruised guy was his brother's friend, Anthony Drakeford. Drake. They had been on the motorway, travelling towards Swansea when they were involved in an accident.

The kid had hesitated when Tracy asked him why they'd been travelling to Swansea and Mackie had held his breath, wondering if he was about to move onto whacky ground. He didn't. They were trying to find Eileen, he'd said. She'd moved out and put the house on the market and Marco wanted to – he stopped himself at this point – wanted to talk to her about it. Mackie was on the point of butting in to ask why the kid was so scared of his brother, but Tracy got in before him.

'So you've been living with your brother, Marco?'

The kid nodded.

'And how's that been?'

The kid looked down at his hands. 'OK,' he said.

Tracy was taking it slowly. Edging her way forwards in a manner that put him in mind of Melody. 'So, what does he do then, Marco?'

'He's unemployed.'

Tracy made a big show of looking at the photographs again. 'He looks quite tough.'

This was a bit of an understatement – as far as Mackie was concerned the kid's brother looked like a complete bastard.

She got there slowly, drawing it out of the kid bit by bit, and Mackie listened, trying not to flinch or let anything show on his face. It was apparent from what the kid said that Marco was a small-time criminal: extortion, robbery, menace, and the kid was an unwilling part of the set-up. Marco was the one in charge, Drake was the driver and the kid was the one – he'd paused here and glanced at Mackie – he was the one who had to get into places, because he was small.

'OK.' Tracy had sat back at that point. She looked knackered. 'So, I've had a word with Mr Carpenter – Mackie...'

She *blah-di-blahed* for a bit about what a good foster carer he was, how experienced, etcetera, etcetera. Mackie knew it was as much for his benefit as the kid's: she was worried he might have changed his mind, throwing her – and Mackie felt genuine sympathy for her here – back into the shit storm that was just another day in her normal working week. The mad thing was, he hadn't changed his mind. The kid's story, he knew, wasn't quite complete. It was the part that he'd left out that had Mackie hooked.

The upshot was the kid was going to stay at Mackie's *for a day or so,* while they tried to locate Eileen. It struck Mackie that seeing as they had nothing to go by other than her name, and the fact she was staying with a sister somewhere in Swansea, this was a bit on the hopeful side.

Deal clinched, Tracy was up from the table and stuffing paperwork into her briefcase.

'Quick word, Mackie,' she said, gesturing to him to come into the hall. She closed the kitchen door behind her. 'This brother. The police were already interested in him. Driving under the influence, or something like that. They're going to be a whole lot more interested when I tell them what the kid has just said. Do you want me to ask for a patrol car, a bit of protection in case he comes calling?'

'Oh. Thanks, Trace. Thanks a bundle.'

She was too beat for sarcasm. 'No, thank you, Mackie ... completely saved my bloody bacon, you have. Right – I'll be in touch.'

21

Sharon and the kid were in full flow when he got back into the kitchen. 'Me and Riley have just been discussing the plan.'

'Right...' Mackie tried to hide the disappointment in his voice – he'd been squaring up for another question-and-answer session with the kid – namely finding out how the drawings came into the equation.

'Hungry work, though, Mackie. Any more crumpets in that bread bin?'

'Toasted teacakes?'

'Bingo! Get them in the toaster and I'll tell you what we're going to do. So ... it's pretty straightforward.' She nodded at the kid and he nodded back. 'Riley is going to come to work with us...'

'Hang on a minute, Sha. To work? Have you lost your marbles?'

'Hold your horses, Mackie boy. Let me finish. He's going to come...' she paused like she was about to pull a rabbit out of the hat, 'on work experience.'

'Oh, right. And how are you planning to square that with Tranter?'

'Faith, Mackie, dear.' She winked at the kid. 'That's the next part of the plan. I'm going to have a word with Arlene.'

Tranter's wife, Arlene, was something of a legend. Along with Bertha, she was the only person who could give Tranter a run for his money. She favoured leather trousers and plastic surgery and, unfortunately for Tranter, was a firm believer when it came to the power of a good function. It was the bane of Tranter's life – and everyone else's. Hobnobbing, she called it. *Not a flaming biscuit, Ken*, they'd once heard her saying to him, *a necessary part of a successful business life.* They'd imagined him stomping around the bedroom as she pointed him in the direction of the shower, leaving her to unwrap his dry-cleaned suit and deliberate overshirts and ties. It was rumoured she made him have manicures. They had their own tanning suite which was what gave Tranter his trademark mahogany finish.

To be fair, Arlene was a businesswoman in her own right: she owned a string of upmarket hair salons which were popular with anyone who considered themselves rich or famous. The secret of her success, she liked to point out, was her attention to detail – and she wasn't particularly talking about the hairstyling. Each salon, she said, whispered *luxury:* the interior design, the fresh bean coffee, the complimentary head massage. In reality, it was the fact she'd gone to school with Catherine Zeta Jones and had – before *Cath* went all Hollywood – cut her hair on a regular basis, that was the real clincher and Arlene milked it like a prize Friesian. She'd had an old photo enlarged onto canvas – her and Catherine as teenagers – and hung one behind the reception desk of each salon; it worked a treat. Making an appointment was not about which day was available so much as who else was booked in.

Arlene didn't style anymore. Her job was all about preserving the image – popping in if a *significant* client was booked in, making sure the magazines were open at the right pages, ready with some high society titbit – and attending functions, which was where Tranter came in. *You've got to look the part, Ken.* This had previously involved a spread in some fancy magazine. Sharon had brought a copy in and they'd all marvelled over it: Arlene draped in uncharacteristic pastels, Tranter perched precariously on the arms of various sofas, looking out, misty-eyed at the view from their seafront veranda.

'No kids,' he'd said. At that point Lauren had just started deviating from the norm: rocking the boat just enough to keep him awake at night. Sharon and Trev had looked at him like they knew what he meant and he'd smiled back because they didn't have a clue. At that point neither did he, really.

The really important thing about Arlene – apart from being able to manage Tranter – was that she loved Sharon. She'd do anything to keep her happy. This was not because she really cared a hoot about her but because she didn't want her to leave. Sharon, she believed, posed no threat. She'd have thought differently if she saw her in action down at the club but that was unlikely to happen. Arlene hired Sharon after she'd got rid of Yvette whose accounting, apparently, wasn't good enough. They all knew it had bugger all to do with her adding and subtracting and everything to do with the fact that she was thirty years younger than Arlene and would have given Marilyn Monroe a run for her money – something Tranter was fond of saying: too fond as it turns out because they all arrived one Monday to find Yvette gone and Sharon in her place.

It went like a dream – 'a fabulous idea,' Arlene said. The Tranter's doing their bit for the community. They could almost hear her writing the press release in the background.

Once it was all settled, the kid excused himself and went for a lie-down, which suited Mackie and Sharon because it meant they could enlarge on the topic of conversation.

Top of Sharon's list was what Tracy had been talking about in the hallway.

'The kid's brother,' Mackie said. 'This Marco guy. The police are interested in him. That's all she told me.'

Mackie followed this up with the question of what they were going to tell Trev.

'No need to tell him any different, is there? The kid's my friend's boy and he's doing a week's work experience. Simples.'

Mackie shook his head. She was forgetting two important details. A – Trev was the one who found the kid; and B – he was Swansea's answer to Hercule Poirot.

'Nah, he'd have us sniffed out in half a minute. He saw the kid, remember?'

'He saw him, Mackie, and then he bloody fainted. I doubt he remembers much about that day at all. Apart from Bertha turning up. Then again, it would be easier if he knew. Not so cloak and dagger.'

This was one of the things he liked about Sharon. She made everything so straightforward. He could have puzzled over what to do for another hour and not come to any conclusion.

'Who'll tell him?'

'For god's sake, Mackie – I'll tell him if you like.'

'Keep it simple, though. Don't tell him about any of the funny stuff – like the drawings.'

'My lips are sealed.' She wiggled her eyebrows at him and ran her finger across her lips.

This led nicely on to the question that had been at the back of his mind since Tracy had left.

'What's your opinion then, Sha, about the drawings?'

'Not sure yet. But I think we need to take it easy on that front – let him bring it up, yeah? Sounds like he's had enough to deal with – we don't want to go bouncing in like a pair of bloody detectives. We'll let him tell us in his own time.'

Which turned out to be sooner than they thought.

The kid didn't particularly need a lie-down, he just needed a quiet place to think. The fog in his head was starting to clear and he wanted to make the most of it. The social worker had told him she would try to find Eileen but he knew his way would be faster. He didn't have his sketchbook or his photograph – or Marco's research – but he had Mackie and Sharon. He took the notepad and pen off the hall table as he passed, climbed the stairs, propped himself up on the bed and tried to bring Eileen back into his mind. He smiled, because there she was after all this time: on the sofa, working on her puzzle book; in the kitchen making the tea; looking up from her knitting to give him a quick smile. He imagined her waving to him, calling out his name ... then, as the humming in his head started, he blew out a long breath, closed his eyes and let himself go.

He is flying. The white room is nothing more than a thoroughfare – a few strides and he is across and out into the open air. He shifts his gaze to the left, then to the right, spreading his arms wide as he scrolls lazy circles in a sky that is the bluest thing he has ever seen. The air is warm and thick as water. He turns onto his back and allows himself to sink into it – then waits.

In the distance a dark shadow is gathering – moving fast and getting closer. Birds. A vast cloud of birds. They wheel towards him and pass overhead in a chatter of noise, arrowing through the sky on wings that barely move. He rolls back onto his belly, stretches out his arms, and follows them until, in the distance, he sees what he is looking for. He approaches slowly because, even though he is still far away, he recognises it. It is the tower in his sketchbook, the one they were heading for before the crash. A small figure is standing on top of it, waving. He smiles and speeds up because even though the tower is already disappearing, he knows he has found her.

22

They were on their second cup of tea when the kid walked back into the kitchen. He looked like he'd just woken from a deep sleep – or rather, that he'd not quite woken and was sleepwalking. He had the notepad clutched against his stomach. He sat down and put the pad on the table.

'Alright, Riley?' Sharon said. 'You look a bit...' She paused to choose the right word. It wasn't easy. 'A bit ... dazed.'

The kid looked at her like he was peering up through a pool of water. He opened his mouth as if he was going to say something, but no words came out.

'Give him a minute, Sha,' Mackie said, as if he had a clue what he was talking about. The kid turned his head slowly and looked at him.

'Can you look at this for me?'

Mackie let Sharon take the lead. All the champing at the bit about wanting to know more about the kid's drawings and there he was, suddenly nervous to look at whatever it was on the notepad. The telephone notepad.

She considered it for a couple of seconds then pushed it towards to him.

'Oh,' he said. 'It's the 3M's Water Tower in Gorseinon.'
The kid's face suddenly cleared. 'Do you know it?'

'Know it? I ought to bloody know it; I've been driving past it on and off this last twenty odd years.' He allowed himself this slight exaggeration – he'd not been able to afford to run a car for years – because the drawing was so ordinary: not an angel in sight. 'It's just down the road.'

The kid made a noise like someone had let all the air out of him. 'Can we go there now?'

'Well, possibly.' He couldn't think of any reason to say no.

Sharon was another story. 'Hang on a minute, this...' she pointed at the drawing, 'this obviously makes some kind of sense to you, Riley, but to be honest...'

Mackie kicked her under the table. *Letting the kid tell them in his own time* had apparently flown right out of the window. She moved her leg and ignored him.

'To be honest, me and Mackie are struggling a bit to, you know – understand.'

The kid looked at her then back at the drawing. 'Could I try and explain afterwards?'

The M4 was busy. The kid was in the back seat behind Sharon, his small white face gazing out at the passing traffic like he was keeping a check on it.

'Everything OK?' Mackie was wondering if he was thinking of the accident; if he was feeling anxious about being on the motorway.

'Yes, thank you.'

'OK, well, keep looking to your right. We'll be able to see

the 3M's any second now. You can't miss it. Hang on; look, there it is, coming up now.'

'Oh, I can see it. Look, I can see it.'

Mackie turned to look at the kid. His mouth was open and he had both palms on the window. As they passed the tower he turned his head to keep it in view. Mackie kept quiet, not sure what was going to happen next. After a few moments the kid made a sound like he was clearing his throat and sat back from the window. His eyes were shut.

'Well?' Sharon said, eventually.

'I don't know.' He had the dazed look on his face again.

'But that was it, yes? That was the tower in your drawing?'

'Yes, but I ... I don't think she was there.'

'She wasn't there. What does that mean, Riley?'

The kid didn't answer.

'OK.' She glanced at Mackie. Raised her eyebrows. 'Perhaps it's time for us to have that chat we were talking about, so you can tell us a bit more about these drawings. Yeah?'

'Alright.'

'Good. OK. Where's the nearest Pizza Hut?'

Mackie should have said something – he knew from experience that Pizza Hut was not the best place to be on a Sunday afternoon, unless you were six years old and having a birthday party. There were at least three on the go. The place was teetering somewhere between party and bun fight.

'Any chance of a quiet table?' Mackie asked.

The waitress gave him a weary shrug. 'Take your pick.'

He surveyed the mayhem – fifty kids off their heads on excitement and Coca-Cola.

'There's a table outside...?'

'We'll have it,' Sharon said.

'I'm just going go to the toilet.' The kid disappeared into the rumpus.

'Don't forget, we're going to go steady with this, Sha. No bloody Scott and Bailey. He might not find it, you know, easy to talk about.'

He was wrong. The kid found it very easy to talk about – laid it all out for them like it was the most normal thing in the world.

'My mum was a clairvoyant.'

That's how he started: *his mum was a clairvoyant.* He said it like he was telling them she was a checkout assistant at Tesco's. Then he described how, one night, he'd discovered that he was too.

'I didn't know what it was. I just ... it was like I sort of floated off ... and when I woke up, I'd drawn a picture. Marco said I had the gift – the same as Mum.'

'What happened to your mum?'

'She died. Ages ago. When I was little. Then my dad met Eileen and we moved in with her.'

'So your dad...?'

'He died too.'

Christ, Mackie thought.

'So then it was just me and Marco and Eileen.'

'So how does it work?' Sharon said when the kid ground to a halt. She was working her way through a slice of pizza.

166

Mackie could see the kid was trying to explain it as well as he could, but it took a bit of following. And a bit of believing. From what he understood, the kid's gift involved coming over all funny, floating off into a white room, seeing things – or people – then waking up and doing a drawing.

Sharon wiped her hands on a serviette. 'So, the drawing is the clue?'

'Yes.'

'The clue to how to find whoever it is you're looking for?'

'Yes.'

'So why didn't it work today?'

'Because it wasn't the right time.'

Mackie would have left it there, but Sharon was on a roll.

'What about that drawing you did for Mackie, then? We went and found the statue, but she wasn't there. His daughter wasn't there. Was that because it wasn't the right time?'

The kid looked at Mackie: he scanned his face from forehead to chin.

'I'm not sure. Not yet.'

Mackie sprang up to get away from the kid's stare. 'I'm just going to the toilet.'

The pandemonium in the restaurant was just reaching fever pitch. The ice cream factory looked like it was on its last legs – he knew the feeling. It was time to go home.

'Well that was bloody interesting.' Sharon was twisting the cork out of a bottle of red. Mackie got two glasses out of the cupboard and opened the back door to let some air in.

'That's one way to put it.'

They'd driven back more or less in silence. A few lame attempts to talk about something ordinary had petered out and left them all to their own thoughts.

'So, are you ready for the rest?'

'What rest?'

'The bit about Eileen. He told me when you went to the toilet. You were gone ages.'

It was true. He'd locked the cubicle door behind him and tried to get his head in order because the kid had just looked at him the way he had in ICU: like he was somehow reading him. And all he'd wanted to do was run.

'Right. Yeah, OK. Do I need to brace myself for more … more weirdness?'

'Unfortunately not.'

The rest of it was your average human misery. The kind Tracy Cooper dealt with day in and day out. Except for the part about Eileen.

'This Eileen woman sounds pretty bloody marvellous,' Sharon said. 'And clever. Putting the house on the market? Good move or what?'

'Dangerous move, given what we know about this Marco bloke.'

'Maybe. But it got the poor kid out, didn't it? Brought him here. Anyway, what about this book full of drawings, then?'

'I don't know, except it sounded pretty important. Like he thought he might pick up some clues up from it and get a better idea of where to find Eileen.'

'Where is it?'

'That's the problem. He doesn't know. It was either lost in the accident or...' and he went as white as a bloody sheet when he said this... 'or Marco still has it. Also, he said something about needing his rucksack?'

'Oh, shit, yeah. Hang on.'

Mackie went upstairs and pushed open the bedroom door, ready to explain himself. Ready to tell the kid the rucksack was still in the Golf, at work. But the kid was asleep. Mackie crept to his bedside and looked down at him. Even at rest his face was furrowed and streaked with worry.

23

Mackie's mobile rang while he was making breakfast. It was Sharon.

'Mackie, all set?'

'Yeah.'

'Have you taken the kid through the plan again?'

'Yeah.' He hadn't. The kid was still upstairs getting ready.

'So he definitely knows what to say if Tranter asks him anything?'

'He does.'

'OK. And you're going to get here early so we can go through the Trev part of the plan?'

'Yeah ... Sha?'

'What?'

'Do we need to synchronise our watches?'

'Fuck off.'

They'd not got to the end of the street before she was on the phone again.

'I've just had a thought. We don't want the kid looking like he recognises the yard. I'm going to have him to myself anyway, it's just if Tranter comes in the office and says anything.'

'Roger that.'

She put the phone down on him.

It was just as well she'd phoned because they arrived just as Tranter got in early. He was pulling in as Mackie and the kid arrived at the yard.

'This the lad, then?' Tranter barked. 'I thought Arlene said he was something to do with Sharon?'

'Oh. Yes, he is. But he just lives up the road from me. Sharon asked me to call for him.' Mackie gave the kid a quick nod.

Tranter stuck his hand out of the window and offered it to the kid. It was hard to tell if it was nerves, or the rush of Lynx that came at them like a genie out of a bottle, but the kid shook it solemnly and then stepped back.

'Thank you for letting me come,' he whispered; Mackie's heart pinged up to his shoulders.

'Oh, you're from up north, are you?'

The kid glanced at Mackie. Two minutes in and they were already off script. Not only that, but the first step of the plan – retrieving the kid's rucksack from the Golf – was completely out of the question.

'Ah, I'm not sure.' Mackie put his hand on the kid's shoulder. 'Sharon didn't say. But no doubt she'll fill us in. So, come on, er, lad...' He directed the kid with a nod of his head. 'We better get over there before she comes looking for us. Don't want you to be late on your first day.' He then steered him across the yard and into the office. He was sweating by the time they got through the door.

'What did Tranter say?'

'He asked the kid if he was from up north. His accent. He was also wondering why I'd brought him in and not you.'

'OMG. Never thought of that.' Anyhow...' She heaved herself out of the chair. 'Come in, Riley. Sit in that corner by the little desk. If Tranter comes in let me do the talking, OK? Right, Mackie, you can bugger off now. Leave me to it. I'll see you at tea break.'

They were busy all morning. Tranter had had one of his *thinking* weekends which usually meant that Arlene had been on at him. He descended on Mackie and Trev as soon as they had the machines started, came marching up the aisle giving them the cut-throat signal to switch off. Mackie stayed in the cab, feeling the last vibrations shake themselves loose out of the metal, then climbed down. He looked at Trev who gave a minute shrug before he hopped down. They approached Tranter side by side. There was something of a showdown about it: him and Trev squinting into the sun, Tranter in his leather waistcoat, scowling up from under the brim of his cowboy hat.

'Alright, boss?'

Speaking without being spoken to? Trev was pushing it.

'None of your fucking business, lad, you're my fucking employee, not my fucking therapist.'

Three fucks in one sentence? Arlene had definitely been at him. Mackie's heart was going like the clappers.

'That business last week with the kid...' Mackie felt his knees give. 'If anything had happened to him, you know, like if he'd fallen, or if he'd fucking died...' He spat this out, his two hands balled into fists at his side. 'Christ, the insurance would have had me by the flaming nadgers.'

Mackie avoided Trev's eye. Tranter's nadgers were not generally a Monday morning topic, although he reckoned they might make a bit of a comeback at tea break.

He was having cameras installed, that's what it boiled down to. And him and Trev needed to clear some space so they could be sited. On top of that he was introducing new safety measures: all new arrivals – regardless of time of day or night – had to be checked thoroughly to make sure there were no stowaways; *plus* weekly checks on all vehicles were going to start at the beginning of August.

'We've got sloppy, lads,' Tranter said. 'Time to tighten things up around here. Right?'

'Right,' they chorused, but Tranter was already walking away. They watched him, still not daring to look at each other, which was just as well because he suddenly stopped and turned.

'Well?' he hollered. They stared at him. 'What you fucking waiting for?' he said. 'Get to it.'

The office was small and warm but the kid didn't mind. There was something about being there that felt familiar – safe. He was halfway through his second hot chocolate, listening to Sharon on the phone, when the humming of his head started. He put down the cup and got himself ready.

The white room is sunny and airy and makes him smile. He knows he doesn't need to linger there because the way is already clear. The door is open and through it, in the distance, he can see a tower. He stretches himself out – a long smooth arrow – and flies towards it. He glances down at the road far below him and follows its twists and turns until he reaches a wide expanse of water – and the tower. He circles the water twice, enjoying the feeling of cool air on his face, then leaves.

The drawing came easily. Like it had been waiting for him. He folded it up and slipped it in his pocket.

24

Trev was loading a Mondeo onto the forklift when Sharon gave them the shout for tea break. There'd been no time for chat because Tranter had been on top of them all morning, conducting the proceedings, so Mackie was in a sweat because he'd not had a chance to action the second step of the plan – priming Trev about the 'work experience kid.'

He didn't dare to broach the subject as he crossed the yard with Trev because he wasn't sure if Tranter was behind them or not. He needn't have worried.

'Who the fuck is that?'

The kid was coming out of the office with the tea tray.

'Oh,' Mackie said, as nonchalantly as he could. 'He's something to do with Sharon. Work experience, I think.'

'Christ, couldn't he think of somewhere better than this?'

When they got to the picnic table Sharon was in position, lines at the ready. 'Trev, this is Riley. Riley, this is Trev. Riley's here to do a bit of work experience.'

She waited as per the plan to see if Trev recognised the kid, but he reached for a doughnut without really paying any attention to him. 'So,' Sharon said, moving swiftly on, 'what's happening?'

'He's getting CCTV put in.' Mackie hesitated. 'Because of...' He glanced at the kid. 'You know, for the insurance.'

'Protecting his nadgers, apparently.' Trev shoved the whole doughnut into his mouth. He chewed it for about two seconds, swallowed and turned his attention to the kid who was sitting quietly, gazing up at the spot where the Merc had been. Sharon gave her nose a gentle tap – the signal that she was about to reveal the kid's true identity – and launched into her preamble. She needn't have bothered.

'So, Trev...'

But Trev wasn't listening. He was still looking at the kid. He turned to Sharon, who was still on her preamble.

'Shut up a fucking minute, Sha. What's going on here?' He pointed at the kid.

'That's not a work experience kid, that's the kid who was in the Merc...'

Mackie folded his arms across his chest. 'Told you. I told you he'd recognise him.'

Sharon ignored him and launched into the main menu. She kept it tidy – the bare facts like she'd said, but Mackie held his breath and watched Trev's face the whole time, wondering what his reaction would be. It wasn't exactly what he'd expected.

'So, what was it like?' he asked the kid. 'What was it like being up there?'

Mackie had expected the kid to look at him or Sharon for some kind of permission to speak, but he didn't.

'It was nice.'

'Nice?'

'Yes. Safe.'

Trev gave this some consideration. 'Hot, I bet, though. So, could you see us, then, down here?'

'Oh, yes. I could see you when you were on your breaks.'

'Ha. I bet we looked like a right sorry bunch of losers, huddled over our tea and a plate of digestives.'

'You didn't,' the kid said. 'You looked like a little family.'

They all sat quiet for a minute or two after that.

'Right,' Sharon said, eventually. 'Times up. Trev – not a word about this to his nibs – especially now his arse is on fire about the CCTV. Get cracking before he sees you slacking. Ha ha, Mackie, I just need to check some paperwork with you, yeah?' They went into the office leaving the kid at the table.

'Everything OK?'

'Yes,' she whispered. 'He's done a drawing ... I wanted to show you it.'

Mackie took the drawing off her.

'You recognise it?'

'Not a clue.'

'Me neither. Oh, hi Trev.' Mackie put the drawing on the desk as casually as he could as Trev came back into the office. Trev was straight on it.

'Sha, do you know where ... oh, what've you got there that's so interesting?'

'Oh, just a drawing. Riley's a bit of an artist, isn't he, Mackie?'

'Let's have a look, then. Oh, yeah. That's pretty good. The kid has a good eye. Is that where he's from, then?'

Mackie and Sharon looked at him. 'What?'

'Merthyr. Is that where he's from?'

'Trev, how the hell has this got anything to do with Merthyr? It's a ... I don't know. What is it, Mackie?'

Mackie shrugged. 'A castle? A lake? I don't suppose it's anywhere in particular,' he started, but Trev whipped the drawing up before he could finish.

'Nope,' he said. 'It's Llwyn-onn. The other side of Merthyr. And it's not a lake, Mackie, it's a reservoir. Look.' He tapped the page. 'That bit of road you can see there, that's the A470 to Brecon. Them two cars parked by here – picnic bench there, isn't it? People like to stop and eat their sarnies.'

'Come off it, Trev. How could you possibly know that? Like when was the last time you went to Merthyr?'

'I go every weekend, actually. Asda's. Mum likes their sausages. And their little pork pies.' Something about this made Trev blush.

Sharon shot Mackie a *whaddyaknow* look. He raised one eyebrow in response. They'd always imagined Bertha had Trev confined to barracks on a weekend – cleaning detail or some such delight.

'What, she actually lets you use the car?'

'Saturday mornings, yeah.'

Bertha, as far as they were aware, was in charge of every aspect of Trev's life. She dropped him at the yard each morning and, if he was lucky, picked him back up at clocking off time. This was where his side-line came in – he was quietly earning himself enough money to get a car of his own.

'OK. So, how can you tell that – wherever you said it was – from a drawing of a reservoir?'

'Well, by this tower here – the castle, Mackie, and the hills, of course.' Trev traced his finger along the line that bordered the right-hand edge of the drawing. Look, that's definitely Twyn Croes, isn't it? Other side of that you've got Pontsticill, haven't you?'

Sharon's chin went south again.

'Twyn Croes. Trev, how the...'

'Oh, well, when I was in the scouts...'

Mackie was wondering how long Trev was going to go on. When Tranter suddenly walked in, he realised his mouth was hanging open and a fair bit of time had passed since Sharon had called time on tea break.

'What the fuck is this?' Tranter hollered. 'The Mother's fucking Union?'

Trev leapt to attention, knocked the chair over then shot off out of range, leaving Mackie and Sharon staring from the chair to Tranter.

'Right,' Tranter said. More of a grunt than a word. 'I'm supposing, seeing as you're still all enjoying tea break at...' he flexed a tanned wrist towards his face, 'at eleven sodding thirty, that everything's ready for this CCTV bloke.'

'Yeah,' Mackie lied. It was safer than saying, 'it is,' because in fact it wasn't. He and Trev still had some clearing to do for the final camera site. 'Right, then.' He bent over, picked up the chair and tucked it back under the desk. 'I'll erm, I'll get back to it.'

25

Mackie was clearing the final spot for the CCTV installation when he saw Sharon coming across the yard. He switched the engine off and jumped down from the cab.

'Everything OK, Sha?'

'Christ, Mackie, I've been on the tannoy this last ten minutes.'

He pointed to the ear defenders hanging round his neck.

'You need to come now. It's the kid. He suddenly went all ... weird. Come on.'

Mackie set off at a sprint. The kid was sitting outside, his elbows propped on the picnic table, gazing up at the sky. Or so he thought, because when he got nearer he realised the kid's eyes were closed. The drawing was on the table in front of him.

'Alright, Riley?'

The kid opened his eyes. 'Yes. But...'

'Is something wrong?'

'I don't know. I think...' He picked up his drawing and stared at it. 'I think it might be time.'

'Christ...' Sharon leaned against the table to get her breath. 'Is he OK?'

'He's fine,' Mackie said. He might have added, *I think,* because the kid didn't particularly look fine. He had the same look about him that he'd had after the 3M's escapade. Like he wasn't quite there.

'So come on, then. Spit it out. What's wrong?'

Mackie looked at the kid. 'Go on,' he said. 'Tell Sharon.'

The kid held the drawing out towards her. 'I think it might be the right time,' the kid said. 'I think Eileen might be there.'

'What, now?'

He gave a small shrug. 'Today.'

Sharon took a sharp intake of breath, looked at Mackie and gave a little shake of her head. 'That's a bit of a tall order, Riley.'

Mackie knew what was coming next because, when it came to tall orders, Sharon was something of an expert. 'Let me have a bit of a think,' she said. 'Go on, bugger off, Mackie. I'll see you at dinner break.'

It came as no surprise to Mackie that Sharon was late calling dinner break. She was no doubt playing it safe because of their extended tea break. When she did call them, however, the jaunty edge in her voice told him he might be wrong.

'Come and get it, boys,' she crooned in her best Patsy Cline voice.

'Thank god for that. Thought her bloody watch had packed in.'

She was waiting for them with a grin on her face. 'Pin back your ears, lads. Do you want the good news or the bloody good news?'

'I'll take anything as long as it involves a sausage sandwich,' Trev scoffed.

Tranter's bad mood, it transpired, had not just been down to the impending CCTV installation. He'd got a function. He'd gone into the office shortly after the kid's revelation and announced he'd be clocking off early. She'd waited until he'd gone then called them in. Enough time, Mackie realised, for her to have more than a bit of a think.

'So...' She put her hands on her hips.

Mackie sat down. The look on her face that told him there was going to be more on the table than a plate of gingers. He was right. As Sharon saw it, Tranter's unexpected departure presented a bit of an opportunity for a well-earned skive and – she looked at Mackie at that point – a bit of a work's outing.

'What's that supposed to mean?' Trev mumbled through a mouthful of bread.

Mackie knew exactly what it meant. He just couldn't work out why she was bringing it up in front of Trev.

'Well, if we set off now,' she continued, 'we could get there, you know, nice and early.'

Mackie was rolling his eyes at her, cautioning her to shut up before she put her foot in it completely. She ignored him.

'Where?' Trev was onto the gingers now.

'Merthyr, of course.' She pulled the drawing out of her pocket. Exhibit number one. 'Here.'

Mackie gave up at that point. He did as he was told and pinned his ears back while Sharon introduced Trev to some of the kid's more unusual talents. He had to hand it to her, she'd given it a lot of thought. Her introduction, where she likened the kid's drawings to a trail of crumbs, struck an immediate chord.

'Like a detective, you mean?'

'Exactly. Like one of your Michael Connolly's. Except the clues are drawings.'

Trev palmed another ginger and gave this some thought.

'Of course, if you think about it, this will be our last chance for a bit of fun. Once that CCTV goes up it'll be like bloody *Crimewatch* round here. We won't be able to move without him seeing us.'

This was a particularly well-planned clincher, as far as Mackie was concerned, because Sharon knew Trev – Sketty's answer to Harry Bosch – loved a bit of *Crimewatch*. She also knew that, once the CCTV was up, his little side-line business would go down the Swanee.

'Is this all true?' Trev asked the kid.

'Yes.'

'So who are you looking for?'

Mackie held his breath, wondering how the kid would explain the next bit – and how Trev would react. He needn't have worried.

'She's called Eileen. She's my stepmum.'

'Ooh. The plot thickens. More *X-Files* than Michael Connolly, actually, Sha.'

'So you're in?'

'Why not. All for one and one for all, and all that. Anyway, it'd be nice to have a change of scenery – and see the reservoir again.'

'Way to go, Trev. *The Three Musketeers* or what?'

'Hang on a minute, Sha. I make that four musketeers.' Trev turned to look at the kid. 'You can't leave Riley out.'

It was a different story when Sharon started in on the next part of the plan.

'Great.' She trilled her fingernails on the table. 'That's settled so, that just leaves one problem. Transport.'

'Well, it's got to be your car, Sha. We can't get there on the bus.'

'Car's in for an MOT.'

'So we can't do it then, can we?' Trev's voice was all disappointment.

'Not necessarily. His nibs isn't here. There's no CCTV yet – we can take Barbie.'

The colour left Trev's cheeks. 'Well, you can count me out, then,' he said. 'No way I'm taking Barbie. Christ. He'd fucking kill us.' He ran his finger round the inside of his roll neck and looked out across the yard at the black Mitsubishi Barbarian which was stationed, showroom style, in its own special spot, diagonal to the fence, where its gleam caught the eye of anyone who came in. They called it Barbie behind Tranter's back because his name was Ken, but also because it added a bit of weight to their side of the scales and took a bit off his. Childish, but hell, it ticked their box.

'But we can't do it without you, Trev,' Mackie said. 'You're the one who knows the place.' This was a weak attempt to remind him that he, with his geographical prowess, was the star of the show. It didn't get him anywhere.

Sharon followed it up with a bit of 'you only live once,' although they both knew this wasn't entirely the case for Trev – all the living he'd ever been granted was the thin slice that Bertha allowed him.

'Yeah, that's my concern. Living.'

'Come on, Trev.' For some reason the thought of an escapade, an adventure, had Mackie more excited than he would have liked to admit. Trev shook his head and folded his arms. You could see the boy in him.

They were getting nowhere until the kid, who had been quiet throughout all this, suddenly piped up. 'I think I might need you to be there, Trev.'

Mackie didn't know what the kid meant but it didn't matter because it did the trick.

'Oh,' Trev said. 'Well if that's the case...'

It was decided that Mackie would be the driver. Decided, meaning that Sharon grabbed Barbie's keys off their hook then set off across the yard at a lick. Mackie didn't quite latch on until she jumped into the passenger seat and Trev slid, like he'd been greased, into the crew cab, leaving him to take the hot seat.

'I can't believe we're doing this,' Mackie said, as he turned the key. Barbie gave a throaty growl and her dashboard lit up like a Boeing 747. Sharon was rooting in the glove compartment. Amazingly, the first thing she pulled out was a pair of gloves.

'Oh, here we go,' she said and brought out a small stack of CDs. 'Right, let's see what the bugger listens to. Hah!' She shuffled through the CDs. 'Crap ... crap ... crap,' until she came to one that passed muster. She manoeuvred it into the slot and, as they turned out of the yard, Sir Tom started on 'Green Green Grass of Home.'

'Nice one, Sha,' Trev cheered from the back. 'Have you got any sweets?'

'Is the Pope a Catholic?' she snorted and produced a bag of assorted toffees.

'Hey, your Lauren would approve of this.' They'd just pulled onto the A465 and Mackie could feel himself settling into the lull of the road. It had been a while since he was behind a wheel, but Barbie didn't notice a thing.

'Wouldn't she just.' He wound his window down and grinned out into the warm air. He glanced at Trev and the kid in the rear-view mirror, the two of them perky in their seats like two kids setting off on holiday. He glanced at himself in the wing mirror and smiled at what he saw. He looked happy. 'Turn that music up, Sha,' he shouted, as Tom launched into 'It's Not Unusual,' because he suddenly wanted to share it all with the world. This feeling of hope, the possibility that they counted for something: he wanted it to pour out over the hills and towns and remind people that this was how easy it could be. Step out of your little box and there it was, waiting for you.

He wanted that drive to last forever.

They quietened down as they started approaching the series of roundabouts that led to Merthyr, then turned onto the A470 towards their destination. Mackie glanced at the kid in the rear-view mirror. 'Everything OK?'

'Yes.' His cheeks had some colour in them which seemed like a good sign.

'Right, we're not far now,' Trev said. 'It's coming up on the left, shortly. Here we are. Can you see it, Riley?'

Mackie pulled Barbie into the layby that ran alongside the reservoir. There were a couple of cars parked further along – just like in the kid's drawing – and Mackie suddenly realised that this could be it: the moment they found Eileen. He looked over the water trying to work out why the thought of it had him feeling panicked rather than relieved. Why he felt so attached to this strange kid – not quite ready to let him go.

But Sharon was all business. 'Right,' she said, climbing out of the truck. 'Bite the bullet time.' She walked towards the nearest picnic bench.

Mackie hung back. 'You're still sure about this, Riley? Sure we're in the right place?'

The kid glanced over at the two cars, tilted his face up to the sky and took a deep breath in. 'Yes.'

'Come on, then. Sharon, you stay here. I'll go over with Riley and see if ... if Eileen is there.' He didn't want anyone to be with him, because if she was there, he didn't know how he would react to simply handing the kid over. He made himself move and followed the kid towards the parked cars. As they got closer, Mackie could see one of the cars was empty. It had a silver screen protector on to keep the sun out. The kid peered in through the passenger window, then looked at Mackie and shook his head.

Mackie should have been disappointed, he knew that, but instead he felt relieved.

'What about that one?' The second car was a little further along. Its rear window was tinted. 'Do you recognise it?'

The kid didn't answer, but the slump in his shoulders told

Mackie he didn't. 'Well, maybe the time's not quite right, yet. Like the 3M's?' He put his arm across the kid's shoulders – he could see he was close to tears. 'Why don't we wait for a bit. Maybe she's gone for a walk or something?' The kid shrugged him off but Mackie pressed on. 'Come on, lad. I'll ask Sharon and Trev to pop into Merthyr. Get us a pizza? I'm starving. We could sit at one of the picnic benches – wait for a bit, you know?' He was jazzing it all up, but he could see the kid wasn't buying it.

'No.' The kid shook his head. 'I just … I just need to be on my own for a minute…' Then he walked away.

Mackie watched him go. Forced himself not to run after him. To run after him and tell him not to worry, that everything would work out OK, that they would find Eileen…

'What's going on?'

Sharon and Trev were coming along the path towards him.

'Nothing. She's not there.'

'Bugger. How's Riley?' Mackie didn't need to answer: they could see him, sitting on a low stone wall, hunched forward, staring at the ground.

'I've told him we'll wait a bit.'

'OK. Fair enough. Let's park ourselves here so we can keep an eye on him.'

Mackie managed to sit for a couple of minutes then got up and trekked towards the kid. He clambered over the low wall and went down to the water's edge. He bent down, selected a couple of flat stones then, without saying anything, sent them skimming across the water.

'Not bad, not bad,' he muttered, like he was talking to himself, then bent down and chose another handful. He gave it another minute or so then turned and offered a stone to the kid. 'Competition?'

It worked. Before long the kid was at his side and the pair of them were grubbing for the best stones and hurling them across the reservoir. Mackie kept it up until his arms were aching. Anyone driving past might smile to see them, he thought. But that was the thing about appearances. You couldn't always trust them. They gave it another half hour then called it a day. Mackie pulled the truck into the traffic then drove, listening to Trev and Sharon's conversation. Trev started it off with a story about a local woman who had made her name with cold water swimming. Not the kind of stuff you see in those fancy books, he explained. *Wild Swimming,* ha ha. What she did went beyond wild, it was insane.

'The Merthyr Mermaid.' He turned and pointed towards the hills that towered in the distance. 'Pwll-Du,' he said, 'just outside of Blaenavon. Did her first ice mile in Keeper's Pond...'

'What do you think of that, then, Riley?' Sharon twisted round in her seat and tossed the kid a couple of toffees. 'Do much swimming yourself?'

'Not really. Just school and that.' He unwrapped a sweet and passed one to Trev, who was already lining up his next story.

It was about how he'd eventually moved on from the scouts and joined the Sea Scouts. *I had a friend in those days*, he'd said, and Mackie missed the next bit because the poignancy of the words caught him unawares. They obviously got Sharon the same way because she launched into a long-winded speech about how Trev did have friends – them. It wasn't that convincing, really, because there was no real evidence to back it up. 'So how come you gave it up, then?' she asked. 'Your sea scouting.'

A no brainer as far as Mackie was concerned – and he was right.

'Mum thought it was a bit too dangerous.'

They all thought about that for a few moments and then Sharon piped up.

'I was a mermaid once, actually.'

'Oh, yeah, well, pass me and Riley another toffee and tell me more.'

Mackie half listened, but his mind was on the kid. How he was feeling because this was his second failed attempt to find Eileen.

'It was at the baths in town,' Sharon said. 'Before they modernised them, yeah? Me and my mates, we had this routine on the top diving board. 'The Tawe Mermaids' we called ourselves. We were fantastic. Drove all the lads mad, we did. God, those were the days.'

After that she cranked the music up and they drove back in silence.

Carol from next door was in the garden unpegging Dougie's work pants off the line when they got back. She nodded at him, then looked at the kid.

'Alright, Mackie?'

'Alright, Carol?' This was usually as far as they went. One of them might throw something in about the weather or work – he knew her from his old days at Tesco's – but nothing beyond that.

'Your Lauren OK, is she?'

'Yeah ... why?'

'Oh. Just wondered. I saw the police were here this afternoon, thought, you know...'

'Ah, no. There was a bit of an incident at work...' He glanced at the kid. 'Probably something to do with that. I'll ring them now when I get in.' He followed the kid up the path and unlocked the door. There was a calling card on the door mat. Mackie picked it up and put it on the hall table. The kid leaned down to look at it.

'Is there a message on it?'

'No. But that's alright. I'll give them a ring after we've had something to eat, yeah?'

The kid wasn't going to leave it at that. 'Do you think it's about Marco?'

'Dunno.'

Mackie wondered if it could be about Eileen but he didn't say it. He was trying to work out how to ask the kid about the way things had gone at the reservoir.

He switched the kettle on. 'Still warm out there, isn't it? How about we sit in the garden for a bit? Get some fresh air?'

This was pushing it, bearing in mind all the fresh air they'd had at the reservoir, but Mackie was reluctant to leave the kid to his own thoughts. Sharon and Trev had kept the conversation going most of the way back and by the time they got back to the yard, the crease had dropped out of the kid's forehead. Now, though, he needed to ask him about Eileen. He waited until they were at the garden table.

'So, erm, any feelings about ... erm ... Eileen today? When we were at the reservoir, I mean?' He took a swallow of tea, passed the kid a biscuit; he was trying to keep the conversation light.

'No. I tried ... but I couldn't see her.'

Couldn't see her. Mackie rolled with it. 'OK. So, like yesterday, you mean? The wrong timing?'

'I don't know.' The kid pushed his drink to one side. The small crease in his forehead was back. 'I'm tired, Mackie. Is it alright if I go upstairs for a bit?'

'What? Well...' Mackie could feel himself hotting up. He'd misstepped, gone in too quick. 'OK then, but ... but I'm going to put a pizza in – I'll bring you some up when it's done, yeah?'

But the kid was already on his way up the garden. He looked like he had the weight of the world on his shoulders.

Mackie was still in the garden, wondering what he might do to perk the kid up when the phone rang. He considered ignoring it, closing his eyes and going to bed himself, but then thought of the police calling card. It was Sharon.

'Well – have you landed yet?'

'What?'

'From this afternoon,' she said. 'From our road trip. Our Thelma and Louise extravaganza.'

'Oh. Yeah.'

'God, it was good, wasn't it? Christ, you know something, Mackie, it made me feel almost bloody human. Hardly been able to sit down. How about you?'

'Yeah, same.'

'Same? You sound like you've just come back from your own bloody funeral.'

'Nah, just – you know, a bit tired. Worrying, I suppose, about ... you know, about Riley. Wondering how I can perk him up, you know.'

'Aha, well, here I am to your rescue, Mackie, dear pal, because I've got a proposal.'

'Not another.'

'Another. And it's probably,' she dropped into her telephone sex-line voice, 'going to involve a bit of Sir Tom.'

He smiled into the receiver. 'I take it you're singing tonight, then?'

'Got it in one. And, wait for it, I've got Barry to reserve a table for you and Riley. Plus,' she did a short trumpet fanfare, 'it's curry night. Much as you can choke down for a fiver.'

He didn't have the energy to think one way or another. 'OK... go on, then. I'll go up and see if I can revive Riley.'

'Fablus! See you at seven thirty. Hey ... bring some wet wipes, Barry won't stump up for serviettes.'

26

It was knocking on eight by the time they got there so the place was already packed. Mackie held onto the kid's arm as they hovered in the doorway, trying to spot an empty table.

'You OK?' The kid had backed up against him as if he was nervous.

'There's a lot of people.' He pointed towards the bar. Sharon was there, talking to Barry, who must have said something because she turned round and waved them over.

'Whaddya think?' She stepped back from the bar with a little jazz hands side shuffle.

'Tidy.' She was wearing a black velvet bodysuit with matching choker.

'I'm hoping it won't get too hot.' Sharon was adjusting the crotch. 'They're gonna go mental, aren't they, Barry?'

Barry gave a small grunt. His eyes were on his optics or, more accurately, on the young barmaid who was on her tiptoes, most of her midriff on show, doling out the happy hour doubles.

'Yeah, mental, Sha.' He pushed away from the bar. 'I'll just go change that whisky.'

'Guess what?' she said, when he'd gone. 'Barry's got a couple of scouts coming in. He's been talking about it for ages but he's done it, so—' She did a half twirl which was enough to let him know the bodysuit was going to pose a bit of a heat issue. 'Tonight could be my lucky night. Bye-bye Tranter's, hello sun, sea and stardom!'

That was far as she got because Barry had taken to the stage and was warming up the PA system. This involved several blasts of feedback that hit the metal plate in Mackie's head like a tuning fork; but it seemed to serve as a sort of signal because everyone suddenly stopped what they were doing and took their seats.

'Ooh, here we go,' Sharon said. 'Come on, your table's at the front. Oh, hang on.' She picked something up off the bar and put it on her head. Pussycat ears on a hair band. Mackie raised his eyebrows.

'I've seen it all, now.'

'Not quite.' She turned to lead the way. She had a long black tail pinned to her backside.

Sharon was right. The crowd went mental. She started with 'What's New Pussycat?', then swung into 'Green, Green Grass', and by the time she hit 'Delilah', the sweat was flying off her.

'She's good, isn't she?' the kid said, once the clapping and foot stomping had died down.

'She's fantastic.' Mackie had swivelled round in his seat so he could scan the audience for Barry's scouts. He didn't believe for a minute there'd be any because that was how it was with him and her – Barry dangled the carrot and Sharon kept believing that one day she'd actually get the bugger between her teeth. Except, deep down, he knew she didn't really believe that at all because he'd met Marsha – Barry's wife. She was cut from the same cloth as Arlene except there wasn't as much of it: she was still part of the 'ladies who lunch' brigade except, judging from the size of her, she wasn't big on the lunch aspect. She sometimes turned up unannounced at the club, aiming, no doubt, to catch Barry *in flagrante delicto* with one of the barmaids, not for one minute suspecting he'd been supplementing her bony bedtime offerings for years with a woman whose generous padding offered all the comforts of a small sofa.

'Well. What did you think?'

Sharon flopped onto the chair next to them. There was steam coming off her.

'You were bloody fantastic.'

'I was, wasn't I? Christ, I'm hot.'

'You certainly are, darling.' She swivelled round. She had a smile on her face and Mackie knew what she was thinking: that Barry had kept his word and she was about to be *scouted*. The bloke put her straight soon enough. 'Not too hot to handle though, I bet.' He patted the empty chair beside him. 'Why don't you come over here and sit next to me?'

'Piss off, Gerry, or I'll tell your Angie what you said. Christ.'

She swivelled back. 'I'm going to have to go and get this bloody thing off.' She tugged at the neckline of the bodysuit, exposing a mound of damp cleavage and releasing a tide of perfume that swamped both him and the kid before they had a chance to move out of its path.

'Follow me,' she said as she hoisted herself off the chair.

'What?'

'Follow me. He'll have the curry out in a minute. It'll be like the bloody goldrush. Come on.'

She twisted her way across the packed floor, dodging tables and stray hands and left them by a set of trestle tables, which, apart from a selection of stained paper tablecloths, were bare. 'Wait here and don't move,' she said. 'And get me a plate too, yeah? I'm bloody ravenous.'

The kid was gazing across at the bar. 'Is Barry Sharon's husband?'

'No. Just a friend. Hey, do you think we should sit back down and—'

He got no further. It was like the starter's gun had gone off: one minute he and the kid were alone at the trestles, and the next, after a kind of synchronised scraping of chairs and tables, the entire club had formed a queue behind them.

'Mackie.' He craned his neck to see where she was. 'Get me a couple of naans, yeah? But no kebabs, OK? Whatever you do, don't be tempted by Barry's kebabs.'

Getting a taxi home had, at the time, felt like a good idea. The kid had scoffed a plateful of curry then gone back for more and Mackie, ignoring Sharon's advice, had been tempted by Barry's kebabs. All in all, by 10.30pm the prospect of a long walk back home sat heavy so Mackie had scooted the kid up to the taxi rank. He thought nothing of it until they'd got settled in the back seat and the driver asked for his address.

'Oh. It's you.' This struck Mackie as a bit odd until he

recognised him. 'I was at your place the other night.' The bloke was eyeing him in the rear-view mirror.

'Oh, yeah.' Mackie was suddenly conscious of the late hour and the fact that he'd obviously been drinking.

'Couldn't get a babysitter, then?' The driver flicked a look at the kid.

'What? Oh. No – it was a family do, you know. Curry night. Good though, wasn't it?' He gave the kid a small nudge and he nodded his head.

The bloke was still regarding him in the mirror. 'The police came round yesterday.'

There was no need for Mackie to panic because the police knew the kid was with him. But old habits die hard. 'The police?' He could feel Barry's curry creeping up his gullet.

'Yeah. A couple of cops. Came by the taxi rank. Wanting to know about pick-ups on Thursday night.'

'Yeah. They've already been round to see me,' Mackie said, swallowing the curry back down. 'Left their card so I could give them a ring. Good to know they're on the ball, isn't it?'

'I'm going to go straight to bed, Mackie.'

'What? Oh, yeah. No problem.' Mackie was considering the police calling card. It was on the hall table where he'd left it. 'Good night though, wasn't it?'

'It was brilliant.'

Mackie knew the kid wasn't just saying it: the night had put a smile on both their faces. The club, the curry, Sharon in action – it had been just what they needed.

'I'll see you in the morning, then. Oh, by the way,' he said as nonchalantly as he could, 'I left a drawing book by your bed – just in case ... you know...'

Mackie made a cup of tea and took it out into the garden. He eased himself onto the bench under the tree and leaned his head back against its trunk and thought about what the day had served up. It was all sitting in his head like a knot he couldn't unravel. He picked at the edges of it: Tom Jones and Barbie; Sharon and the Merthyr Mermaid; Trev and his boats; until he reached the tangle in the centre of it all. *The kid.*

The kid was sitting on the edge of the bed, trying to understand what was happening. It had happened twice now: a drawing he thought would lead him to Eileen, but led him nowhere. Mackie hadn't been able to get the rucksack from work but he was starting to think that the photograph he had tucked inside it wouldn't help anyway – it didn't when he was in the Merc, so maybe it never would.

He'd known as soon as they got to the reservoir that he'd made another mistake. Eileen wasn't there; she never had been. He'd looked out over the water trying to bring her to him and studied the tower at the far end of the reservoir, searching it for clues, but nothing had happened.

He could no longer ignore the feeling that he had all day – that Eileen was slipping away from him – and somehow, this was OK. He just didn't understand what it meant. Nor did he understand what he'd seen when he was watching Sharon on stage. He'd thought at first that the shadow hanging over her was a trick of the lighting but realised, as she grinned her way through her repertoire, that it wasn't. It was attached to her, like a small grey cape. And it was weighing her down.

He went to the window, pulled back the curtains and looked out. He traced the line of rooftops and chimneys etched against a sky that was stretching towards night. He followed a tapering line of birds as they passed, silent and intent, nodded at a half-moon rising out of a bank of cloud, then lowered his gaze to the garden.

Mackie was sitting under the tree, staring out into the dark. The kid swallowed hard.

It was just like the drawing he'd done in his sketchbook.

He gave a small nod of recognition and suddenly everything made sense. It was alright. Everything was as it should be. He was meant to be there – with this tree, these people. He didn't know why yet, but all he needed to do was wait and the answer would come. He gave another small nod – of acceptance – and felt the confusion that had been weighing him down all day slip from his shoulders; and, like it had been waiting, the humming in his head started up.

The whole of Swansea is laid out before him as he sails out through the air – his arms outstretched like some gliding bird. He circles Mackie's house then, guided by nothing but a faint breeze and the trace of moonlight across rooftops beneath him, heads off. On and on he flies, enjoying the cool air, smiling into night clouds that dissolve as he passes, until his eye is caught by a gleam of light in the distance. He pulls in his arms and, like a dart, flies towards it. He lifts his face and tastes the salt in the air. He is heading towards the sea.

The tower is very tall and he thinks, at first, it is in the water. A lighthouse maybe. But he is wrong. As he gets closer he realises that although the sea lies on its one side – a wide open expanse that tells him nothing – its other side looks down on rows of boats. He can hear the water lapping against their sides, the wind tapping out soft rhythms against their empty masts. He pulls himself away and flies back.

27

There was a *fresh-start* feel to the next day. Mackie felt it as soon as he woke up: something like the excitement at the beginning of term, the pleasure of making the first mark on a clean page, packing fresh exercise books into a new satchel. It hadn't even been marred by the phone call to the police.

He'd got up early and decided to make the call to the police which he somehow hadn't got round to the night before. This had been prompted partly by the conversation with the taxi driver: he was pissed off that he'd not just told the bloke to wind his neck in, instead of flipping straight into his 'guilty as charged' mode. Mostly, though, he just wanted to know why they wanted to talk to him.

It turned out the kid was right. It was about Marco: less of a talk and more of a heads-up, he'd thought, when the call was over. Tracy Cooper had obviously enlightened them about the real motive behind Marco's search for his younger brother. They suspected Marco now had transport because a CCTV camera had captured a car theft in progress and the guy in the frame matched the mugshot they had of him. There was nothing to worry about, the officer assured him, because Marco didn't know where he lived – or that he had the kid staying with him. *Nevertheless* – the word hung between them until Mackie, his new satchel still swinging on his shoulder, batted it away 'I'll call you if I need to,' he said and hung up.

The kid came down five minutes later, smiling. Mackie was going to tell him about the conversation with the police – the veiled warning – but something stopped him. He didn't want to take the shine off the day – or the smile off the kid's face.

'Number one job as soon as we get in today, Riley. We must get your rucksack out of the Golf, yeah?'

'Erm, yeah. OK.'

'What have you got there?' A needless question because Mackie could see what it was: the drawing book he'd left on the kid's bedside table.

The kid held it up to show him. 'Whose is it?'

Mackie looked at the cover. Lauren went for simplicity when it came to gender stereotyping: she bought one of each and let the twins do the choosing. The trucks and tractors on the cover had it singled out as Tylo's.

'It belongs to my grandson, Tylo.'

'Oh. Does he live here, then?'

'Sometimes. He's not here now though; he's with his mum.'

'Your daughter?'

'Yep. Lauren.'

The kid nodded at this and sat down at the table. 'You found her, then?'

'What? Oh, yeah. I did. I should have told you – I didn't think you'd remember ... Anyway...'

'Was she in the sea?'

Christ. 'Well, yes, funnily enough, she was... Anyway, I wonder what today will bring?' A casual opener Mackie thought, hoping it would prompt the kid to stop asking questions and maybe show him whatever it was he'd drawn. He didn't. He put the book to one side.

'So, where is she now?'

'Lauren? Oh, she's on holiday. In Cornwall. With Tylo and his sister, Amber. They're twins, they're nearly five...' Mackie left it at that. He didn't want to talk about Lauren. He wanted the fresh start to stay with him, not for it to be muddied by the usual background worry about her and the twins.

The kid nodded, then filled his bowl with cornflakes and set about them like he'd not eaten for a week.

The fresh start to the day feeling lasted until Tranter arrived: the screech of tyres as he came through the gates was a kind of shorthand to warn them he was in a foul mood. He'd got the dogs in the back of the car, all barking their heads off which added to the general feeling of threat. They all kept their heads down until he'd disappeared into his den, which meant that tea break was delayed; Mackie and Trev were watching the clock a full hour before the microphone crackled and Sharon's voice sailed through the air.

'Thank god for that, Sha. Thought you'd bloody forgot. Oh. Only gingers again?' Trev palmed a handful and slotted one into his mouth.

'Thought I'd wait 'til he'd stopped prowling around. No point rattling his cage.' Sharon shifted the plate out of Trev's reach.

'What's up with him?'

'Not a bloody clue.'

They nodded into their coffee mugs, like they were considering something of import – world poverty maybe, or the strength of the pound against the Euro.

'Anyway.' Trev reached over for another biscuit. 'What about yesterday? Bloody good or what? We should do it more often, you know. Go out together, like mates.'

'But we are mates, Trev,' Sharon said.

This wasn't really true, Mackie thought. There was a world of difference between being a mate and just being someone you worked with. For him, Trev had always been in the second category, so from that point of view the trip to the reservoir had been an eye-opener – a glimpse of a Trev he'd never seen before or bothered to ask about.

'In fact, we're more than just mates. What was it you said, Riley? We looked like a little family.' Sharon smiled.

Trev turned to the kid. 'Well, you've proper perked things up around here, you have. Got anything else up your sleeve?'

To Mackie's surprise, the kid got up and went into the office. He came back a minute later with Tylo's drawing book in his hand. 'I did this,' he said, then opened it to a page and passed it to Trev. Trev let out a noise somewhere between a snort and a cough. Mackie's first thought was that he'd fallen foul of a ginger nut.

'Fuck me ... sorry, Riley, but look at this.'

Mackie tried to tell himself he was wrong, but the lurch in his chest as soon as he clapped eyes on the drawing told him he wasn't. A view through a window might sound pretty generic, but Mackie knew there was only one place in Swansea that had a view like that: the Meridian Tower. Or, to be more specific, the swanky eating place on its twenty-third floor.

'What is it, Riley?' Mackie asked, which was a bloody stupid question, but he was trying to buy himself some time.

Trev was straight on it. 'Don't be an arse, Mackie. You know where that is. It's the Meridian Tower down at the Marina...'

'The restaurant on the top floor, to be precise,' Sharon added.

'So, is this...' Trev was all excitement. 'Is this like yesterday?'

The kid didn't actually answer; that's what Mackie remembered later. He neither confirmed nor denied what the drawing was about or who it was for. It was Sharon and Trev who simply picked it up and started to run with it, not knowing at that point it was going to change everything.

By the time dinner break came round, Sharon had it all settled. Mackie jawed his way through a cheese sandwich and listened to the plan. She'd buffed the impending trip to the tower (*definitely on, Mack, straight after work – hot irons and all that*) into some million-dollar film production: the magnificent view, the Marina ... the scones. The kid was completely sold – all smiles and nods, and Trev was nothing short of tap dancing. It was a losing battle before he even started.

'I'm just not sure, Sha ... I'm a bit knackered to be honest...' In terms of a strategy, it was hopeless, but it was all he'd managed to come up with because Tranter had been on his back all morning.

'Oh, come on, Mackie.' She turned to Trev and the kid. 'It'll be great, won't it, boys?'

'Yeah, come on, bud, don't let us down. Don't be a party pooper.'

'Sharon.' He left Trev and the kid at the table and followed her into the office. 'Do you think it's a good idea, roping Trev in, I mean?'

'What? Oh, I didn't need to rope him in. He's all for it. Got all misty-eyed about it if I'm honest – said he used to spend a lot of time down the Marina when he was younger. It seemed mean not to invite him along – he's one of the gang, after all.'

One of the gang. This was Sharon all over: she loved a waif and stray. The kid was a typical example – once she'd learned about his predicament, she was straight in there. Scooped him up like he was a chick out of its nest. It was to do with how things had been for her when she was growing up, he knew that, but he loved her for it.

'So, what has Riley said about it? Does he think Eileen will be there?'

Sharon considered the question a moment. 'Come to think of it, no. He didn't say anything about Eileen.'

'So, what if it doesn't work again? You saw how he was yesterday at the reservoir.'

'You're overthinking it, Mackie. He enjoyed the club after, didn't he?'

'Well, yes...'

'So, there you are, then. Go on, bugger off and stop worrying so much.'

Mackie set off across the yard, chiding himself for not coming up with a better argument, because it wasn't really the Trev aspect of the trip he was worrying about: it was the Meridian Tower.

Don't be a party pooper. Trev didn't know it, but he had it in one.

Lauren's twelfth birthday. The tower had just been completed so Mackie had pushed the boat out, so to speak, and booked them in for a birthday tea. *Table at the front?* the girl had said on the phone. *Why not?* he'd replied, with the confidence of a man who didn't know what the hell he was talking about. *Why not?* He soon bloody found out. He survived the shock of stepping out of the stairway and emerging into the restaurant – an experience he could only liken to his foolhardy attempt at Vertigo in Oakwood Theme Park – but following the waitress across the floor, which seemed to be moving slightly, was more than he could manage.

'Come on, Dad.'

Lauren was already at the table but he was lagging several yards behind, holding onto the back of a chair.

'Look.' She was at the plate glass window, pointing one way and then the other. 'You can see everything, Dad. Look.' She turned to her right. 'You can see the sea,' she said, then swivelled to her left, 'and the Marina.'

She was right, but all he could see was the height, the drop, the water below. And all he could think of was Sandra.

Once the waitress had helped him peel his fingers off the

back of the chair, he crossed the space on legs he couldn't feel and sort of threw himself down at the table. He managed an hour by keeping his eyes fixed on his plate and cup and avoiding any sideways movement of his eyes or head. Then, after concocting some story about another birthday surprise, he made his escape. And he'd never been back.

28

Afternoon tea break brought good news. The trip to the Meridian was off. Tranter had arranged for the CCTV fitters to come and give everything the final once over and someone needed to stay back late. Mackie had his hand straight up.

'Just go without me,' he chirped.

'Don't be dull, Mackie. You've got to be there for...' she cocked her head at the kid, 'for Riley.'

'Well, someone's got to stay.'

'I'm not bloody staying,' Trev said.

'We'll just have to go another time, then.'

Mackie waited to see what the kid's response would be: whether he'd pipe up and say the time was ripe, *now,* but he didn't say anything.

'Mind you,' Mackie was casting around for some silver lining to lift the general gloom that had descended, 'It'll give us a chance to move your stuff, Trev. The camera they're going to put up in the corner is going to be a bit of a problem, isn't it?'

Trev folded his arms across his chest. 'Wow, Mackie. That's brilliant. A trip out or an hour moving my stuff.'

Mackie didn't say it, but it would also give him a chance to get the kid's rucksack out of the Golf. It was a win all round, as far as he was concerned.

'You could put your stuff in the old bus instead, Trev. That would be a good place,' the kid said.

They all looked at him.

'What?'

'That bus behind all the tyres ... the cameras won't be able to see it. And it's bigger than ... than the Transit...' He trailed off.

'Oh.' Trev put his hands on his hips and gave them all an exaggerated nod. Mackie suspected pantomimes had been on Bertha's allowed list. 'There's the bloody mystery solved, then.' He raised his eyebrows at the kid. 'I think you owe me a quarter of midget gems and a packet of Curly Wurlys...'

'And a bag of crisps...'

'Thought I was going proper mad, I did. Right, Mackie, you deal with the CCTV blokes when they come. The kid will be helping me – paying off his debts. Meet me at the Transit, kid, as soon as Tranter's buggered off. Right?'

'Right.'

They all helped in the end. As soon as Tranter had gone, they formed a conga line and passed the spares out of Trev's Transit and piled them up by the tyre stack.

'Here, Riley. Look at these.'

It was the hubs off the Merc.

'I reckon it's these that saved your life.'

'I know,' the kid said.

'Plus those bloody midget gems.'

Mackie knew Trev was making a joke out of it, but it was true. If it hadn't been for Trev's little side-line the kid might

211

still be in the Merc now. It would have gone in the crusher and no-one would ever have known where the kid had gone. The thought made him shiver.

'Right, so...' Mackie was washing the dishes and the kid was wiping down the table. 'Shall I go and get your rucksack?' He said it casually, as if he'd not been thinking about the rucksack since the moment they'd got in. He'd managed to retrieve it from the Golf at the end of the day and now it was hanging on the banister. But the kid hadn't mentioned it. Mackie was preparing himself for a talk. Not his usual skirting round the edges of things that Melody had disapproved of, but a proper talk where you asked and said things that actually moved everything forward. Moving forward had never really been his forte.

'OK.'

Mackie went into the hall, unhooked the rucksack and took it into the kitchen. It was very light, so light he was worried it was empty – that whatever was so important to the kid wasn't actually there anymore.

But the kid didn't seem worried. He unzipped a compartment in the lid, took out a small photograph and handed it to Mackie.

'Ah. Is that her? Is that Eileen?'

'No. It's my mum. And me.'

It was a photobooth shot – just a single frame cut from a strip. Although the shot was under-lit it was obvious the two people in it – a dark-haired, serious looking woman and the small child looking up at her – were related.

'You look very young.'

'It was just before she died. I was nearly two, I think.'

Mackie knew this was the point where he could choose to back off: to trot out some small sympathy and move swiftly on. He thought of Melody.

'Do you want to talk about it?' he said. And to his surprise, the kid did.

Afterwards, when the kid had gone upstairs, Mackie took his coffee out into the garden. What had surprised him the most about the kid's story was how similar it was to his own – and Lauren's: mothers who died young, bewildered fathers left to raise the children. There were some differences, of course: the kid's mum had been married before – a violent marriage she managed to get out of, but not before she had a baby: Marco. The kid had never met Marco's dad but he knew a lot about him because Marco talked about him all the time: none of the bad stuff like why his mum had run away from him, just stuff like how great he was, how he was going to find him and move in with him.

The other difference was that the kid's dad had fared better than many because he'd met Eileen. Ironic, really, because when he died Eileen ended up raising two boys and neither of them were her own. Except, from where Mackie was standing there was nothing ironic about it at all, because wasn't that the modern way of doing things? None of the wife and two kids, tea on the table, job for life normality his own father would have known. Now it was all mix and match kids and partners, zero contract hours and ready meals. No wonder the kid had looked down on them from the Merc and thought they looked like a family.

The kid was waiting. He knew the white room was not far away, that he could close his eyes and there it would be. He just wasn't sure what it was going to show him. He had the photograph in his hand and many thoughts in his head: thoughts of Mackie and Sharon and Trev – and the tower, because, he still didn't know what had drawn him there – or who. He didn't know if he'd gone there for one of them, or all three of them. He only knew he hadn't gone there for Eileen. She was still far away. He thought about the tree in Mackie's garden and reminded himself of what he understood when he saw it. He was in the right place. He was with the right people. He settled back against the pillows and let himself go.

He knows without opening his eyes that someone is there with him. The air is not still but moves round his face, soft fingers of a familiar fragrance. He opens his mouth and pulls it down into his lungs, swirling it round his chest and into his heart. *Eileen,* he thinks, smiling. But he is wrong.

He opens his eyes and his mother is standing in front of him.

She smiles at him then holds out her hands, palms up, and leans forward to cradle his face. Her breath is the sound of a large ocean. She bends lower until her mouth rests on his head and he waits for her to speak. She says nothing but straightens up and walks away, turning once to beckon him to follow. She takes his hand as they walk through the doorway and together they glide through a sky that stretches out, warm and cloudless, above a land that rolls beneath them in a patchwork of green fields and hedges, small roads and scattered houses.

She releases his hand and points ahead – to something that she can see, but he cannot. Then she smiles at him and sends him on. He travels quickly, eager to be back at her side. He can see it now, in the distance but getting closer. There is no tower: just a wide river, a stone bridge. He looks back at his mother to check he is in the right place – but she has gone.

The kid woke, smiling. His mother had gone, but the time he had spent with her had left him feeling hopeful. Hopeful that he hadn't lost his way, that he was using his gift – the one she had given him – correctly. He pulled in a long breath, searching for some small trace of her scent, then lay for a long time, retracing their journey through the clouds. Eventually, he looked at the drawing he had done and realised, with a sharp pang in his chest, it was for the one person he had not been thinking of. It was for Marco. He studied it and understood what was going to happen. Marco needed the drawing.

It would bring Marco to him.

He put it down on the bedside table, rolled onto his side and waited.

29

Mackie was up early again – mainly because he'd not exactly gone to bed. The kid had gone upstairs after their 'talk' and Mackie, feeling like he'd taken a small step in the direction of not being so bloody scared about 'meaningful conversation' had cracked a beer or two and fallen asleep in front of the telly. He was filling the kettle and mulling over what he was going to tell Sharon about it all when he heard the front gate go. He assumed it was the postman – maybe a card from Lauren and the twins – so it was a surprise when someone knocked at the door. He clicked the kettle on and went to answer it. There was a bloke on the doorstep.

'Where the fuck is he?'

Mackie stepped back into the hallway, his hand still on the door latch.

'What?'

'Riley,' he said. 'What the fuck have you done with him?'

'Riley?' Mackie said. 'Who are you?'

He was stalling because he knew who the bloke was – the same *fuck-you* look on his face as his mugshot. It was Marco – smaller than Mackie had imagined but the wire in him unmistakeable: some tightness in his face and voice, like he was waiting for an excuse to let fly. What he couldn't work out was how he'd found them.

'Never mind who I am, you fucking paedo. Just hand him over.'

'I don't know what you're talking about, mate.'

But Marco just smiled. Mackie could see how someone might be afraid of him. The guy's eyes were set deep in his face, dark and dead like they'd already seen too much.

'I think you know exactly what I'm fucking talking about, *mate*.'

'How d'you know where I live?'

'I got your address from the hospital, didn't I?'

Marco stepped forwards and Mackie could tell he was being measured up. He brought his fists round in front of his body. Marco laughed.

'Don't even think about it, Grandad,' he said and put his hand flat against Mackie's chest. 'Give me the kid and there won't be any trouble.'

'Like I said, I don't know what you're talking about.'

He lowered his head and shook it slowly. 'You're making a big mistake.' He gave Mackie a slight push.

'I need to tell you something,' Mackie said.

'Oh yeah?' He brought his face up closer.

'Yeah. I used to fight. I was a boxer.'

Marco stepped back and studied Mackie's face. 'Well good for you, old man. Problem is – I still do fight. And I don't need no fucking gloves.'

He pushed Mackie again: there was enough behind it to send him off balance. Mackie grabbed his shoulder and dug his fingers in. He was muscle as well as wire. Marco spun round and took a loose shot at Mackie's face. Mackie answered with one on the side of the head – diluted it a bit. Just a taster. Marco laughed or snarled, and got stuck into Mackie's ribs: short punches that landed quick but had no real weight behind them. All arm and no shoulder. Mackie spun round and looped his arm round his neck.

'I've warned you, son,' he said and gave Marco a couple of jabs to the kidneys. Half-hearted but he felt them.

Marco grunted then threw his weight forward, broke free of Mackie's arm and came at him like someone had flicked a switch. It was a big mistake. Mackie let him get a couple of hits in then slugged him good and hard on the jaw. He went straight down, no messing. One minute he was like a bloody wind-up toy, the next he was getting cosy with the skirting board.

Mackie stood back and waited to see what Marco would do next, wondering whether he was going to have another go. He inched himself onto all fours, making a big deal of it, then, with no warning sprang to his feet and lunged at Mackie. His hand was only inches from his face when Mackie realised he was holding a knife. He jumped back and drove his left fist into Marco's small hard belly and, as he doubled over, gave him another on the chin. The knife skittered across the floor and he went down again. This time he looked like he might stay down.

'What's happening?'

The kid was on the landing peering down. Mackie stepped over Marco and hurried up the stairs towards him. 'It's nothing. Go back in your bedroom a minute, I'll...'

But Marco was up again. He let out a howl, grabbed Mackie

from behind and dragged him down the stairs. 'I'm gonna kill you ... you fucking lying paedo. Riley, get the fuck down here, now.'

'Look, can't we just talk about this...'

'That's right, not so fucking clever now, eh, *mate?*'

Marco spread his feet wide and put his fists up in front of his face. There was blood trickling from the corner of his mouth and down his chin. Mackie shook his head.

'Look, lad...'

But Marco was bouncing towards him. He took a couple of poky jabs and then Mackie decided enough was enough. 'Sorry about this,' he said and pulled his arm back.

'Too late for that, Grandad, you're gonna get ... ooof.'

He went over like a felled tree, taking the hall table with him. Mackie looked over his shoulder. Riley was still at the top of the stairs. He was holding his drawing book. 'I'm sorry,' Mackie said. 'I didn't want to hurt him. He just wouldn't stop.'

He looked back at Marco: he was rolling his head from side to side like he was trying to click it back in place. Mackie bent down and picked up the knife. 'Are you OK?' he said. He could see the fight had gone out of him but he still kept his distance.

'Keep the fuck away from me.' Marco rolled onto all fours then pulled himself upright with the banister. 'Where the fuck did you learn to do that?' he said, rubbing his chin. He glanced up at Riley. 'I've been looking for you.'

'I know,' the kid said. He held his book up. 'I was waiting for you. I've done you a drawing.'

Marco gave Mackie what he supposed was meant to be a smile. There was some triumph in it. 'That's my boy,' he said and held his hand out, inviting Riley to come down.

'Hang on a minute.' Mackie positioned himself at the bottom of the stairs. 'You don't have to do this, Riley. You don't have to go with him.' But the kid was already walking down. He reached out and put his hand on Mackie's shoulder.

'It's alright, Mackie. I'm not going with him.'

Marco gave a snort and gestured impatiently for the book. The kid slid past Mackie and handed it over, then sat down on the bottom step. The hall looked like someone had driven a car through it but the kid didn't seem to notice.

'It's on the last page. You can tear it out and take it with you if you want.'

Marco swiped through the drawings until he came to the last one. He regarded it for a moment or two then slapped the page with the back of his hand. 'What the fuck's that supposed to be? That's not going to help me find the bitch and you fucking well know it.'

He took a step towards the kid and Mackie eased himself down the last couple of steps and stood between them.

'It's alright, Mackie, I'll need to show him.'

He got up, picked his way through the broken table and photo frames and walked into the kitchen. Mackie and Marco looked at each other then followed. The kid sat down then pulled out a chair for his brother. Mackie, for the sole reason of introducing some sort of normality to the situation, put the kettle back on. When he turned round the kid had the drawing spread out on the table. He was tracing his finger across the page, talking quietly.

'I don't know what you mean.' There was something in Marco's voice that suggested shock. A kind of winded edge to it. 'How? You were supposed to be finding Eileen ... not ... Fuck me.' He put his hand to his forehead and bent over the picture. 'That one there? You're sure?'

The kid nodded.

'When?'

The kid studied the drawing again. 'Now, I think.'

'Shit.' Marco scratched his head. 'So ... if I go now, he'll be there?'

'Yes.'

'Right. OK...' He picked up the drawing and rolled it into a tight tube and pushed his chair away from the table. 'I'm going, then,' he said.

'OK.'

Marco turned to Mackie. 'He needs help to find someone,' he said, pointing at the kid. He put his hand inside his jacket and pulled out a large brown envelope and threw it on the table.

'That's all I've got,' he said. 'But it might help.' Then he gave the kid a small punch on the shoulder and left.

They sat for a while when Marco had gone: the kid had picked up the envelope but hadn't opened it. He was turning it over and over in his hands. Mackie was waiting for the air in the kitchen to settle and for his head to go back to normal.

'Sorry about Marco,' the kid said, eventually. 'Sorry he hurt you. He's...'

'Angry?' Mackie wanted to add *fucking psycho*, but didn't.

'Yes ... but—'

'You don't need to make excuses for him, lad, there's nothing about him I haven't seen before.'

'He's scared, mostly.'

Mackie let out a snort. 'Scared? He didn't exactly look scared to me. What about this?' He held the knife up. He'd closed the blade but he still didn't like how it felt in his hand. 'I don't think your Marco's scared, Riley, I think he's bloody dangerous. Anyway ... we'll just have to leave everything as it is. I'll have to get myself cleaned up. I've got to get to work.'

It was the last thing he'd wanted to say, or do, but it turned out to be good move: it got them out of the house, which still seemed to be vibrating at some wild frequency. It also gave Mackie a chance to walk some of the shock out of his system, and to talk to the kid some more. The drawing he'd done for Marco had been about his dad.

'He talks about him all the time but he hasn't seen him for years,' the kid said. 'He doesn't even know where he is.'

'Except now.'

'Yeah, now he does.'

'So that's where he's gone? To find his dad?'

The kid nodded. Mackie mulled it over a bit. 'Do you think it'll work then, the drawing?'

Mackie didn't want to push it but the drawings the kid had done so far had been pretty unsuccessful.

'I think so.'

'So, what about Eileen?'

'I already told you – we moved in with her after our mum died. A long time after.'

'No, that's not what I meant. I meant why can't you find her?'

He shrugged. 'Marco used to do that bit, he called it his research.'

Mackie nodded. 'Is that what's in the envelope, then? Marco's research?'

'Probably.'

'Well, we can look at it when we get home, eh? You never know, it might tell us where Eileen is.'

Mackie left it there. He had his jolly voice on but he felt knackered. The adrenaline that had kept him ahead of Marco had seeped away and left him jittery and, if he was honest, close to tears.

30

'Well, smack my bloody arse – what the hell's happened to you?'
Sharon was up off her wheelie chair the minute she saw him.

'It's alright, Sha. I'm OK. It looks worse than it is.' This was
a lie – his head was banging like a gong. 'It was Marco. We've
just had a visit from Marco.'

'Oh my god, Mackie. Here, sit down.' She pulled out a chair
for him. 'What happened?'

'Mackie won.' The kid smiled.

Mackie resisted the chair and gave a small laugh. 'Well, let's
just say we sent him on his way. The kid gave him something
he needed and he buggered off.' He didn't tell her Marco had
brought something. That there was an envelope waiting for
them when they got home.

'Gave him something?'

'Yeah – tell her, Riley.'

'I did him a drawing and ... and he went away.'

'A drawing?' Sharon asked.

'Yep. Of his dad. He's gone to find him.'

'Tidy. So, how are you both feeling?'

Mackie hesitated – there was a *toe-in-the-water* edge to her
voice.

'Well...'

He got no further, for she was the bringer of good tidings – namely that Tranter had phoned to say he had a migraine and wouldn't be coming in. This would normally have had Mackie whistling a happy tune but he knew, from the look on her face, where she was headed.

'So...' she said, looking at the kid. 'Back to yesterday's plan. Are we going for morning coffee or afternoon tea?' She leaned over and switched the microphone on. 'Oh, Trevor?'

Mackie was still trying to work out how to extricate himself from the part of the plan that involved travelling up to the twenty-third floor of the Meridian Tower. The general air of glee around the idea of the journey did not extend itself his way. Trev and the kid were in the back, Sharon was driving and he was looking out of the window trying to hear himself think above the trill of excitement coming from all corners.

'They do a cracking muffin,' Sharon was saying. 'Or we could do the morning coffee special. God, I could get used to this.' She wound the window down and the air streamed in and lifted her hair away from her face; she suddenly looked so young. 'Feel that sea breeze, Mackie. Christ, I love it.'

He turned to the window again as they started approaching the town centre. The sun was lending a kind shine to buildings that had long passed their usefulness – whole swathes of glass and steel that ought to have been taken down years ago. Remodelled. Wetherspoons was already doing a brisk trade: a mix of late lunch punters, happy hour regulars and the poor buggers who'd been there most of the day.

The tower was shining like a beacon: more glass and steel but new. Modern.

'You come here much, Mackie?' They were at the lights and Sharon was tapping her false nails against the steering wheel.

'The Marina, yeah. Not as much as I used to, I suppose.' After Sandra died he and Lauren used to go down every weekend, pottering along the quayside, paddling in the grey sea, sheltering behind the sea wall with their sandwiches – anything to keep them out of the house.

'How about you, Trev?' The lights changed and they moved forward.

'Used to, but not now. I've been back a few times, but mother ... well, she was very *anti* about the development and all that so...'

'She boycotted the place, then?'

'Yeah.'

Mackie knew she wasn't the only one: a lot of people objected to the development of the Marina. It turned out they had a point because, lovely as it was, a lot of the apartments were still empty or had been snapped up by portfolio holders for student accommodation.

'Shame. Doesn't know what she's missing.'

'You know it well then, Sha?'

'Very well.' She turned to Mackie and lowered her voice. 'The Tower. It's our place. Mine and Barry's. Marsha can't do heights, see.'

He didn't really know what she meant but he didn't care. 'I'm not that good with them myself,' he said, seizing the

226

opportunity to get his cards on the table. 'So I thought, I'd probably wait downstairs while you three go up.'

'Don't be so bloody dull, man. It won't be the same without you. You've got to come with us, hasn't he, Trev?'

'What?'

'Mackie. Says he doesn't like heights. Wants to stay outside while we go up. I'll look after you,' Sharon said. She was reversing into a space that was marked reserved.

'Honestly, Sha, I'd rather wait … hang on, I don't think you can park here. 'It's…'

'Reserved.' She winked at him.

Barry? he mouthed and she nodded. The happiness on her face made him want to cry.

She took Mackie's arm as soon as they were out on the tarmac and half-marched him towards the entrance lobby.

'Now, you'll be fine. We'll look after you, won't we, Trev?'

Trev was holding the door open and had him through it and into the lift before he got a chance to say anything.

'Houston, we have lift off,' Trev announced as the lift doors closed. It didn't help. The kid cwtched closer. Mackie could feel the warmth of him against his skin. 'You'll be alright, Mackie,' he said, as the lift jerked itself loose from the ground floor and began its climb. Mackie wobbled his head at him like a drunk.

It wasn't quite as bad as he'd remembered: it was busy, which cut out some of the feeling of openness, and they were given a table in the middle rather than at the edge. Sharon had the menu open before they all sat down.

'What's on the menu, Sha?' Trev was swivelling his head round like it was on a stick. 'God, this place is ... it's unbelievable, isn't it?' Then he launched into a bit of a history lesson about the docks which Mackie couldn't concentrate on because the kid had got up and taken himself over to the windows that looked down onto the sea. He was gazing out with a look on his face that was, Mackie reckoned, edging towards weirdness. He forced himself to get up and go over.

'Alright, Riley?' He kept his eyes on the kid's face and away from the view.

'Yes. Are you?'

'Sure. It's not quite as bad as I remem— as I thought it would be. Have you seen the other side?' Mackie nodded towards the windows on the other side of the restaurant. 'Come on.'

Before he knew it, Trev, evidently spotting an opportunity to extend his history lecture, joined them. 'See over there?' He had his hand on the kid's back. 'See that big red ship...?' and off he went. Mackie made it through 'Lightship 91, Helwick' but sidled off halfway through 'Tugboat Canning.'

'Christ almighty,' Sharon said. 'I'm going to put him forward for sodding *Mastermind*. How does he know all that stuff?' She was looking round for a waitress.

'Anyway, did the kid say anything while you were over there with him?'

'No. Nothing – although he had a bit of a look to him, you know? A bit faraway?'

'He'll have a faraway look on his face by the time Trev shuts up. Oh, hang on.'

'I was just telling the kid about the museum,' Trev said. 'I thought we could all go over there, see the boats and all that, you know?'

'Well, you can count me out of that little excursion.' Sharon stuck her hand up to summon the waitress. 'I'm not leaving here 'til I've had my full scone quota. Why don't you take Riley, Trev? Mackie can stay here with me. How long will you be, do you reckon?'

'An hour, tops?'

'Okey-doke. See you outside in an hour, then.'

Mackie was on the verge of objecting when he realised the option of enduring another hour in the tower was vastly more attractive than the option of enduring another hour of Trev's pontificating.

'OK, is that OK with you, Riley?'

It was hard to read the expression on the kid's face.

'Yeah. It's fine. The boats sound ... interesting.' He got his drawing out of his pocket. 'I think, you know...'

Mackie got up and took the kid to one side. 'Eileen, you mean? In that case I'm coming with you...'

'No, Mackie.' The kid was shaking his head. 'It's not Eileen. I'm not sure. But I want to go. With Trev. You stay here with Sharon.'

He gave Mackie thumbs up and followed Trev towards the lifts.

'Right.' Sharon stood up and brushed the crumbs off her belly. 'We've ticked the scone box. Now – I've got something to show you. Come on.'

Mackie assumed that whatever it was she was going to show him was outside, but the lift stopped on the sixth floor and Sharon got out.

'You'll like this.' She dropped him a wink.

He followed her down the corridor until she stopped outside a closed door and rummaged in her handbag.

'Here we are.' She held out a key card, slotted it above the handle and the door clicked open. 'Welcome to the lurve nest,' she said, standing to one side so he had to squeeze past her. She followed him in. It was big and modern, more like a hotel than a home. But gloomy.

'Hang on. Wait 'til you see this.' She went across to the bed and picked up a remote control, then aimed it at the window blinds. They went up silently and Mackie's mouth dropped open.

'My god, Sha. It's ... it's...' He went over to the window.

'It's lush, isn't it?'

'It's incredible. So this is...'

'Barry's. Mine and Barry's. This is where we, you know ... meet up.' She went across to the bed and smoothed the bedspread. 'We're going to live here one day,' she said. 'When he's left Marsha. Until then, well, we have to make do. Here, come over here...' She swung her legs up onto the bed and patted the space beside her. 'Come and look at the view from here.'

Mackie lay down next to her, slightly alarmed by the thought that he was on Barry's side.

'See? Isn't it amazing?'

It was. A floor to ceiling of sea and sky.

'See the ships? That'll be us one day. Cruising. I'll be

singing. Barry, managing the bar. God ... hey. Come and have a look at this.' She swung her legs back onto the floor and levered herself up. 'You won't believe your bloody eyes.' She crossed the room and opened a door. Mackie peered over her shoulder.

'Ta da!' she said and flicked a switch. The lights came on, low and moody, revealing a vast bathroom. 'Nice, eh?' She nudged him in the ribs and pointed to the corner. 'Jacuzzi bath, plus...' He followed her finger to the other side of the room. 'His and hers washbasins ... Oh.'

She went across to one of the basins and picked up a small jar. She unscrewed the lid and held it to her nose. Mackie knew from the look on her face that it wasn't hers.

'Alright, Sha?'

'What? Aw yeah, fine, I ... my face cream. I was wondering where I'd put it.' She screwed the lid back on and put the jar in her bag, then went over to the bed. She pulled the covers back and looked at the sheet, then picked up a pillow and took a sniff. Mackie didn't say anything. She went to the window and stared out.

'We ... we better make a move,' Mackie said, eventually. 'The hour must be up.'

'Yeah, we better.'

She didn't move.

'Should I go on my own? Do you want to stay here a bit?'

'Not really.' She turned to look at him. Her cheeks were wet.

'I'm sorry, Sha.'

'Yeah, me too.'

31

Sharon drove them back in silence. She turned down Mackie's suggestion of going in and opening a bottle or two and dropped him and the kid off at the end of the road.

'Is Sharon alright?' the kid asked.

'She will be. She's ... you know...'

But he didn't really know because he'd reacted to Sharon's discovery in his usual manner: he'd made the right noises then left it alone. He'd thought about it all the way back – told himself it was because the kid and Trev were there – but it was more than that. It was like a habit he couldn't get himself out of. He fancied himself a counsellor but couldn't even talk to his best friend – to anybody, really. Not about the stuff that really mattered; the stuff that dragged you down. *Talking is good for you, Mackie,* Melody used to tell him. *Burying things isn't. So* he'd always smiled in agreement – and kept the shovel hidden.

With this in mind he decided he was going to get the kid to open the envelope as soon as they got in. He'd forgotten that they hadn't cleared the mess up.

'Oh, shit.' Mackie stepped through the door onto broken glass. 'Hang on, Riley.'

He steered the kid through the debris and got the dustpan

out of the cupboard. The envelope was on the table where they'd left it.

'Look, I tell you what, why don't you have a bath or something? I'll get this mess cleared up and then we'll ... then you can show me that envelope, yeah?'

Mackie watched as the kid threaded his way through the debris in the hall then, as soon as the bedroom door closed, he picked up the envelope. It was grubby but blank, front and back, and sealed. It had been opened, but now it was stuck down with what appeared to be hospital tape. He held it up to the light but got no clue as to what was inside. He decided he'd wait until the kid was there and dropped it back on the table. Then he took his phone outside and tried Sharon. She didn't answer.

The kid was stood at the bedroom window. He could see Mackie in the garden below, sitting beneath the tree. It was a very beautiful tree – but sad. Like Mackie, it was guarding some secret it longed to be rid of. He reached for his pencil and a sheet of paper then closed his eyes.

The white room was waiting for him. He glanced round to make sure it was empty then walked towards the door. He pushed it open and stepped out into a dark rainy sky.

Although the sea is far below him he can feel the sting of salt water in his eyes and the lashing wind against his face. He can hear the thunder of pounding waves and the struggling thrum of a boat engine. He can hear the slamming of car doors, the thud of running feet, loud voices calling into the night. And above it all, he can hear the sound of a baby crying.

He looked down at the piece of paper, and saw that it was blank. It did not surprise him because he knew the drawing Mackie needed was the one in his sketchbook.

By the time the kid reappeared, Mackie had cleared up the hall and was part way through making the tea.

'Sausage sandwich?'

'OK.' The kid sat down. 'What are these?' He'd picked up the photographs that Mackie had rescued from the debris of glass and splintered wood.

'My photos, they were in the drawer.' He leaned over the kid's shoulder.

The kid looked up at him then back down at the photos. 'No.' He picked up another photo. 'It wasn't that daughter I saw, it was this one.'

Mackie gave another small laugh which got snuffed out before it hit the air – because the picture the kid was holding up was the one of Sandra.

'Oh.' Mackie took the photo out of his hand. 'That's not my daughter,' he said, 'that's Sandra. My wife.'

'She was the one who was in the sea.'

Mackie tried the half laugh again, for his own benefit more than anything because his head had suddenly started to hum.

'No. You've got it wrong. That's my wife, Sandra. She's ... she died. A long time ago.'

The kid closed his eyes and kind of tilted his chin towards the open door. He breathed in deep a couple of times then looked at Mackie.

'I'm sorry.'

Mackie turned his back on him and fussed over the frying pan. The hum in his head had risen a notch. More like a bell, an alarm bell.

She was the one who was in the sea.

Mackie turned off the gas and wandered out into the garden, walking slowly, because the kid's words were picking at his edges and he could feel himself starting to unravel.

He breathed in deep and went out to the Rowan. He noticed how its higher branches were moving in a breeze that he couldn't feel; how its top leaves looked dry, like they were already veering towards their autumn colours; how its berries were already forming. How he'd planted it after Sandra had died because he needed it as a reminder of what he'd lost.

And what he'd let go of. It was as if the thought quietly prised some lid off him. As if everything he kept stowed beneath it suddenly rose to the surface. He felt her name rise in his throat. *Elise.* He closed his mouth against it, breathed deep, felt the flutter of her in his head, his chest, his heart.

'Are you OK, Mackie?'

The kid was coming down the path towards him, treading carefully. He had a mug of tea in one hand. And the envelope in the other.

The kid sat down on the bench beside him. Mackie took a gulp of tea and watched as he peeled off the tape, eased up the flap and tipped the contents of the envelope onto his knee. There were several printed sheets, a folded scrap of paper, a page that looked like it had been torn out of a telephone directory – and a sketchbook. The kid laid everything but the sketch book to one side.

'This is it.' Mackie didn't know whether he was referring to the sketchbook or what was about to happen next. Mackie's first thought, as the kid turned the pages, was that Sharon had been right. The drawings were like a trail of breadcrumbs, landmarks that Marco obviously used to plot their route – the forecourt of a filling station; a barge moored beside a café terrace; a huge red brick building with a name – Pryce Jones – mounted on the roof.

His second thought was that he wasn't going to dwell on what the kid had said about Sandra's photograph. The sketchbook was the important thing: it was obviously the missing link and now the kid had it back they could help him pick up the trail of breadcrumbs again and do what he'd come there to do – find Eileen.

'So,' he was buoyed up by this idea, 'I guess it's the drawings nearer the end that are the important ones? As you got closer, I mean.'

'Yes.'

'Come on, let's have a look, then.'

The hesitation on the kid's face should have warned him: the way he paused for a moment with his hand on the page before he passed the book over; the way he leaned in as if to lend some kind of support. But at that moment Mackie was all for getting to the final clue.

The drawing was framed on all sides, as if he was looking through a window down onto a small garden. At the bottom of the garden, standing by a closed gate, was a tree.

'Oh.' Mackie reached out and touched the page then sat back again. He wiped his hands on his jeans then across his forehead.

It was his tree. The kid had drawn his Rowan tree.

He made himself pause for a moment then pulled the drawing closer to check, but the stretching curve of its trunk, the network of slender branches and small sprays of leaves and berries that were reaching upwards into a sky that was veering towards dark, told him he was not mistaken.

'That's...' He pointed at the small figure sitting beneath the tree staring out into the dark.

The kid nodded. 'Yes. That's you.'

Mackie couldn't say afterwards how long he'd sat there trying to grab hold of something to anchor him: something that wouldn't just keep him in the moment but would make the moment stop right there.

'What does it mean?' he said, eventually.

'It means I was meant to come here. This is where I was meant to be.'

'But ... why?'

'Because of this, I think.'

Mackie watched as the kid traced his finger down the trunk of the tree; as he followed the weave of its unseen roots that spread, like an echo of the branches, into the earth – then stopped at a small dark shape cradled in the rooty tangle below.

His heart gave a small ping.

'What's that? What is it?'

'It's a box, I think,' the kid said.

Mackie let out a small gasp and felt something in his chest release. He blundered up off the bench.

'What do you mean, a box?' He could hear the wild edge in his voice.

'I'm not sure. I think it's a secret ... Mackie...'

'I'm OK, I'm OK, just give me a minute, I'll— '

Mackie rushed into the kitchen, closed the door and clamped his arms around his chest. He held on but it was hopeless: something had broken loose and was rising like a small bubble to the surface, up towards the air, the light, forcing its way through his throat and into his mouth. He clamped his lips tight and stumbled to the sink and drank down a mug of water. Then another. *No*, he wanted to shout. *I'm not ready for this.* But who was going to listen? He had no Melody to smile her encouraging smiles, no psychiatrist to help him navigate the road ahead. He splashed some water on his face, sat down, then shut his eyes. The box. He imagined he had it in his hands. Its lid was still closed as he knelt down and tucked it back into its nest of roots and scraped the dry loose soil over it. He tamped the earth down with his hands and feet then added another layer until all traces of it had disappeared. Until all traces of his baby daughter, Elise, had disappeared.

He went to the back door to let the kid know he was going to bed, then took himself up the stairs before the kid could tell him anything else.

He is wading into a calm sea hauling the small dinghy behind him. He nods as the sky darkens, recognising that is the moment the sea will start to swell. He grips the rope tightly and wills himself forward, waiting for his feet to leave the seabed, forcing him to swim. He glances over his shoulder at the dinghy: it is following smoothly in his wake, slick with water and gleaming in the moonlight. There are a few moments of calm before the waves swell higher and he feels the first tug of panic pressing out of his chest and into his throat. It's alright, he shouts and, as the words fly out into the air, he realises he's off script. He has no time to think about it because the sea suddenly rises up into a wall of water, and he is thrashing towards it, trying to clear the top before it tumbles under the pull of its own weight. The dinghy is tilting precariously but he holds on, urging it to follow, until, with a feeling that is familiar and terrifying, he starts to slide down the face of the wave and into the trough beneath.

There is a moment when everything seems to stop and the wave hangs suspended above him before something in it gives and it crashes down. It's alright, he shouts again and his voice rises above the water and into the sky. He turns to the dinghy, knowing that it will be empty, but this time – this time – he doesn't wake up. No. He dives beneath the waves and, ignoring the salt-water sting, scans the murky water. He swims beneath the dinghy, diving deeper because its cargo cannot have sunk far. He will be able to find it. If he just keeps looking, he will be able to find it.

He lay for a while longer thinking about the dream, his Aberystwyth Angel, the Rowan tree – the box buried in its roots – then he turned on his side and thought about the kid sleeping in the next room. He would get up early, he would make them breakfast and then he would talk to the kid – ask him what he needed to do.

The kid was not asleep. He was thinking.

He was thinking about Trev and how he felt when he was with him at the Marina; he was thinking about Mackie and the box buried beneath the tree; he was thinking about Sharon, and what he saw while she was on stage – the pale grey shadow floating behind her like it weighed nothing at all when in fact it was holding her down like a lead weight.

But most of all he was thinking that time was running out. That it wouldn't be long before he had to leave. He got his paper and pencil ready, closed his eyes and, knowing this would be his last chance, got ready to go to the white room.

He looks around for a moment, breathing quietly, anticipating the breeze on his face and, when it comes, gets up and follows it to the door. The air is cool and damp and thick with night and, he discovers as he launches himself forward, has a current to it. He relaxes into the flow waiting to see where it will take him. He rolls onto his back and sees that the sky above him is speckled with stars and reaches his hand up as if he might touch them. He does not know if this reaching changes things but all of a sudden the air beneath him changes to water and he begins to pick up speed. He flips onto his belly and tries to see what is ahead but it is too dark and everything is too fast and he realises he is no longer going with the flow, but out of control. He spreads his arms out wide and tries to turn against the current but still he surges on, the noise of the water louder and louder, like thunder in his ears. He lifts his head clear and screams for help but it is no good because the water is no longer carrying him; it is pulling him under, closing over his head, filling his mouth, his lungs...

'My god, Riley, what's going on?'

The water had gone. The light came on. Mackie was stood beside the bed.

The kid wanted to say he was dreaming but he couldn't get his breath. He leaned back against the pillows and closed his eyes.

'Were you dreaming?'

The kid nodded.

'Do you want a glass of water?'

The kid shook his head then shuffled down the bed and pulled the covers up as if he was going back to sleep. He felt Mackie stroke his head then heard the light switch. He waited until the door closed then sat up, reaching for his sketchbook. He studied the two drawings for a long time. *They are what he expected.*

32

Mackie didn't get up early next morning, nor did he make breakfast, because both he and the kid overslept. He woke to the sound of voices outside his window – Dougie next door setting off for work. He leapt out of bed, roused the kid, and the two of them half jogged to the yard clutching pieces of toast. There was no real opportunity to talk about the events of the night before. This was something of a relief to Mackie because, in the broad light of day, what had happened now felt more like a dream than reality.

It was apparent as soon as they got to the yard that something was amiss. The office was still locked up. Mackie looked through the window, but the computer wasn't on and there was no sign of Sharon's jacket or bag.

'Strange,' he said to the kid. He walked across the yard and looked down the first aisle but there was no sign of Trev, either. He had a sudden illogical panic that he'd got the time wrong. Lauren had landed herself in trouble like that once – so wasted she took the twins to school at 8.30pm one night. She'd have got away with it except the headmaster was working late preparing for a concert and waylaid her as she was hanging their coats up in the cloakroom. Social services were round next morning.

'Where is everyone?' The words were no sooner out of his mouth when Tranter came into view. He was giving it large as soon as he spotted them.

'Oh, well, I see we're not quite the Marie fucking Celeste, then,' he boomed, striding across the yard. 'Glad to see I've got at least one bloody hand on deck.' Mackie was taking bets in his head as to what he was going to say next, seeing as he'd got himself onto a bit of a nautical theme.

'Well? What the fuck's going on? Jumped bloody ship, have they?' Tranter stuffed his hand in his waistcoat pocket and pulled out a bunch of keys. There was something different about him.

'No idea.' Mackie stepped aside as he barged past, his hands balled into fists and his chin poked forward. Then he clocked it: his hair. Arlene had been having a go at it: his signature ponytail had been teased out and lacquered into a kind of triangular Mississippi mudflap. Its bottom edge could have scraped ice off a windscreen.

'Where's Sharon, has she rung in?' He was taking a chance because Tranter was already fumbling with the keys and his bald patch, which had more shine to it than usual, was changing colour.

'Rung in? What the fuck is that? We're not at fucking school. *Rung in*. Christ.'

He fumbled a bit more then threw the keys at him.

'She spoke to Arlene, apparently. Last night. Needed the day off. That's all I fucking know.'

'What about...' Mackie stopped, wishing to god he'd never started. 'What about Trev?'

'What about him?' Tranter put his hands on his hips and spread his legs.

'Er ... I haven't seen him yet. Just wondering... Is he in?'

'Is he in? How the fuck do I know – I don't keep a fucking register, do I?'

The kid gave the back of his legs a small nudge: Trev was walking in through the gates. He saw the three of them and, before Tranter had a chance to turn round, dodged behind the tool shed. He stuck his head back out and gave a small wave.

'Oh, sorry, yeah. I must have missed him. He's in the diesel shed.'

'Well, thank Christ for that. Right, get the fucking door open, then.'

Mackie pushed the office door open, pausing for a couple of moments to let the heady mix of Sharon's perfume dissipate. He motioned to the kid to sit in the corner, then turned to the computer, trying to look like he knew what he was doing. He fished in the drawer for a pen then clicked on the answer machine. Tranter eyed him for a few moments more then, suitably convinced, backed off.

'Right. I'll leave you to it. I'm in my office if you need me. And tell Trev I want to see him.'

'Yeah, will do.' His heart was chuffing like a steam train. He waited 'til Tranter was halfway across the yard then switched off the answer machine and swivelled round to the kid. 'Can you do me a favour?'

'Yeah.'

'Go find Trev for me, tell him I need to see him.' Mackie

glanced out of the window. 'Here, take this.' Mackie passed him a piece of paper and a pen. 'If Tranter sees you, tell him someone's rung in wanting a Corsa wing mirror. Yeah?'

He watched the kid go, then turned back to the answer machine. Seven messages. He was praying that one of them was from Sharon because her absence was messing with his head. This was guilt largely because, despite knowing what had happened at the apartment, he'd not checked on her the night before – he'd tried once, but then got so caught up with everything that happened, he'd not tried again. He played the tape through twice but there was no message from her. He then tried her on his mobile and got voicemail. He could feel himself sinking.

Where are you? He tapped the message in, added a couple of upbeat emojis and sent it. Nothing came back. He sat down at the desk, fired up Google mail, then ran through the inbox, looking for her name. It wasn't there. He was just getting up when a new message dropped in. It was from the CCTV company – a short message to say they would be arriving earlier than arranged: 10.30am instead of 11.45am. Mackie sank a little further. Their jaunt to the tower meant he and Trev still had one more post to fix ready for the cameras which meant – he glanced at the clock above Sharon's desk – they only had one hour to get it done. He checked his mobile one last time then, with a heaviness in his chest that was making his throat ache, he set off to find Trev. He met the kid halfway there and followed him back to the diesel shed.

'Alright, Mackie?' Trev said.

'Not really.' Mackie half closed the door behind him. 'Sharon's not in and...'

'Oh, she said she's got something on...'

'What?' Mackie felt the stirrings of relief, but it was mixed with something more complicated. 'You've spoken to her?'

'Yeah. Last night. Rang her, didn't I?'

'Oh. Was she OK?' He couldn't help it. He should have been grateful but instead he felt— *put out. Guilty.*

'Sounded it.'

'OK, good. What's she got on, did she say?'

'Dunno. Something to do with Barry, I think.'

'Ah, OK. Of course.' He smiled and let the relief kick in. *Barry.* She probably had his balls in a bag already.

'You OK?' Trev was eyeing him up.

'Yeah, fine. We overslept and I was ... you know, a bit worried about Sharon ... but, anyway, the CCTV blokes will be here in an hour. We need to get that last post in and then...'

He didn't get chance to say much else because Tranter suddenly appeared in the yard. He walked towards the office then stopped, hands on his hips again, swivelling this way and that. His new hairdo stuck out behind him like a small rudder. Mackie told the kid to stay in the shed then called out to Tranter. He came striding towards them.

'And what, pray tell, are you two cretins up to?'

'Just coming to find you, boss,' Mackie said. 'The CCTV blokes are coming a bit earlier. They had a cancelled appointment, they...'

'What time?'

'Half ten.'

Tranter shot his arm out then pulled it back to consult his Rolex. 'Sodding hell. Right. Is everything ready? You got all them posts in?'

They nodded. Safer than saying 'yes'. They hadn't done the post that would give a view of Trev's new stash van.

'Right. Let me know when they get here.'

They watched 'til he was out of sight, then Trev turned to Mackie and grinned.

'What the fuck's going on with his hair?'

They were at the top end of the last aisle – the kid was with them – heading for Trev's new stash van when there was a sudden crackle of activity from the office microphone. Mackie's heart gave a hopeful lurch.

'Mackie. Where the fuck are you?' It was Tranter.

'Here we go.' Mackie spun on his heels and left Trev and the kid behind as he half jogged to the office. He slowed down as he cornered round the last aisle because he could see the CCTV blokes had already turned up. He avoided Tranter's eye and walked straight up to them.

'Alright?' he said to the nearest one. 'Want me to show you where they're going?'

'No, Mackie, he wants you to stand on your head and whistle fucking Dixie, you dull arse. Get a move on, for Christ's sake. And tell the fucking Scarlet Pimpernel, wherever the fuck he's vanished to this time, I want to see him in the office now. Pronto.'

Mackie raised his eyebrows in a way he hoped posed the

question without actually having to say anything because he didn't have a clue what Tranter was on about.

'I mean Trev,' he hissed. He turned to the CCTV blokes and held his arms out wide as if to say *give me strength*, then wound his head round to look at him again. 'Well? What the fuck are you waiting for? These lads haven't got all fucking day. Go on. Piss off, for Christ's sake.'

The bloke fell in beside Mackie with a bouncing lollop that put him in mind of Shaggy from *Scooby Doo*. His mate was younger. He had the look of someone on a government scheme. Neither of them spoke and he could sense their embarrassment.

'Don't take any notice of Tranter.'

'No shit, man. That is some wound up dude. Is he always like that?'

'Nah. Bit of a bad hair day.'

He gave them a tour of the yard, pointing out the sites for the cameras, then left them to it and went off to find Trev. He was at the new stash van chatting to the kid.

'Trev. What's going on? We need to get cracking – the CCTV blokes are already here.'

'Aw, me and Riley were just catching up. Boat talk, you know, after the Marina yesterday.' Mackie felt it again. That pang of displacement.

'Also, the boss wants to see you. Pronto.' Normally this would have had either of them up and scurrying, cap in hand, towards whatever vitriol Tranter was waiting to dole out; but Trev didn't move.

'I was just telling the kid I went back afterwards. I'd forgotten how much I used to love that place.'

'Trev,' Mackie said, putting a bit of an edge in his voice. 'You'd better get over there. You know what he's like and...' That was as far as he got.

33

The kid suddenly gave a small gasp and shot a terrified glance over Mackie's left shoulder. Mackie froze, expecting to hear Tranter's voice in his ear any moment. When nothing happened, he turned round slowly to see what the kid was looking at. There was no one there.

'What is it?' Mackie said, turning back to him. 'Oh, shit. Trev. Quick.'

The kid had slumped back against the van. His face was slack and his eyes were half open and flickering. He was making a noise somewhere between a moan and a hum as Mackie ran over and put his arms round his shoulders.

'Riley.' The kid weighed nothing at all. 'Riley.'

'I think he's having a seizure. I'll go get some water.'

'No. Hang on, Trev. Let's give him another minute. He'll come round in a minute.'

He sounded a damn sight more confident than he should. 'Riley, come on, son. It's Mackie, Ah. Here we go.' He felt the kid stiffen under his arms then he suddenly opened his eyes and stood up straight. His face was white.

'It's Sharon.' He put his hand over his eyes and made a small noise in the back of his throat, then stumbled to his feet. 'It's the sea. She's going in the sea.'

Mackie swore that for a few moments he lost himself completely. The kid's words catapulted him so far he thought he would never find his way back. It was the kid's hand on his arm that brought him down.

'We have to go, Mackie. We have to go now.'

'But where is she? Do you know where she is?'

'The same place as yesterday.'

'What?' Mackie squawked, but the kid didn't answer. He was already ahead of them, threading his way back through the stack of tyres and out into the aisle.

The two CCTV blokes stood back and watched, open-mouthed, as the kid legged it across the yard with Mackie and Trev in his wake.

'We've got an emergency,' Mackie yelled. 'If the boss asks, tell him we've got an emergency.' Then he slowed down. 'Trev, we've got no car, we...'

'Follow me,' Trev shouted, and sprinted towards the gates. His car – Bertha's car – was parked across the street. He had them rolling before Mackie got his door closed.

'Slow down, Trev,' he said, as they hit the town centre traffic. 'Oh shit, no.' He looked in the wing mirror – a police car was racing down the outside lane, its lights flashing. 'Move over, move over,' Mackie shouted. 'Oh, Christ, he's going to pull you in, Trev. Oh.' They watched as he overtook and raced off towards the roundabout. He'd no sooner disappeared than another siren blared out behind them and an ambulance swerved past.

The kid suddenly stuck his head over the back of Mackie's

seat and pointed at the windscreen. 'Follow them, Trev,' he shouted. 'Follow them.'

'What?'

'Keep up with them. They're going to Sharon.'

Mackie's heart nearly flipped through his mouth but Trev didn't hesitate. He dropped a gear, wrenched the wheel hard to the left and took off after the ambulance. As they approached the roundabout a fire engine fell in behind them and the traffic parted and they all veered right in a blare of light and noise that bounced off the steel and glass buildings and funnelled into Mackie's head like it was a lightning rod. Trev straightened into the approach to the lights and the Tower came into full view.

'Where is she?' Mackie yelled. 'Can you see where she is?' He could barely hear his own voice for the ringing in his ears.

'It's OK, Mackie. We'll just follow this lot,' Trev said.

'But can you see her?' he yelled. 'Is she in the sea?' He got hold of the door handle. He wanted to get out of the car and run. Run and find her, get to her. *Stop her.*

'She's on a ship, I think.' The kid's voice sounded far away and Mackie knew without looking that his eyes were closed and his chin was lifted.

'A ship? Christ almighty.'

'Hold on,' Trev said. 'Here we go!' He yanked the wheel to the left and they skidded into the Marina entrance. People were standing back from the road, watching as they sped by. Mackie opened his window and craned his neck to get a better view of what was happening up ahead. There were more blue lights. More sirens.

'I think we're stopping,' Trev said. The ambulance in front was slowing; its brake lights were on. 'Oh, wait a minute.' It wasn't stopping, it was being waved through by the police car in front, onto the pedestrian walkway. Mackie could see blue and white police tape, a crowd of people being herded back by a small policewoman, faces at apartment windows, people leaning over their balconies—

'I can't follow him. We'll have to get out.' He nudged the car onto the pavement but Mackie was off and running before he'd switched the engine off.

'Which way, which way?' Mackie shouted. The kid was behind him, at his heels. He caught up and took hold of his hand and somehow managed to pull him to a halt.

'There.' He was pointing between two buildings. 'That's where she is.'

Mackie gasped and then his knees gave way.

'No. No.' He grabbed hold of a metal railing and pulled himself upright, willed some strength back into his legs, then set off running again because it wasn't a ship the kid had pointed to, it was a sail: the one that held up the Sail Bridge.

'Sorry, sir.' The first cop they came to didn't stand a chance of stopping them; they nearly had him over as they flew past towards the bridge.

'Sharon, Sharon!' Mackie as yelling at the top of his voice and he didn't care.

'Sir.' A pair of cops stood in his path but he dodged round

them and kept running. He didn't know where the kid or Trev were at that point because all he could think of was her. Her, with every beat of his heart, every thud of his feet on the boards. 'Sharon—' He hollered her name until it was all he could hear. A cop stepped forward like he was going to try and stop him. 'Where is she? Where is she?' Mackie yelled. 'I'm her friend. I'm her best friend— ' The cop said something into his radio then fell in beside him as they started the approach onto the bridge.

And then something in Mackie's head shifted and everything slowed down.

'Sharon.' His voice was a whisper.

She was about a hundred yards ahead of him. She had her pink sequins on.

She was on the wrong side of the railings.

'Sharon.' He said it louder, but the wind whipped his voice away. She was holding the railing with one hand, looking down into the water.

'Don't,' he called. 'Don't do it. I'm here. I'm here.' But she didn't hear him. She couldn't have heard him because the next thing he knew she let go of the railings and fell into the water below.

'She's in, she's in,' the cop was yelling into his radio. 'Sir, come back, it's OK, we've got— '

But it was too late. Whatever he was going to say didn't reach Mackie because he was running; and then he had his hand on the railings and he was vaulting over and up into the air where he seemed to hang for a moment before dropping like a stone into the sea. The water closed over his head and he thrashed his arms to stop himself sinking too far. He opened his eyes and searched the water around him, looking for some sign of her: a flash of pink, her blonde hair, her face. Her lovely smiling face. He rose to the surface, grabbed a lungful of air, then dived again. He wasn't going to lose her; he wasn't going to let her go. He swam deeper, swivelling his head left then right, feeling the pressure in his chest, the need to breathe tapping at the back of his nose and throat. He went a few more strokes then tucked himself into a ball, turned and shot himself up towards the surface. He was pulling in another breath ready to dive again when someone grabbed him round the neck. He struggled for a moment until a voice eventually penetrated the noise of the water which seemed to be in his head, as well as all around him. 'I'm a police diver, sir. Relax. We've got her.'

'Is she ... is she OK?' Mackie spluttered.

'She's OK. Come on. Relax. Let yourself go limp, yeah? Here we go now, I'm going to tow you to the dinghy.'

Mackie twisted his head round so he could see the man's face. 'You've definitely got her?'

'We've definitely got her. Come on.'

It was OK. They'd got her. She was safe. Mackie lay himself back in the man's arms and wept.

34

Mackie was counting on his fingers. The small movement was rustling the silver space sheet that was still draped over him underneath the red ambulance blanket. He could hear the doctor talking to Sharon in the next cubicle. He'd been given something. *This will help you relax*, the nurse said, as she put it in. He couldn't stop shaking, even after the cold had worn off. *The shock*, she said. The shock of the sudden activity, the adrenaline, the chill of the water – but, as the medication hit and the middle of his chest dissolved into a warm pool, he'd stopped listening and started counting.

It was twelve days since they'd found the kid. Only twelve days.

'Right. Let's see how you're doing, shall we?'

The doctor pulled back the cubicle curtain and frowned down at him. Mackie watched his face as he took hold of his wrist and fixed his eyes on the clock on the opposite wall. Old school, Mackie would have guessed: gaunt, still tall despite the stoop his body had long since succumbed to, his hair arranged artfully over the top of his head. His face had a yellow tinge, like he didn't see enough daylight and, although it was unnaturally smooth and tight across his cheekbones, his skin hung thin and crepey round his throat.

'Is it OK?'

He'd dropped Mackie's wrist and was writing something on a chart at the bottom of his trolley.

He peered at him over the top of his half spectacles. 'OK, is not a term we use in this department, Mr Carpenter. Misleading, uninformative and completely inappropriate in a clinical situation, no?'

'Right. Erm, but what about Sharon?' Mackie nodded his head towards the curtain separating them.

The doctor folded his specs and slotted them in his top pocket. 'I assume you are referring to Miss Devereaux?'

'Yes.'

'In which case I have to inform you that I am not at liberty to discuss either her condition or situation with you.' He gave a small sniff. 'Suffice to say she will probably sleep for some time.'

'We work together.' Whatever he'd been given was loosening his tongue. 'This isn't like her,' he said. 'It's out of character.'

'Splendid, but as I say—' He turned, ready to leave.

'But I'm worried about her. I think...'

'Not your job, old chap. Nor mine. Someone will be down to see her shortly.'

Someone. The psychiatric team, he meant. They'd be down with their assessment sheets, totting up the likelihood of a repeat performance.

He swished the curtain closed behind him and left Mackie looking at the ceiling. He could feel the meds rippling out of his chest and up into his head, teasing the knots out of his brain. He let his eyes close and before long he was thinking about the kid again, about the Rowan tree, the box – his Aberystwyth Angel. He laced his fingers on his chest and smiled up at the ceiling, nodding his head like some happy drunk, and whispered the words he'd learned by heart as a child.

Hebrews thirteen, verse two. Be not forgetful to entertain strangers; for thereby some have entertained angels unawares.

'Is that you whispering, Mackie?'

'What? Oh, shit. Sharon.' The curtain between them swished back and there she was. 'You're supposed to be on the trolley, not...'

'On the trolley? Off my trolley, you mean!'

She let out a loud cackle that, even to his addled brain, had some manic edge to it. Her hair was damp and flat and he could see her scalp through it. She saw him looking and clamped her hands over her head.

'For god's sake, don't look at me hair. Lost me bloody wig, didn't I? Damn thing's probably on its way to Cork.' She belted out another loud hoot. 'And this,' she said, pointing at the hospital gown which was stretched like a drumskin over her belly, 'what the fuck is this? Like ... where the hell are my clothes?'

'No idea. But they'll be wet. Sha ... are you OK?'

'Just dandy.' She stuck her hands on her hips and stared at him. There was some wildness in her eyes that made him wish the doctor would come back.

'Well, come on. Get up. Don't want to hang around here for the rest of the sodding day...'

'But ... haven't they given you something? I mean, they gave me something to, I don't know, relax me.'

'Don't think so. But then again, two bottles of Prosecco is pretty relaxing, isn't it? Come on, Mackie old boy, shake a bloody leg.'

'But the doctor said someone was coming to see you.'

'I know. Someone from the psychiatric team.' She crafted a pair of air quotes. 'But I don't need to see them, do I? So I'm not hanging around, am I?'

'For Christ's sake, Sha, you just jumped in the bloody Marina.'

'That's true.'

'So, you know ... they'll want to talk about it.'

'Well, I don't want to talk to them, do I? I want to talk to you. And the kid. Where is he, by the way?'

He was with Trev. Mackie remembered them standing by as he got loaded into the back of the ambulance. Trev had leaned over and put his hand on his arm.

'He's with Trev. They've gone back to the yard.'

'Shit. What's he going to tell Tranter?'

He hesitated. 'He's going to say you'd ... erm, broken down, we had to come and get you. I didn't know...'

'Broken down.' She rolled the words round her mouth like they were a flavour.

'On the roundabout ... your car was blocking the roundabout...'

'Good thinking there, Mackie. Bloody good thinking. Right, my clothes, where are they? Aha, here we go. Soaking. Ah, well.' She lifted her hands to the neck of the gown.

'Sha.'

'What?'

'Close the bloody curtains, for god's sake.'

She let out a low chuckle and wiggled her backside. 'You don't want to smack my arse, then?'

The taxi driver's face dropped like a badly-timed soufflé when he pulled up outside the hospital and Sharon stepped forward out of a small pool of water. Despite the fact she was shoeless (her best pink pair, she'd taken them off before she jumped) and dripping wet, Sharon acted like everything was normal; she calmly whipped out the bin bag her clothes had been in, spread it on the back seat and climbed in before he had a chance to say anything.

'Where to?' he said, looking at Mackie, not Sharon.

Sharon leaned forward with a small squelch and reeled off her address, then sat back and looked at Mackie. 'Christ, I'm gagging for a cuppa.'

He was still trying to decide whether or not she was OK. She'd convinced the A&E staff, but they didn't know her. They'd finally acquiesced because she'd accepted an appointment card for the Mental Health Crisis Team but that got tossed in the bin as soon as they were outside. She was humming now and looking, apart from the obvious, like her usual self. Better than her usual self, actually.

'I can't believe you did that.' She leaned into him and took hold of his hand. 'I can't believe you bloody jumped in to save me. Hah. Just goes to show.' Her eyes filled with tears and she turned to look out of the window. There were a lot of things he could have said but he didn't say any of them.

'Right,' she said, once they were in the house. 'You get that kettle on. I'll have the first shower. Here,' she unhooked a dressing gown off the banister, 'get your wet stuff off and put that on. Don't suppose your mobile's working?' He slipped his hand in his wet jacket pocket and pulled it out.

'No chance.'

'Here, use mine, then.'

'What for?'

'To ring Trev. Let him know what's happening. Tell him to come round here after he's finished, yeah? Him and the kid.'

'Sure.'

He took his time. After she'd gone upstairs Mackie went into the kitchen, stripped his stuff off and slipped into Sharon's dressing gown. This was more comforting than it ought to have been bearing in mind the pink velour and fur trimmed hood. He caught a glimpse of his reflection in the window as he was filling the kettle. A sort of cross between *Snow White* and *Frozen*. Amber would have loved it. He went through to the hall and got the phone. He could hear Sharon upstairs singing above the steady patter of the shower. She'd got Nancy Sinatra's boots on big time. He didn't know whether to be amazed or concerned: she'd just been fished out of the Marina and she was acting like nothing had happened.

'Well?' She padded into the kitchen five minutes later. The bits he could see of her looked pink and scrubbed. The rest of her was covered by a furry onesie. Tiger print. She looked like a kid on her way to bed. 'What did he say?'

'Couldn't get through.' This wasn't strictly true. He hadn't actually phoned: there was a feeling in his head like his brain had disconnected from its moorings and was bumping softly round the inside of his skull. It wasn't entirely unpleasant. 'I'd better go for a shower,' he said. 'Have you got ...' he picked up a fold of the dressing gown, 'anything else I can put on?'

'I've left something out for you. I'll put your stuff in the washer ... go on, bugger off.'

Twenty minutes later he shuffled back into the kitchen.

'Ooh, take a look at you! Warm now, I bet.'

'Well, yes, but—' He put his arms out. 'Really, Sha? This is all you had?'

'You just don't recognise a good thing when you see it, Mack. Baloo's my favourite.'

'Baloo.' He looked down at himself and shook his head. *Jungle Book*!'

'I know, I know. I just never had myself down for...' He grabbed a handful of loose fur. 'For this.'

'You need to start living a bit, pal. Anyway, coffee's in the garden. Come on.'

He followed behind as she *conga'd* through the kitchen and out the back door. He smiled, but he was worried. *Denial,*

Melody would have called it – this dizzying, *let's-move-on* cheerfulness. He was wondering when it would stop and she would crash back down to earth. He was wondering if he'd be able to cope with it.

'Did you speak to Trev, then?'

'Sure did. After Tranter bent my bloody ear.'

'He went for it, though? The story. You breaking down?'

'Apparently so. Not a happy bunny, mind you, according to Trev. Anyway, they're coming round after work. Trev and Riley.'

'Right.' Mackie swallowed hard. 'That'll give us chance to talk, then.'

'OK.' she tucked her tail to one side and lowered herself onto the swing seat. The framework groaned, then settled a little lower on its haunches. 'Come on, then. Next to me.' She patted the small space beside her.

35

'So,' she said, after a few sips. 'Who's going to go first?' That threw him.

'Go first? For god's sake, Sha, you're the div who's just got fished out of the Marina. It's you who needs to do the bloody talking. Not me.' *Christ.*

She weighed this up for a while then narrowed her eyes at him. 'Oh yeah?'

'Yeah.' Mackie folded his arms across his furry belly and looked away.

'Fair enough. But one question before I start, OK?'

'OK.'

She picked up her tiger's tail and started twirling it round her fingers. 'How did you know? Where I was, like, and … well, you know … what was going on?'

'Well—' He was going to give her the whole hog, but she cut him off before he got started.

'It was the kid, wasn't it? Tell me it was the kid.'

'It was the kid.'

'I bloody knew it. I bloody well knew it.' She raised her two palms in front of her. 'Who the hell is he, Mackie? How does he do it?'

'Christ knows,' he said, realising that as far as his angel theory went this was a pretty neat answer.

'Well I felt it, you know. Felt him. When I was on the bridge. It was like his voice was just behind me.'

'What? Telling you to jump?' His voice came out sharper than he'd intended.

She gave a low chuckle. 'Believe it or not ... yes. Anyway,' she took a slurp of her coffee, 'are you sitting comfortably?'

'More or less.'

'She paused and considered her fingernails. 'I thought it was real, Mackie. Me and Barry. I think it probably was. At first. But that jar of cream in the bathroom...?'

'It wasn't yours.'

'It wasn't mine, so...' She gave a short laugh. 'I phoned him last night. Said I'd got the day off. Said I could meet him at the apartment if he was free. Not one to turn an offer like that down, our Barry. Thought his luck was well in. Anyway, I was on the balcony with the Prosecco when he arrived...'

He'd been full of himself, she said. And full of Viagra – probably taken it on his way up in the lift. Had his pants half off before he'd noticed the jar of face cream on the table beside her. Exhibit number one. 'I had to hand it to him, considering his pants were round his ankles and things were getting a bit *strained:* he played it cool. Ignored the jar, kicked his pants on the floor and started on the buttons at the back of my top'.

He stopped in his tracks, apparently, when Sharon picked the jar up and took the lid off. *Oops,* he'd said. Oops – a word that might describe some minor stumble – not a revelation that was going to take the floor from under someone's feet.

'The daft thing is, Mack, I could have coped with most things. Like if he'd lied or made an excuse or apologised even. But he didn't. He laughed, then said, "Sorry love, but what did you expect?" What did I expect? I said. What about the cruise ship, our plans, our future together? That really tickled him. "Come on, darling, a cruise ship wouldn't look twice at you. Although", and this really amused him, "I hear whale watching is popular on those northern lines".'

'God, Sha, what a wanker.'

'Mad, isn't it? And I thought he liked me like this.' She patted her belly. 'Said he liked a bit of padding on a woman so I just started eating and before you know it, it was bye-bye anorexia, and hello obesity. And all that crap about talent scouts? Made up, all of it. Pure fabrication. *Crazy Sharon*. Christ, I made him a fortune. His Girl Friday, that's what he called me in private.' She gazed off into the distance and gave a small chuckle. 'The jar belongs to Miss Tuesday, apparently. So I threw it at him, which gave me a certain amount of satisfaction although not half as much as dropping his pants off the balcony. He left in a bit of a hurry after that and I thought *sod it* and opened another bottle of Prosecco. Then I had the idea.'

'The idea?'

'Yep. It was Aberystwyth that started it.'

'Aberystwyth?'

'You're starting to sound like a sodding echo, Mackie. Shut

the fuck up and listen. So, it kind of started in Aberystwyth when we saw that group of women coming out of the sea. You remember?'

He chanced a small, 'Mmhh.'

'Well, that's what got me thinking. Do you remember the old baths in town? Before they modernised it?'

He nodded although he didn't have a clue where she was going.

'Did you ever go off the top diving board?'

'I was more of a wave machine fan. Or that funnel thing that dropped you in the pool.'

'Well, on a Saturday afternoon I was the queen of that top board. I was telling you all about it when we were coming back from that reservoir. It was Trev and all his talk about the Merthyr Mermaid. It made me remember, see? Me and the girls, we'd lounge around the poolside all glammed up with our bikinis rolled as small as we could get them. 'The Tawe Mermaids' we called ourselves. When we'd got enough attention we'd all file up onto the diving platform and faff around for a bit like we were, you know, scared. Then Fi and Dee would do this double act backflip into the water, and, as soon as they surfaced, Cerys would fly out into a swallow dive while I climbed the last rungs up to the top board where, like Olga fucking Korbut, I would go up onto my hands, balancing until it felt like the whole bloody place was holding its breath. Then I would launch myself up and out and arc through the air clean as a knife and hit the water like a torpedo. It was fantastic. I was fantastic.'

'So, what you're saying...' He was struggling to stick with her.

'What I'm saying. Mackie, is that I lost it. I lost all that part of myself. After I quit Uni, the girls went on without me, you know. Not their fault – I kind of took myself out of the picture and they just carried on. We met up a couple of times but it didn't work. I mean, Cerys was teaching, Ffion was a midwife in London and Dee was waiting for an Australian visa; and then there was me, Mrs fucking Shrek, pushing paper for Tranter all week and shagging someone else's husband on a weekend. They didn't have a clue what to say to me.'

She stopped talking and closed her eyes and, for a moment, he thought she'd fallen asleep. Then he suddenly realised she was crying.

'Come on, Sha, it's time to think about moving forward now. Not looking back.' She shook her head and wiped her eyes with the tiger's tail.

'But that's it, Mackie. I did want to go back. Queen of the fucking top board. It was like I suddenly realised that was where I'd left myself. My proper self. I know it sounds soft, but going back? That's what I suddenly wanted to do.' She took a deep breath.

'Anyway – as I was saying, there I was on the balcony, two bottles down and thinking about that diving board and before I knew it, I was downstairs, outside and heading for the Sail Bridge. I didn't have a plan. I just wanted to see if the *feeling* was still there. And it was, because the next thing I know I'm climbing over the railings and judging the drop, like I might, you know, really do it. I think that's when people started noticing me. I don't know how long I was there but I suddenly realised the police had turned up and there was a bloke in a dinghy shouting at me through a loudspeaker. I tried to tell him I was alright – I wasn't committing suicide or anything – but he couldn't hear me. And then,' she picked up her tiger's tail and started twiddling it again, 'that's when things got slightly weird because, and don't laugh at me, Mackie, I swear to god I heard the kid's voice, right behind me.'

He leaned forward in his seat. 'Go on.'

'It was like he was right there, whispering in my ear.'

'What did he say?'

'He said, *jump*. So I did. And this is the really crazy bit: as I launched myself into the air it was like something slipped off my shoulders. I actually felt it, Mackie. It slipped off and when I surfaced it was like my whole body was singing. Then the bloody diver grabbed me and spoiled the moment, but Christ, you should have been there.'

'I was there.'

She smiled. 'You were there.' She patted his hand. 'And that's something I'll never forget.'

'So,' Sharon said, after a while. They were still wedged in side by side swinging gently. 'I've shown you mine – it's your turn to show me yours.'

He didn't know where to start. *The Rowan tree? The box? The whole truth and nothing but the truth about the night Sandra died?*

He started carefully. 'The kid's got his sketchbook back. Marco brought it. It's full of drawings.'

He bought himself a bit of time outlining the various

drawings in it – the barge, the store sign – and said she'd hit the nail on the head with the trail of crumbs idea.

'Anyway, the last drawing was a bit of a shock. I was expecting some kind of revelation, you know – the final clue to finding Eileen...'

'But? I can feel a 'but' coming.'

Mackie got up off the swing. 'Yeah. There's a 'but'. A pretty big one, actually. I don't know, Sha, it's too weird. He ... he'd done a drawing of the tree in my garden.'

'OK. So he'd done it while he was staying with you, you mean?'

'No. It was already in the sketchbook. I watched him untape the envelope. The drawing was already in there.'

She puffed her cheeks out and raised her eyebrows. 'And what did he say about it?'

'He said...' *Christ.* 'He said he was meant to come here. He said this was where he was meant to be.'

'My god. OK. So that's weird, then. Here as in the yard, you mean? Or here as in your garden?'

Mackie hadn't considered that one. 'I don't know.'

'So did he say why he was meant to come?'

Mackie sat down on the cane chair opposite Sharon and put his head in his hands. 'Yeah.'

'This is about your Sandra, isn't it?'

He looked across at her. 'Sort of.'

'Well, hold the front page! Let's go in the kitchen. I'm going to put the kettle on.'

36

Sharon knew about Sandra – or thought she did. She knew that she had died when Lauren was young, but she didn't know how she'd died. It was sudden, that's all Mackie had told her. An accident while he was working away – keeping the edges blurred, mainly because, at that point, his own edges were still pretty blurred. There was only so much revelation he could cope with. And somehow, he'd parked it there. Or buried it.

Mackie took a deep breath followed by a mouthful of tea.

'There's things about me that you don't know, Sha. Things from the past.'

He could hear the wobble in his voice. 'Sandra didn't just *die,* she ... erm ... she killed herself. It was ... god. Hang on a minute.'

He couldn't remember the last time he'd said the words out loud. He reached across for the tea towel and mopped his forehead with it.

'I don't really think she meant it to happen, she ... she wasn't well. So she didn't really know what she was doing, I think.'

Sharon propped her elbows on the table and rested her chin on her hands. The kitchen was still and quiet, like it was holding its breath, waiting for him.

'We'd been married nearly four years. Lauren was almost

ready for school and Sandra was expecting again. I was working on the roads. A big outfit. I was doing a load of overtime because we'd had the chance to buy our council house and we'd gone for it. Anyway, everything was fine. The baby was born...' He stopped there because he could feel the ache starting up in his throat. 'And everything was fine, and then ... then it wasn't.'

Sharon sat quietly while he told her the rest. How, afterwards, they'd said it was post-natal depression. But undiagnosed. How he'd not realised because he was working away a lot of the time – there was a big night job on in Bristol and he was only home at weekends. How he'd just thought she was tired. He told her about the night he was on the tarmac lorry and the boss came for him, said he needed to get home because there was something wrong with his wife: she'd left Lauren with a neighbour and not come back.

'What about the baby?' Sharon spoke softly, like she was scared of interrupting the flow.

'Elise,' Mackie said. 'Sandra had taken Elise with her.' He swallowed down a mouthful of tea. 'Anyway, when I got home the police were waiting for me and I ... I thought they must have found her and they were dropping her off. But they weren't. They were waiting for me. *Get in, Mr Carpenter*, they said. *Get in quick,* and they put the siren on and pulled away before I'd got the door closed properly. So that's when I knew, really. That things were, you know, bad. But they wouldn't tell me anything, just kept saying to hold on, that we'd be there soon, so I sat holding onto my seat belt trying to work

273

out where we were going, but in my head I was shouting her name. *Sandra, Sandra.* Then we stopped and I recognised where we were ... It was the Mumbles... the pier in the Mumbles.'

'Christ, Mackie. You are shitting me?'

But Mackie was no longer listening, he was no longer there. He was running through the dark, his feet thudding on the damp boards, salt spray on his face...

'She was already in the water when I got there. They had divers in.'

Sharon put her head in her hands. 'Oh shit, Mackie.'

'I set off running but they grabbed me and held me back. It was alright, they said. They'd got her.' *Got who?* Mackie had shouted. *Who have you got?* They looked at him like he was mad. 'Your wife, sir. We've got your wife.' *But what about my daughter? What about my daughter?* He was screaming at them and he couldn't stop because he could tell by the look on their faces they didn't know about his daughter, they didn't know about— He paused because he didn't want to choke her name out.

They didn't know about the baby. They didn't know about Elise.

After that, everyone started running. He got to the railings and looked down into the water and it was lit up and he could see someone laid out flat in the bottom of one of the dinghies. *Sandra* he yelled. *Sandra. Where's the baby?* He climbed up onto the railing and swung his leg over, then someone grabbed him and pulled him backwards. *Let me go,* he shouted. *I need to find her. I need to find her.*

'I thought she was in the sea. I thought my daughter was in the sea.'

Sharon grabbed hold of his arm. 'You thought your daughter was in the sea? Like the kid...'

'Exactly. Like the kid said!'

'For Christ's sake, Mackie, why didn't you say, why didn't you tell me?'

'Simple, Sha: because it was too bloody painful. Because I'd buried it a long time ago and I couldn't face digging it all back up. But now...'

Telling her the rest came easy – like a bottle that had been uncorked – it just poured out of him. He told her about the ambulance, the hospital, the race down the corridor, intensive care. How he'd thought, afterwards, that it had all been a show because Sandra must have been dead when they got her out of the water; that they were clinging on to the hope they might revive her not realising that he believed – he knew – that they could do it. They couldn't, of course. Before he knew it they were talking about oxygen starvation, nature taking its course, organ donation and then, at some point in the middle of the night, they switched off the machine. She went straightaway. The machine stopped and so did she.

You can't blame yourself, Mackie. That was Melody, months later. Earnest from the get-go. He remembered nodding like he was agreeing with her because he didn't want to burden her with the weight of his guilt. He wanted to carry that all on his own. And that is what undid him. There's only so much one mind can cope with and in his case, he tipped easily. He spent the rest of that night at the hospital and when he woke next morning, there was a sound in his head he'd not heard before. Like a radio out of frequency. He remembered getting up and walking from one end of the corridor to the other trying to tune it in. *What is that fucking noise?* That's what he shouted as he strode past a nurse, banging the top of his head with his fists. *Can't you get them to switch it off?*

It turned out that they could switch it off because the next thing he knew he was staring at blank walls in the acute psychiatric ward at Cefn Coed, lulled by a cocktail of medication and the sound of his own breathing. *Nervous breakdown prompted by shock and grief.* Layman's terms. With a few knobs on. Worrying knobs like thinking the metal plate in his head was picking up radio signals, like thinking they were lying to him and Sandra was alive and trying to find him. Enough to introduce him to the realities of Section 63 of The Mental Health Act anyway. But Elise? They didn't talk about her and he didn't ask. Couldn't. His only thoughts, as he lay staring at the ceiling was that she was in the sea. Eventually, they put him out of his misery. Told him Elise wasn't in the sea – she was in foster care, like Lauren. A different family – one that specialised in young babies. He'd often wondered if things would have been different if he'd known straightaway – if he'd known Sandra had wrapped her in a warm blanket and laid her on a bench; that a policewoman had shone her torch across the small bundle of her then shouted out into the dark, her voice choked with tears.

They kept him for three months: a regime of medication that kept his head quiet and some fairly intensive grilling courtesy of Dr Peart – a clinical psychologist? Psychiatrist? He didn't know the difference but it didn't matter to him, because he eventually agreed to discharge him with *ongoing support* – cue Melody – and he went back home thinking it was all over, only to discover his struggles had just begun.

'For the sake of brevity let's just say I lost the house and almost lost Lauren.'

Eventually, with Melody's help, he got rehoused, and he got Lauren back. Elise was a different story. His background health – by which they meant Cefn Coed – and the challenges of his new situation meant that they couldn't recommend her immediate return, that the case would be reviewed once things had settled. It never happened because in some low moment he gave in. He gave in and gave her up.

Adoption. It's the right thing to do, Mackie. That's what Mary Kavanagh said after the meeting. The right thing to do? All he remembered was getting up from the table and walking out of the room, then going home and gathering her few things into a box.

There weren't many: her wristband from the maternity unit; the Babygro they'd brought her home in; a pair of bootees Sandra had knitted. The next morning, he and Lauren went to the garden centre and when they got back, he dug the hole, put the box in the bottom and planted the tree.

'So, it was her tree? Elise's tree.'

He nodded. 'And somehow the kid knew that. That picture

of the tree? He'd drawn it, roots and all, and guess what was tucked away in the soil?'

'The box?'

'The box.'

'So, what now?'

'I'm going to ask him to help me find her, Sha. Find Elise.'

'Sounds like a good plan,' she said.

'Sounds like the only plan.'

'Well, I reckon you won't have long to wait. They'll be clocking off any minute.'

37

It had gone half past five. Mackie was beginning to wonder what was taking Trev and the kid so long when Trev suddenly barrelled through the back door and out into Sharon's garden, breathless, like he'd been running. He didn't see them, at first, tucked away on the swing.

'You're late.'

'What the fuck?' He took a step back. Then he saw them. 'Oh Christ. I'm not interrupting anything, am I? It's not feeding time at the zoo?'

'Ha ha. Cuppa?'

'No.' He arranged himself in one of the cane chairs opposite. He had *news* written all over his face.

He took a couple of deep breaths and for a moment Mackie thought he was going to burst into song. 'So? Have you seen it yet?'

'Seen what?'

'YouTube ... you've only gone viral, Sha.'

'Viral? What are you on about, Trev?'

'Your bloody nosedive. Somebody posted it, didn't they? And you, Mackie. Fuck me. You went over those railings like Daniel fucking Craig. It's all over the bloody Internet. Here, have a look ... oh.' He grabbed Mackie's phone which was propped up on the table, a nod in the direction of trying to dry it out. It dripped onto his lap.

'It was in my pocket.'

'No worries ... hang on.' He got his own phone out and started speed scrolling.

'Trev,' Mackie said, unconcerned at that point. 'Where's the kid?'

Trev glanced up from the screen. 'Oh, he's gone ... Right, here we are...'

'Gone?' The word gurgled out of his throat. Mackie struggled to his feet. 'What do you mean, he's gone?' It must have been the crack in his voice because Trev stopped what he was doing and looked at him.

'Oh, sorry, Mackie. I thought you knew. She tried to ring you – she left a message. Oh, yeah...' He nodded at the dripping phone. 'It was the social worker. She turned up at Tranter's. She took him.'

'Wait a minute, Trev.' Mackie was concentrating hard on staying upright. The inside of his head was firing in all directions. 'What do you mean she took him?'

'To Eileen,' he said, and Mackie's knees buckled. 'They found Eileen.'

'Mackie.' Sharon levered herself off the swing and got hold of his arm. 'Come and sit back down. You look awful.' She steered him back to the swing seat and propped a cushion behind his head. 'Right, Trev,' she said, when she had him arranged to her satisfaction, 'I'm going to make us a cuppa, then you're going to put that bloody phone away and tell us exactly what happened.'

There wasn't much more for Trev to tell. A car had pulled into the yard and a woman had got out: Tracy Cooper (from the description Trev gave) and she'd chatted to the kid – and then to Trev.

'So, Riley,' Mackie could barely say it, 'he just left? Went with the social worker?'

'Yeah. But, like I said, she tried to ring you.'

'He didn't say anything about ... me?'

'No, but he gave me this...' Trev searched the pocket in his jacket and pulled out a piece of folded paper.

'Oh, thank god.' Mackie was up off the seat, by his side and reaching for it before Trev had it unfolded. 'Did he leave it for me?' He didn't listen to Trev's answer because he knew it had to be for him. *I was meant to come here,* the kid had said. *This is where I was meant to be.* And he'd come because of the box – because of Elise...

But the drawing made no sense. No matter which way he looked at it, it made no sense at all.

'It's a boat,' Mackie said. 'A boat called 'The Sea Scout'? He looked at Trev.

'Yeah. I know. The kid gave it to me.'

'To you. *For you,* you mean.'

Trev nodded and took the drawing back.

'Do you ... but why, Trev? Why has he done you a drawing of a boat called 'The Sea Scout'?'

Trev shrugged. 'He said it would help me find someone.'

'But...' Mackie glanced over at Sharon like she might help him take it all in: the kid going off with the social worker; a drawing for Trev, not for him. 'I didn't know you were looking for someone, Trev.'

'We're all looking for someone, Mackie. Isn't that what it all boils down to?'

Mackie dropped his chin onto his chest and let this sink in.

Sharon got hold of his hand. 'Don't worry, Mackie. He'll be in touch.'

'But my phone,' he said.

'Bugger the phone. He knows where you live, doesn't he? He knows where you work. There's probably a message on your answer machine. Come on. Chin up. He'll get in touch.'

But what if he didn't? Mackie wanted to say. *What if the kid simply disappeared from his life?*

'Yeah. You're probably right, Sha. I'll go home and check the landline. That'll give you and Trev a chance to catch up. How's that washing doing?'

'It's in the tumbler. Won't be far off, but I was going to put something in the oven, make us a bit of—'

'Nah, I'll get straight off. Been a long day and all that.' He gave her an unconvincing smile, picked up his phone and headed towards the kitchen. He took his clothes out of the drier and went to the bathroom and, as soon as the door was closed, he burst into tears. *The kid had gone.* He'd gone before he'd had the chance – or the guts – to talk to him properly, to tell him what it was *he* needed. And why? Because he was a fool and a coward, that's why. Sharon? She'd jumped in the bloody Marina – no messing there. *Jump*, the kid had said, and she'd bloody well jumped. And now Trev, all lit up and ready for action with his drawing. *But what about him?*

He closed the front door behind him and the empty house wrapped itself round his shoulders like a damp blanket. He shrugged it off when he realised the message light on the answer machine was flashing. He pressed play then sat on the bottom stair and waited. *You have two new messages...*

The first was from Tracy Cooper. 10am – around the time they were racing towards the Marina. They'd found Eileen, she said. Chirpy, like it would be the good news he was waiting to hear. The second one was a little later. Tracy again, saying she'd be picking the kid up from Tranter's – she'd catch up with him there.

He listened to the machine making its little reset noises then went into the kitchen and cracked a beer. The kid's sketchbook was on the table. He took it outside, settled himself under the tree, opened it to the last page and ran his fingers over the paper. He traced the swirl of leaves the kid had drawn, the sweep of branches, the tangle of roots, Elise's box – and let them rest on the man sitting on the bench. Him.

It was a simple drawing, nothing more than a silhouette, really, but the sadness in the slope of the shoulders – his shoulders – was palpable. He gazed up into the dark, tracing the tops of the chimneys, following a line of clouds backlit by a brightening moon and knew it was time to do something about that sadness.

It was time to let it go.

With that thought, he closed the sketchbook – and the telephone rang...

It was as easy as that. This is what Mackie was thinking as he walked up the path and through the kitchen, because he knew – knew for certain – that it was going to be the kid on the other end of the line. That the kid – with his *magic*, had sensed the decision he had made and was ready to help.

'Hi, Dad. It's me.'

'Lauren.' His heart dropped and took his voice with it.

'The one and only. Don't sound so pleased.' There was an edge to her voice that said she'd had a drink or two.

'Sorry. I was expecting...' He trailed off.

'We're home.' There was an exclamation mark in the way she said it.

'Great.'

'Thought we might pop round. The kids are dying to see you, aren't you, kids? Kids, it's Granddad...' He could hear the twins whooping in the background.

'It's not a good ... I was just going...' He trailed off again and plonked himself down on the bottom stair. She wasn't listening; she was still talking to the twins. 'Go on, get your things ready ... are you there, Dad?'

'Yeah, but...'

'Right. We're setting off now. See you in five. *Amber, what the fuck?*'

He put the handset down and leaned his elbows on his knees. He was still there ten minutes later when the twins shot in through the front door.

'Where's Mummy?' he said, after he'd managed to untangle himself from them.

'She's getting our stuff.' Amber perched herself on his knee.

'Oh? What stuff?'

'Our jamas of course, Granddad.' She poked him in the ribs like they were sharing a little joke.

'Your jamas? Och, hello.' Lauren swept in through the door. She smelled of wood smoke and salt. She was carrying the twins' rucksacks.

'I'm just going out.' He blurted it, before he lost his momentum.

'Nice to see you, too.' She dropped the rucksacks by the hall table.

'What's happening? Where's ... where's Eddie?'

'He's outside, waiting.'

'Waiting for what?'

'Oh Christ, Dad. I can see you're going to be bloody awkward. Kids, go and put the telly on, I need to talk to Granddad a minute.'

She waited 'til they'd gone then propped herself against the front door. 'Come on, Dad. I've told Eddie it'd be OK. That you'd have them for a couple of days so ... so we, you know, can have a bit of time to ourselves.'

'I can't, I've got work. You know that, Lauren. I've got to work.'

'You could ring in, make an excuse. Come on.'

He shook his head.

'Oh, for Christ's sake, Dad. Don't be such a fucking knob.

This is really important to me. Eddie, he's ... I want it to work...'

'Then make it work. That's up to you, Lauren, not me.'

'Oh,' she said, putting her hands on her hips. 'Good advice, Father. *Make it work.* How the hell am I supposed to do that when I'm up to my eyes looking after those two all the time?'

There was a lot he could have said to that but he held his tongue. The twins hadn't put the telly on. They were in the kitchen doorway, listening.

'Please, Dad. Just one night. Jan could have them tomorrow.' Her voice was wheedling.

'Jan's on holiday.'

'Oh, so what exactly am I supposed to tell him? What am I supposed to say to Eddie? That you've let me down? Because that's what you're doing, Dad. You're letting me down.' She paused to measure what effect she was having then, confident her words were hitting home, forged on. 'And the twins,' she lamented. 'You're letting them down too. I've told Eddie how much they love you, how good you are.'

'I'm sorry, love, but the answer is still no. I can't have them.'

'Fine. Right. Seems like I've got no choice, then.' She yanked the door open and disappeared up the path. He listened to the up and down of her voice then heard an engine start up. He waited, readying himself for the next round, because he was holding on with his fingertips and knew what her next gambit was going to be: *if you won't have them I'll take them to Lloyd's.*

He suddenly realised that several minutes had passed and

she still hadn't come in, so he poked his head through the doorway and scanned the garden for her. She wasn't there.

'Lauren?' He walked down to the gate and checked the street. The van had gone and so had she.

He marched back into the house and grabbed the phone, jabbing at the numbers. He got her answer machine. 'Lauren, get yourself back here. Now. Do you hear me?' She'd laugh herself silly when she heard that one. He banged the phone down and slammed through to the kitchen.

'What was that noise, Granddad?' Amber came into the kitchen, trailing the throw off the sofa behind her.

'What? Oh, nothing. I ... I dropped the phone.'

'Has Mummy gone?'

'Yes.'

She gave this some thought. 'We're hungry.'

'Right.'

'And,' she kicked her trainers off, 'my feet are dirty.'

He forced a smile. She wasn't convinced. She sidled up beside him and put her arm round the back of his legs.

'Are you sad, Granddad?'

'Sad?' It came out in a sort of hiccup. 'No, I'm not sad. Come on, I'll...' He levered himself off the chair. 'I'll run the bath *and* –' he could hear Mr Jolly in his voice and it made him want to cry, '*and* I'll put some pizzas on, yeah?' *Pizzas. It was his bloody answer to everything.*

'Yeah. Yeah.' She gave a little jump and punched the air. 'Tylo, come on. Grandad's doing pizzas and we're having a bath.'

When they were in bed he took himself back out into the garden to think. To consider his options. There were two, as far as he could see. He could choose the easy one: slot into his usual groove, toe the line, maintain the status quo – and carry on being the sad bugger who sat on a bench under a Rowan tree, too scared to make a change. Or he could get off the bloody bench and move on.

He pressed his back against the wooden slats and thought of the hours of support they'd given him; he rested his hand on the bench arm, paused for a moment to feel its familiar grain under his fingers, then he got to his feet and walked away.

38

Mackie phoned the yard early the next morning to let Tranter know he couldn't come in. He reacted to the news like he was auditioning for a movie.

'You. Fucking. What?'

'I'm sorry, boss.' He didn't know what else to say. He'd hoped Sharon would pick up.

'Well, I reckon that's the end of the line for you and me then, son, isn't it?'

'What?'

'Told you the other day, didn't I? If you're *too busy*—'

'No ... no, I'm not. I'm not too busy ... it's just...'

'Forget today, then, I'll see you tomorrow morning.'

'Thank you, boss. I won't let you down again.'

'Too fucking right you won't. Sharon.' His voice faded as he turned away from the receiver, but it didn't matter because Mackie heard him clear enough.

'Get Mackie's P45 ready. He's picking it up in the morning.' Then the line went dead.

When the phone rang a couple of minutes later he was still sitting at the bottom of the stairs staring into space. He looked at it but didn't trust his legs to get him up.

'The phone's ringing, Granddad.' Tylo came down the

stairs. He touched his shoulder as he went past, then, before Mackie realised what he was going to do, picked up the receiver. 'Oh, hello Mummy. Yes ... no ... erm, yes.' He glanced at Mackie then passed the handset over. Mackie held it to his ear but didn't say anything.

'You there, Dad?'

'Yeah.'

'I bet you're mad with me?' He could hear the grin in her voice. He didn't reply.

'Are the kids OK?'

'Yeah.'

'Oh, for god's sake, Dad. Quit the bloody sulking. It was only one sodding night. I mean, is that too much to—'

'He's sacked me.'

'Pardon?'

'Tranter. He's just sacked me.'

'Piss off. You're saying that to wind me up.'

He shook his head.

'You are, aren't you? Winding me up?'

'I'm not, no.'

'What? For one day off? Don't be so dull. He's not allowed to do that ... Eddie, my dad said he's had the sack. That's not allowed, is it?' He listened to her chuntering on, wondering, seeing as she'd never had a job, how she suddenly knew so much about employment rights. 'You've got to fight it, Dad.'

This made him smile. She'd never seen him fight; she'd only seen him give in. He gave her the number of his spare mobile.

He didn't bother explaining what had happened to his normal one and she didn't bother asking.

He didn't know how long he sat there. Long enough to unnerve the twins who quietly shuffled themselves either side of him and sat patting his back. They eventually took off into the kitchen, emerging ten minutes later with a plate of biscuits and a mug of milk. They handed it over like it was the crown jewels, then stood watching him. Mackie took a sip of milk and bit the corner off a custard cream. This earned him a small nod from Amber who leaned over and helped herself to a fig roll. Tylo palmed a couple of bourbons and, seemingly satisfied that all was now well with the world, they tootled off into the sitting room and put the telly on. He was thinking he might as well go and join them when someone rang the doorbell.

He straightened himself up and went to the door and saw Sharon's beehive teetering on the other side of the glass.

'Alright, Mackie?' She bustled past him, trailing a cloud of body spray. 'Oh, that's what it's all about,' she said, as the theme tune to *Peppa Pig* floated out of the sitting room. 'She's dumped the kids on you again.'

'What you doing here, Sha? Why aren't you at the yard?'

'Skiving. I'm not actually here, am I? I'm on my way to the bank.' She plonked herself on a kitchen chair. 'I was going to ring you and then I thought, sod it. I'll pop in. So ... what's going on?'

He looked at her. 'What's going on, Sha? You were there, weren't you? He's given me the bloody sack.'

'No – I know that bit. He was already in when I arrived. In my bloody office on the computer. So I made a quick excuse, didn't I. Said I needed to sign some papers at the bank and got out before he had a chance to object – or ask me about yesterday. And Christ knows what Arlene's done to his bloody hair. But, anyway, work aside…'

'Work aside?' It came out a bit falsetto. 'I think the sack is hardly something to class as an aside, Sha.'

'Point taken. But come on. He was in a shite mood. He'll have changed his mind by teatime. Sod work for the minute. I want to know what happened when you got back last night. Did the kid get in touch with you? Was there a message?'

'Yeah. Two messages from the social worker, like Trev said.'

'And the kid?'

He shook his head.

'Have you tried ringing her, then? The social worker?'

'Christ – no, I haven't.' He'd been that sidetracked by Lauren and Tranter he'd not thought of it.

'Get to it then, Mack.' He trotted to the phone, suddenly full of something that felt like hope and listened to the usual loops of The Verve, pen in hand, ready to take down Eileen's contact details.

"Tracy Cooper is out of the office until Monday. Please contact the duty social worker."

'Out of the office,' he mouthed, then left a short message on the answer machine.

'So…' she said, peering round the kitchen, 'where's this sketchbook, then?'

Mackie slid open the drawer in the table. 'It's here.'

She went through the drawings one by one, taking her time. 'Looks like they came down the A483, because that's in Newtown,' she said, pointing at the Pryce Jones sign, 'and that hotel is in Llandrindod. God, hell of a gift, isn't it? Ah, there we go. Your tree.' She lowered her face to the drawing. 'Oh, look, Mackie,' she said, pointing at the sad bugger on the bench. 'That's you.' She paused a moment, then looked at him.

'That's me,' he said.

That used to be me, was what he should have said, because here was his cue to air his bold decision from the night before. He should be telling her how he'd got up from the bench and walked away from it, full of nothing but good intentions.

'And that's Elise's box.'

'That's Elise's box, yes.'

'Have you decided what you're going to do?'

He thought for a moment before answering. He remembered the certainty he'd felt the night before – a certainty that had him off the bench and walking away from it.

He knew it was up to him to stay off it now, despite the fact that Lauren had nudged him so neatly into his usual groove; despite Tranter capping it all off by sacking him.

'Yeah. I'm going to do what you did yesterday, Sha. I'm going to trust the kid and take the bloody plunge. I'm going to open the box, let it all out. It's been weighing me down far too bloody long.'

'What? Mackie – you're not going to ... dig it up, are you?'

'No. It's already been dug up in a way, hasn't it, Sha? The

kid knew about it, I've told you about it – all I need to do now is...' He searched for the right word. 'Open it back up, confront what's in it...'

'What do you mean?'

'I definitely want to find her, Sha. I want to try and find Elise.'

'What about your Lauren, then? Will you tell her about it?'

It was a good point and he'd already thought about it.

'No. She was too young to remember.'

'So...?'

'So I'm going to play that bit by ear. She's ... you know what she's like, Sha. Sees herself as the main act, doesn't she? I'll choose my timing. Try and find Elise first, then see what happens after.'

'Fair do's. Right. My time's up. I'll phone you later, then. And...' She grabbed him awkwardly and clutched him to her bosom. He breathed in the heady mix of her while she patted his back with her big hands. He could hear her heart beating and the air coming into her lungs and he could have stayed there forever. Eventually, she let go and pushed him back so she could see his face. 'It'll be alright, the kid won't let you down.'

39

They were on the motorway. The soft rubber ripple of the tyres coming up through the seat carrying the hum of the road, like a song, into his head.

The kid wanted to sleep but, although his eyes were heavy, it would not come.

Eileen was sitting beside him and the sun was spilling through the windscreen, lighting up her face and her hair. The radio was on and she was tapping her fingernails on the steering wheel in time with the music. The kid looked out of the window then turned to look at her. She smiled at him, took her hand off the wheel and put it on his arm. He smiled back then returned to the window. He was thinking about Sharon and Trev. But mostly he was thinking about Mackie. He had tried the number that Trev gave them but nothing happened: a blank silence that he listened to, imagining the loose end of his connection waving blindly in space, searching for some answering signal. He closed his eyes and, even though they were travelling north and every minute was taking him further away, he tried to see the path that would somehow close the gap between him and Mackie. But if it was there, he could not find it.

They would not be going back. Eileen had told him this.

The thought twisted itself round in the kid's stomach because he had not intended to leave Mackie yet. He knew that although Mackie was almost there, he still needed him.

When Sharon had gone Mackie stayed in the kitchen, leafing through the sketchbook. He was thinking about the kid and wondering if the kid was thinking about him when he was suddenly struck by what he'd just said to Sharon. *He was going to choose his timing.* A small click in his head, like the sound of something falling into place, took him upstairs. He slid his Aberystwyth Angel picture from beneath the pillow and, before he knew it, and without the aid of any helter-skelter, he had the answer he didn't even know he was looking for. It was obvious – the 3M's and Llwyn-onn had been unsuccessful because the kid had got the timing wrong; so what if the Aberystwyth trip had been the same? The next step was small – but monumental: what if they'd not only been there at the wrong time, but they'd also been looking for the wrong daughter?

He had to speak to Sharon. He was halfway down the stairs when the phone rang.

'Mackie.' It was Sharon.

'I was just about to phone you, I've just had this...'

'Mackie, can you come into the yard?'

'What? What's wrong?'

'Nothing. Nothing's wrong. It's the kid. I think he's left you something. Just seen it now when I got in. An envelope with your name on.'

'An ... an envelope?'

'Do you want me to open it?'

'No. No, Sha. Don't open it. I'll be there as quick as I can. Alright?'

He keyed in Jan Jeary's number then remembered she wasn't there. He stuck his head round the sitting room door. 'Time to get dressed, kids. We're going out.'

'Where are we going, Granddad?'

'Ooh, it's a surprise.'

They were off the sofa and up the stairs in a flash.

'Kids!' he yelled after them. 'Put your cowboy outfits on, because we'll be going on a bit of a trot.'

Sharon was off her chair and out of the office as the three of them cantered into the yard. 'That was bloody quick. Oh, I see...' She gave the twins the once over. 'You came in on the Pony Express.'

'Sure did, Sha.'

It felt more like he'd flown there. Or maybe swam. Whichever it was there was a lightness to him he'd not felt for years. The kid had left him a drawing. It was all he could think of as he'd jogged along behind the twins.

'Where is it, then?'

She handed it over. 'Shame I didn't see it earlier. I'd have brought it round with me.'

Mackie was going to say something about timing, but decided to save it 'til afterwards. He perched himself on Sharon's wheelie chair and opened the envelope.

'My god, Sha.' His hand was at his throat, his heart was bouncing against his ribs. 'I was right, I was bloody right.'

She took the drawing off him and studied it for a few moments. 'Well, I can see the angel statue, but otherwise it's not making much sense.'

He was about to start telling her about his dreams: the dinghy, the rope on his shoulders, the wall of sea, when Tranter suddenly walked past the office window.

'Oh, bugger. He was supposed to be out 'til ... all right, boss?'

Tranter stood in the doorway surveying the scene. 'What's all this, then? No one told me we'd started running a flaming creche, or,' he said, peering at the kids, 'should I say, a bloody corral.'

'Mackie's just come in for his papers, like you said?'

This threw Mackie, but not half as much as it threw Tranter. It was the question mark she'd put at the end that had dropped the ball neatly in his court.

'His papers. Yes. Well.' He hooked his thumbs into his belt loops and cleared his throat. 'So ... anything to say for yourself?'

This, Mackie realised, was his opportunity to plead his case but try as he might, he couldn't think of anything to say.

'I'm sorry, boss.' He gave a small nod towards at the twins. 'Sorry I couldn't come in. But I had my hands full.'

'Mm. Seems to be becoming a regular occurrence round here, doesn't it, Sha?'

'What's that, boss?' Sharon swivelled her seat round like she hadn't been listening.

'Getting let down. People just buggering off with no warning.'

'Oh, yeah.' She caught Mackie's eye as she swivelled back and gave him a wink.

'Nevertheless,' Tranter said, like he was a Radio 4 presenter. 'Nevertheless, I've decided to give you another chance.'

'What? I'm not sacked, you mean?'

'No. Not for the moment.'

'Right, so...'

'But,' he said, and this was where Tranter went wrong, or right, depending on which way you looked at it. 'No more of this fucking days off shit. From now on you toe the fucking line, right?' He jabbed his finger at the floor to illustrate his point.

Mackie looked down at the floor and imagined his toes pushed up against some invisible line. It was a chalk line, perhaps, or a length of rope, maybe a thick chain rusted with age or even a line of bricks set side by side. Whatever it was he'd been pushed up against it for a long time. He looked Tranter in the eye, took a deep breath and then stepped over it.

'Thanks, boss.' His voice was shaky but he stuck with it. 'I'll have a think about it and let you know, if that's alright with you.'

Sharon let out a small gasp.

'Good, glad we understand each other, now piss—' Tranter put his face through a series of double take contortions. 'What the fuck did you just say?'

'I said I'll have a think about it. Anyway, better get these two off.' He glanced down at Sharon and returned the wink, then spun on his heels and exited stage right. He went across the yard like Torville and bloody Dean and was halfway to the car when his mobile rang.

'Dad, it's me.'

'It's you. Good. Where are you?'

'Well, that's why I'm ringing ... I was thinking—'

'Are you at home? At yours?'

'Well, yes, but we were thinking that ... well, seeing as you're not working...'

'Stay there, I'm on my way round.'

'But Dad.'

He cut her off.

Small steps. Melody had always loved them. *One day at a time, one step at a time.* It became his mantra as she helped him piece together the safe, slow progress that kept him on track as opposed to veering off into the wild and uncharted territory that led to Cefn Coed. He learned to shuffle willingly through a life designed to keep his feet on the ground and his head out of the sky.

But that was then.

He could feel it as he walked the twins to Lauren's house. The feeling of release. Of moving forward, bounding ahead. His feet leaving the ground.

'Where are we going, Granddad?'

'Home.'

'Home? You mean to your house?'

'No,' he said. 'To your house. To Mummy.'

Eddie's van was parked outside when they got there. The

engine was running. Lauren was coming down the path with a suitcase, something of a quick getaway about her. 'Oh – hi, Dad.' She put the case in the van and slammed the door shut. Then she turned to face him. 'You got here quick.'

'Yeah. Thought you might be setting off somewhere, didn't want to miss you. Hi Eddie. Nice dungarees.'

'Thanks, man. Good to see you.' He sauntered over and took hold of his hand. 'A real bummer about your job, though. But, hey, thanks for saying you'll—'

'Ed.' Lauren gave him a small shake of her head. 'I've not told him...'

Mackie knew what that meant but ignored it. 'Their stuff's still at home,' he said, looking at the twins. 'But it's only pyjamas.'

Lauren was straight in. 'Oh, well, that's handy, because we were going to ask you...'

'No.' His voice was loud and the twins looked at him.

'You don't know what I was going say.' She slanted her head on one side, amused.

'It doesn't matter. The answer's still no.'

She folded her arms across her chest and dropped her hip. 'But you're not working now, Dad...'

'No, and neither are you, so ... come and give me a kiss, kids. Have a good time, wherever it is you're setting off to, Lauren. Send me a card, yeah? I'll see you all when I get back.'

'When you get back? What do you mean? Where are you going?'

He ignored her and spun, for the second time in less than

half an hour, on one heel and *glided* away. He turned after a few seconds and, with a smile like a man unhinged, threw them a cheery wave and walked off. He didn't know where the hell he was going, but now he was moving forward there'd be no stopping him.

40

'Christ, though, Mackie. I wish I'd taken a photo of his bloody face. *I'll have a think about it and let you know.* I nearly wet my knickers.'

They'd just opened the first bottle and were going strong.

'What you going to do, then?'

Mackie had been thinking about it on and off all day. He'd got back from Lauren's and spent a long time looking at the kid's drawing. It was a snapshot of the dream that had been plaguing him all these years: a night sky; a lone man walking into the sea towing a small dinghy; a rising wall of water rolling in from a dark and stormy horizon; and – watching it all from her plinth, her wings outstretched as if she were ready to fly to his aid – his Aberystwyth Angel.

The drawing had made him feel invincible – like he could do anything. He settled for cleaning the house – set about it like it was some kind of ritual: changing the beds; cleaning the windows; washing the kitchen floor; scrubbing the bathroom. Then he'd sat out in the garden, watching the sheets blow on the clothesline, thinking about what he would tell Tranter.

'I'm going to take him up on his kind offer,' Mackie said.

'What – you're not going to leave?'

'Nope.'

She swiped the back of her arm across her face. 'Well, thank god for that, Mackie. I thought you were going to abandon us.'

'It did cross my mind, I'll be honest. But I started thinking about what the kid said.'

'About us being a little family, you mean?'

'Yeah. About us being a little family. But also that stuff about him being meant to come here. I think we need to give up with all that "we're on the scrapheap" malarkey, Sha, because maybe we're not. We work in Tranter's scrapyard – and I think that's exactly where we're supposed to be. The kid found us because we were in the right place – and look what's happened since...'

'Like me jumping in the Marina, you mean?' Sharon was grinning.

'Exactly – although I fail to see what's so comical about it.'

'Sorry. It's the wine.' She gave a fake hiccup. 'It was bold, though, wasn't it?'

'Bold? It was bloody bonkers.'

'Yeah. *Crazy Sharon* – Barry had it spot on there, didn't he? How much time have I wasted on that prick? Mind you, when it comes to bonkers, I reckon I'm in pretty good company. What about you with all your trees and hidden boxes and bloody angel statues? And Trev – let's not forget about Trev...'

'Oh, I was going to ask you about Trev,' Mackie said. 'I've been thinking about him. Yesterday morning before, you know, before it all kicked off...'

'He had Bertha's car.'

'Yeah. He did. That's never happened before, has it? Plus, Tranter wanted to see him.'

'Well, pour me another glass, Mackie, my dear, then pin back your ears.'

Sha took a sip of wine. 'Remember I said he'd got all misty-eyed about going to the Meridian tower?'

'Yeah.'

'Well, it seems there was a good reason.'

Walking round the Marina with the kid had apparently been something of a trip down memory lane for Trev. It had taken him back to when he was a teenager – to the time when he had a friend: a mate called Clive. They were at school together. Two misfits who, by the sound of things, somehow fitted each other. They did scouts together, then Sea Scouts – inseparable, by the sound of it – until Clive went off to university, leaving Trev at home with Bertha.

'So, the kid obviously picked up on all this. You saw the drawing he did?'

'Yeah,' Mackie said. 'The boat: The Sea Scout.'

Trev had been unable to get the drawing out of his mind so, when he got home, he'd spun some tale saying he needed the car because Tranter had asked him to work late. Then he went back to the Marina and sat watching the boats and reminiscing about happier times.

'Anyway, he lost track of time and Bertha phoned Tranter at home and gave him a bollocking for keeping Trev back so late.'

'Poor bugger.'

'Who? Trev or Tranter?'

'Trev, of course. I mean, Sha, it's all very well for us poking fun at the woman from a safe distance, but can you imagine living with her?'

That was where Bertha's car came back in, apparently. The reason Trev had it parked – thank god – outside the yard was that he'd stood up to her. Told her if she wouldn't start letting him use the car, then he'd have to start looking for somewhere to rent that was nearer to work. It did the trick.

'No wonder he wasn't bothered about seeing Tranter yesterday, then. He was probably still running on pure adrenaline from standing up to Bertha.'

'Exactly ... anyhow, let's have another look at your drawing.'

Mackie slid it over. He'd had it waiting for her when she arrived and he'd spent the first half hour explaining it to her: telling her about the dream – how it had plagued him for years – and how it had come the night before she'd gone into the Marina. He'd told her how he was going to phone Tracy Cooper first thing Monday morning to get a contact number for the kid. He'd told her how he knew what he needed to do – he just didn't know when he needed to do it.

'Can I go with you, when you go, Mackie?'

'Really?'

'Yeah, really.'

'OK, Sha. That'd be ... yeah.'

They sat for a few minutes in silence after that.

'Right, that's me proper knackered. I'm off home to my bed.' She hauled herself out of the chair.

'We haven't finished this, yet,' Mackie said, picking up the wine bottle.

'Nah. Turning over a new leaf, aren't I? Diet starts tomorrow and all that. Anyway, goodnight, pal.' She leaned down and wrapped her arms round him. 'Sleep tight.'

Mackie swirled his wine and let his eyes trace the outline of the Rowan tree. Its branches were stretched out and still, and backlit by the streetlight, it looked unreal, like it was part of a stage set.

41

Monday morning.

'What a difference a day makes...'

'Oh my god, here we go,' Trev said.

Sharon was doing a bit of a song and dance routine when they got to tea break: small *cha-cha-cha* shuffles as she put out the cups. She grabbed Trev before he had a chance to sit down and twirled him a few steps. He made a fuss but didn't put up much resistance.

'What's got into you this morning, Sha?'

'I've joined a group, haven't I.' She threw in a bit of a shoulder shimmy that gave her bra a run for its money.

'A group? Singing, you mean?' asked Mackie.

'Nah, I've quit all that, remember?'

She'd been on the phone the day before relating the conversation she'd had with Barry. Short, basically. And final.

'What kind of group, then?'

'OK. Here we go.' She smoothed her top down, got herself all lined up straight, then put three fingers up. 'Three words.'

'Oh, Sha. Not fucking charades.'

'Play the game, young Trev, play the game ... right, first word...'

Several minutes later, when they'd only got as far as, "the", they gave in.

'It's a swimming group,' she grinned. 'An outdoor swimming group. The Gower Mermates. Went for my first dip yesterday, didn't I? Hey, hang on – I'll show you.' She went into the office and brought her mobile out. 'What do you think of that, then? Baywatch eat your fucking heart out.'

Mackie looked at the photo. Sharon in a red cozzy, her hair hanging round her shoulders, dripping wet – smiling like he'd never seen her smile before. He could feel himself filling up. 'Oh god, Sha. Look at you. You look so ... so happy.'

'I was ecstatic, Mackie. Absolutely ecstatic. Mind you, my bloody minge was numb for hours.'

She went back into the office and came back out with a punnet of grapes. She plonked them on the table and sat down.

'Hang on a minute, Sha. Where's the biscuits?'

'New regime from now on, Trev. Healthy eating, isn't it?'

'Healthy eating? Come off it. I'm bloody starving ... we're starving, aren't we, Mackie? You can do the fruit, Sha – we need our biscuits.'

'Oh, thank you very much, Trev. What happened to, "all for one and one for all?" Do the musketeers only rock up when there's a ginger on the go? Anyway,' she said, 'how did your weekend plans go?'

'I don't have to do charades, do I?'

'No, for god's sake, Trev. Just tell us.'

Trev's weekend, it transpired, had been as exciting as

Sharon's and, amazingly, had involved the sea. He'd put himself forward for RNLI volunteering.

'A lifeboat man, Trev?' Mackie couldn't quite believe what he was hearing.

'Where did that come from?

It turned out Trev had applied before – when he was eighteen – and Bertha had somehow scuppered it for him. But he'd applied now because of what had happened at the Marina. He'd watched as the lifeboat swung into view and stood by as the police divers had dragged him and Sharon out of the water – and he'd turned to the kid and said, *That's what I wanted to be once.*

'It was the Sea Scouts that clinched it, I think,' Trev said. 'The bloke said they had a lot of people turning up because of that telly programme, but when I mentioned I'd done Sea Scouts I could tell he started taking me seriously.'

'So – are they going to have you?'

'Yeah. Timed it perfectly, as luck would have it. The new training course starts this Saturday and I've got myself a place on it. I wouldn't mind telling the kid about it. Did you manage to talk to him yet?'

'No. I left a message for the social worker. Asked her to ring me here.'

'We don't know how he is, then, the kid?' Trev said.

'No.'

'I wonder if he'll come back?'

'I hope so,' Mackie said. But he didn't really think so. He reckoned that if the kid was in his Merc now – looking down on them – he'd know his work was done.

Mackie was on the de-polluter when the microphone crackled into life and Sharon's voice sailed out over the yard.

'Call for Mr Mark Carpenter. Mr Mark Carpenter, we have a call for you...'

He snatched a handful of paper towels and wiped his hands as he headed for the office. *Social worker*, Sharon mouthed as she passed the handset to him.

'Hello? Tracy?'

'Mackie. Hi. How's things?'

'Yeah, OK, you know. Thanks for phoning back, I ... oh, hang on.' He took a pen and the telephone pad from the desk, went outside and sat down at the picnic table. Sharon watched from the office doorway. When the conversation finished she came and sat beside him. She picked up the telephone pad and looked at the blank page.

'Well? You didn't write anything down, then?'

'No. Eileen's taken Riley back up north. She can't give me his contact details.'

'But? Come on, Mack, there's got to be a "but" here.'

'But she's taken my new mobile number. She's going to pass it onto him.'

'Did she say anything else?'

Mackie nodded. 'Yeah, she said the police had picked Marco up.'

'And...?'

The grin on his face was giving him away. 'And ... Riley had given her a message to pass on to me.'

'Come on, I'm all ears, pal...'

311

He gave her a small nudge in the ribs. 'He said to make sure I'd found the drawing he'd left in the office – and he'd be in touch when it was the right time.'

'Top marks, kid! Bloody top marks. And you'll be ready?'

'I'll be ready.'

It comes on suddenly. The kid is in bed when it starts. A low hum at first, like maybe it's the sound of traffic and has nothing to do with his head, but then gradually rising with an insistence he recognises. He grabs his sketchbook then rests back, breathing, and allows the sound to fill him until it is lapping at the lining of his skull. When he opens his eyes he is in the white room. It is warm. The breeze that is coming through the open door strokes his face and he smiles into it as he steps out into the welcoming air. He stretches his body into a long smooth line and flies like a small bright arrow through clouds that part before him, revealing a way ahead that is shimmering with sunlight. He casts his eyes to the left and then to the right: a small bird, easy in flight, waiting for his destination to show itself. There is no hurry; instead, a sense of joy. Of hope. And he knows – even before his pace slows and the clouds beneath him start to thin – what is waiting for him. Who is waiting for him.

The kid slows to a halt and peers down through the gap in the clouds and there he is. Mackie. His head is tilted back, he is looking up, and his two arms are in the air, waving at him. 'I'm ready,' he is shouting. 'I'm ready.' And the kid smiles and waves back.

42

Mackie was in the kitchen when the kid's phone call came.

It was early – nowhere near light. He'd got up because the application form had been playing on his mind. It was Sharon and her Mermates, Trev and his lifeboat training that had spurred him on. He'd got in touch with Cruse – asked them about the possibility of training as a volunteer bereavement counsellor. They'd had the form to him two days later. He'd just completed it when his mobile went off. He took the stairs in giant strides, grabbed it off the bedside table and, breathless, smiled into it.

'Mackie, it's me.'

'Yes.' Mackie's heart was a leaping thing in his chest.

'It's time.'

'Right.' His voice wavered.

'Will you be OK?'

'Yes.'

'Keep your phone on.'

'OK … Riley, what if I don't recognise her…?'

'Don't worry. You will…'

And then he was gone. Mackie keyed in Sharon's number.

'Riley's just phoned. It's time.' He'd already got the bag in his hand, the one he'd had waiting all week like an expectant father, he'd thought, as he'd packed spare clothes, a toothbrush and toothpaste, a book, a packet of sweets – then slipped in the application form – and his Aberystwyth Angel.

They arrived before the town had woken properly. Their presence was noted only by a solitary man who gave them a brief nod, then returned his gaze to the point where his fishing line met the water.

Mackie settled himself in his seat and looked out through the windscreen. The beach was deserted. A great rolling surf, skimming with gulls, pounded a shoreline that was littered with seaweed and driftwood. A line of low cloud hung above the horizon, backlit by a sun he could not see.

'Are you ready?' Sharon asked. He nodded. He was ready. Ready and waiting. Waiting in the airlock that gathers as you close one door and wait for the next to open. He had the keys to that door with him: two envelopes. In one, his application form and in the other, his Aberystwyth Angel.

'Come on, then. Let's go and have a look at her.'

He tucked his phone in his pocket, turned his collar up against the blow of the Aberystwyth seafront and walked alongside Sharon until she came into view. He fixed his eyes on her, noting, as he got closer, the delicacy of her stance; how lightly, despite the bronze that made her, she perched on her plinth, wings outstretched, leaving him to wonder whether she had just landed or was about to leave. Her name was Victory. He stopped at the foot of the plinth and gazed up at her; under his breath he muttered small thanks for showing him where he needed to come. Then he turned and headed back to the car to wait.

They waited as the morning eased into waking. A single jogger padded by, then an elderly couple muffled against the wind, their small dog trotting gamely in their wake. A car passed and then a van and he wound down his window. Before he knew it, the town was up and about and the quiet of the early morning was swallowed by the sound of people, traffic, the busy gulls ... then eventually, his phone.

'It's time, Mackie.' That's all the kid said. And then his phone gave a small ping and a message came in. Like he was in a dream, Mackie turned to Sharon.

'This is it.' He opened the message. It was a photograph – a photograph of a drawing. Mackie enlarged it then showed it to Sharon. The kid's drawing was lined on all four sides, as if it was a view through a window – or a windscreen. Mackie looked at the view through the windscreen then back at the drawing. They were a perfect match – almost, because the kid's drawing had an extra element and Mackie knew that was what he was waiting for.

They appeared within a minute or two. Still a long way off but he could tell straightaway it was them. Three figures bent against the sea wind, walking towards the car. Girls. He consulted the drawing as they neared, concentrating on each figure until, as they passed, the girl in the middle suddenly looked at him and he knew the kid was right. He hadn't needed to worry about not recognising his daughter because there it was in the tilt of her chin, the angle of her cheekbones.

Her hair was long and black like Sandra's and, as she swept back, he dropped the phone and something in his chest shifted. It shifted then, like treasure long lost, it rose to the surface, up through his throat and out through his mouth and into the air.

'Elise,' he whispered. 'Elise?'

His hand reached for the door handle because he wanted to get out of the car and follow her. He wanted to run behind her shouting, *It's me, It's me.* But he didn't. He'd decided he was going to do it the right way. *Use the official channels, Mackie.* That's what Tracy Cooper had advised, and that's what he was going to do. All he wanted now, as he turned in his seat, wiped the tears from his eyes and watched her walk away, was to know that she was alive – and that he had found her.

'That was her, Sha. That was her!'

'Well done, Mackie.' She took his hand in hers. 'Bloody well done.'

It was hard to say how long they sat there, but when Sharon turned the key in the ignition, Mackie assumed they were heading back home. He was wrong.

Sharon reversed out of her space, turned the car round and headed towards the far end of the seafront. Mackie looked at her as she parked the car outside a large hotel.

'What we doing?'

'Well – I'm not sure this is the right term for it – but I think your Melody woman would have called it something like closure. Come on.'

She got out of the car and went round to the back.

'You've not done anything daft, Sha, have you?' She was pulling a large bag out of the boot. 'You haven't gone and booked this fancy hotel or anything?'

'God, no, Mackie. It's a lot dafter than that. Here, grab this and follow me.'

Then she set off towards the beach. She chose a spot, took the bag off him and started unpacking it. 'Here, that one's yours.' She handed him a towel.

'Ah. Hang on a minute, Sha. You're not thinking that I'm...'

'That's exactly what I'm thinking, Mack. Come on, get your kecks off.'

'I can't. I haven't...'

She reached into the bag and threw a pair of swimming trunks at him.

'Tesco's finest.' She smiled then started peeling off her clothes.

She had her Baywatch cozzy on underneath.

'Right, last one in's a stinker.' She gave a whoop and set off towards the waves.

Mackie watched her for a few moments, then he looked up at the sky; smiled up at it and went running after her.

And before he knew it, he was wading into a calm sea hauling the small dinghy behind him. He felt the tangle of seaweed round his legs as he strode out, deeper and deeper until his feet left the seabed and he was forced to swim. He glanced over his shoulder at the dinghy: it was following smoothly in his wake, slick with water and gleaming in the sunlight. He glanced at Sharon.

'Come on, Mackie. It's time to let it go.'

He nodded, then, feeling the tug of the rope on his shoulder, dived down through the water. Down and down, to the sound of his beating heart, to the sound of thudding feet and sirens, to the sound of his own voice crying out into a dark night. Down and down until he felt the rope slip from his shoulders – and the weight he'd been dragging half his life simply vanish. He turned himself in the water and opened his eyes and looked up at the surface: the sun waiting for him, Sharon waiting for him – a whole bloody future waiting for him. He braced his feet against the seabed and launched himself towards it.

About the Author

Kathy Biggs is originally from Yorkshire. She took a summer job in Mid Wales in 1985 and never left. She has two grown children and lives with her husband, Paul. After studying a number of Creative Writing courses linked to Aberystwyth University, she discovered a talent for writing. *The Luck* was her first novel, published by Honno in 2022.

Acknowledgements

A massive thank you to all the team at Honno Press, especially my editor Gemma June Howell, Lynzie Fitzpatrick, Rebecca Parfitt and Janet Thomas, whose guidance and support has been invaluable. Thanks also to Elaine Canning, as well as Osian Grifford and Liz Gordon for the brilliant book cover. My thanks to Jonathan Davies at AJT Recycling, Swansea for his technical knowledge and advice, and to Cath Pendleton (The Merthyr Mermaid) and the Gower Mermates for their inspiration. Thank you to my family and friends and writing buddies for being so encouraging and to my local community – neighbours, bookshops, libraries and press – for embracing me so warmly.

Lastly – but mostly – to Paul, my husband and main man. Always there and always smiling. Thank you, love.

ABOUT HONNO

Honno Welsh Women's Press was set up in 1986 by a group of women who felt strongly that women in Wales needed wider opportunities to see their writing in print and to become involved in the publishing process. Our aim is to develop the writing talents of women in Wales, give them new and exciting opportunities to see their work published and often to give them their first 'break' as a writer.

Honno is registered as a community co-operative. Any profit that Honno makes is invested in the publishing programme. Women from Wales and around the world have expressed their support for Honno. Each supporter has a vote at the Annual General Meeting. For more information and to buy our publications, please visit our website www.honno.co.uk or email us on post@honno.co.uk.

Honno
D41, Hugh Owen Building,
Aberystwyth University,
Aberystwyth,
Ceredigion,
SY23 3DY.

We are very grateful for the support of all our Honno Friends.